## MORE THAN PARTNERS

"Who do *you* think I am?" Josh asked, his gaze meeting hers across the table.

Emmie's breath caught in her throat at the look in his eyes.

"I know who you are—" she began, a shiver of sensual awareness trembling through her. "You're my partner."

"You're right," he said. "We're in this together."

"The ranch or the line shack?"

"Both."

Again they were laughing, and Emmie was glad. For a moment there, she'd been caught off guard by the way he'd looked at her, and she wasn't quite sure what to make of it.

"How long do you think we'll have to stay here?" Emmie asked, wanting to change the direction of the conversation.

"The storm doesn't look like it's showing any signs of letting up, so we may have to spend the night."

# Bobbi SMITH

# WANTED: The Texan

LEISURE BOOKS          NEW YORK CITY

*This book is dedicated to everyone at*
*Dorchester Publishing. You're awesome!*

A LEISURE BOOK®

January 2009

Published by

Dorchester Publishing Co., Inc.
200 Madison Avenue
New York, NY 10016

ISBN 10: 0-8439-5851-0
ISBN 13: 978-0-8439-5851-5

Visit us on the web at www.dorchesterpub.com.

# WANTED:

## The Texan

# Prologue

It was a hot, miserable day, and the weather matched rancher Hank Ryan's mood as he followed his wife, Sarah, and their eight-year-old daughter, Emmie, to the waiting stagecoach.

"You're sure you want to do this?" he demanded, his tone edged with anger and frustration.

Sarah was trembling as she spun around to face him. The fire of her desperate need to flee the untamed, savage West burned in her eyes as she stared up at him. "Hank, don't say another word! I'm leaving and I'm taking Emmie with me—I have to go. I can't stay here—not after all that's happened. . . ." The memory of the horrifying Comanche raid that had left their neighbors slaughtered and some of their own ranch hands dead sent a shudder through her. She couldn't stand living in terror, never knowing when there might be another attack.

Emmie looked from one of her parents to the other, trying to understand why her mother was taking her back East to live. She'd heard them arguing heatedly the past few days, but until this moment, she'd never imagined her mother would really go. She knew there was danger from the Comanche, but she also knew her father would protect them. He always had. Tears welled up in her eyes, and she ran to him and wrapped her arms around his neck as he bent to pick her up. She clung to him in desperation. "Papa, I want to stay with you!"

Hank held her close, loving her, as he told her, "I want you to stay, too, but for now, you have to go with your mother."

"But Papa—" she cried.

It was painful for Hank to take Emmie's arms from around his neck and set her in the stagecoach, but he managed. He faced his wife again, trying to ignore the sound of his daughter's weeping. "You know what we agreed on."

Sarah gave a tight nod. "Emmie will be allowed to visit you every summer."

"Make sure you keep your word." It was an order.

There was no hesitation as Sarah nodded again, and their gazes met for one last time. She knew her husband well, and she knew he would do exactly what he'd threatened to do if she didn't uphold her part of their agreement. If she failed to send Emmie back to the Rocking R every summer, he would cut off all her funds and leave them destitute.

"Good-bye, Hank," Sarah said in an emotionless voice. Then she quickly turned away.

"Good-bye, Sarah." Hank stepped back and made no offer to help her climb into the stagecoach. She'd chosen to leave him. She had chosen go back East.

Hank remained where he was to watch as the stagecoach pulled out.

"Papa! I don't want to go!"

The sound of Emmie's cry tore at his heart as they drove off, but Hank turned away. He was aware that some of the folks from town were watching him, but he didn't care. Though there would be talk, it didn't matter to him. All that mattered was keeping the Rocking R going. He had big plans for the ranch. He was going to make it one of the most successful in the area.

But right then he needed a drink.

Hank headed for the saloon.

# Chapter One

It was almost dark when Josh Grady rode into town. The long hours in the saddle and the unrelenting heat had taken their toll on him. He was tired and would have liked to just enjoy a drink at the saloon, but he was in Big Rock on business. Reining in before the High Time Saloon, he tied up his horse and went inside.

"What'll it be?" the barkeep asked, eyeing with interest the tall, lean, dark-haired stranger who'd just come to stand at the bar.

"Whiskey," Josh answered.

The barkeep made short order of serving him and then watched as his customer drank the liquor down real quick.

"I'd say you were a thirsty man." He chuckled.

"You'd be right," Josh agreed. He shoved the empty glass back for a refill and tossed some coins on the bar.

"I ain't seen you around before." The barkeep wondered what business the man could have in Big

Rock. Everyone in town had been tense ever since the bank robbery.

"I just rode in."

"Well, enjoy your stay."

"I plan to do just that. I heard you had some excitement around here a week or so ago."

"Bad news travels fast," the barkeep commented in disgust as he wiped down the bar with a clean cloth. "The Barton boys robbed the bank and shot the teller. Killed him. The town sheriff got a posse up and went after them murdering thieves, but they couldn't track them down. Ned and Tom Barton were too slick for them. They got clean away."

"I hear there's a reward posted for bringing them in."

The barkeep suddenly looked at the stranger with more interest. "There sure is, a real good one. And it don't matter if they're dead or alive. Why are you asking?"

"I thought I just might give it a try."

"I don't know who you are, but the bank teller was a friend of mine. If you bring those killers in, your drinks will be on the house here every night. What's your name? I'm Al."

"Nice to meet you, Al. I'm Josh Grady."

"I've heard of you." Al looked at him with new respect. "Talk has it you're one of the best bounty hunters around. I suppose if anyone can track them down, it'll be you."

"I'll do my best." Josh drained the last of his whiskey and set the glass down. He wanted to do a little gambling, but time was of the essence. The Barton boys already had a big head start, and he needed to get after them first thing in the morning. He wanted to talk to the law in town before he rode out. "Which way is the sheriff's office?"

"Just down the street about three blocks."

"Thanks."

As Josh turned to go, Al called out, "Good luck."

Sallie, one of the saloon girls, came up to the bar to speak with Al. "Why'd the stranger leave so quick? He sure was a good-looking man. I planned on getting him upstairs a little later. Is he coming back?"

"Not anytime soon."

"Who was he?"

"That was Josh Grady, the bounty hunter, and he's going after the Barton boys."

Sallie looked intrigued and disappointed at the same time. "Al, why don't we put up a wanted poster with my face on it and see if he'll come back and 'track me down'?"

Al laughed as she moved off to work the tables.

*Ten days later*

Ned and Tom Barton sat around their campfire, celebrating their good luck and sharing a bottle of whiskey. They had no doubt now that they had made a clean getaway.

"Yeah, things are working out just fine." Ned grinned drunkenly at his brother as he took another swig from the bottle. They'd been living a life of crime for a few years and believed they were getting real good at it.

"Not if you're hogging all the whiskey, they ain't," Tom said. He snatched the bottle away from Ned and drank deeply.

Both men were laughing.

"They sure weren't expecting us at the Big Rock Bank," Ned bragged.

"And that posse gave up real easy."

"Almost too easy, but I'm not complaining."

"Me, either," Tom slurred, patting the cash-filled saddlebags that lay on the ground next to him. "I'm looking forward to spending this money and enjoying myself with some pretty gals once we get to Black Spring."

"I like the way you think," Ned agreed. He knew the saloon girls in Black Spring were always more than eager to please a man who had money. "Let's head out early in the morning, so we can cover some miles tomorrow." He grabbed the bottle back and drained the last of the whiskey before tossing it aside.

"Thinking about them little gals, I'm ready to ride out now, but drunk as I am, I'd have some trouble finding my way."

Ned grinned. He knew how right Tom was. They had both had more than their share of liquor.

Tom fell back on his bedroll and closed his eyes, while Ned got up to stagger off and relieve himself before bedding down for the night.

The sky was moonless, and Josh was grateful for the cover of darkness as he moved silently across the rugged terrain. He'd left his horse tied up farther back and was making his way toward the distant glow of the outlaws' campfire. He'd been tracking them for days, and he was certain that tonight he would finally bring them down.

Josh drew his gun and stayed low as he closed in. Taking cover behind some nearby rocks to check out the campsite, he couldn't believe his luck. One of the men had already bedded down, and the other had moved off into the darkness on the far side of the small clearing. Josh was glad to see the discarded whiskey bottle on the ground near the fire. If they were liquored up, they'd be moving a little slower, and it would make the outlaws' capture easier for him. Josh knew that now was the time to act, while they were separated.

Josh silently made his way around the campsite and closed in on the drunken outlaw just as he was starting back. Josh did not want to give him the chance to yell out to his brother, so he pistol-whipped him from behind. The outlaw fell heavily and lay unmoving on the ground. Josh holstered his gun, and, using the length of rope he'd brought with him, he quickly bound the man's hands tightly behind his back. He recognized Ned Barton from the wanted poster, and was ready to go after his brother, Tom, when a threatening voice spoke from behind him.

"Hold it right where you are!"

Josh looked over to find the other outlaw standing there with his gun drawn, and knew he had to act fast. He went for his own gun and dove for cover. The outlaw fired, and the bullet slammed into Josh's shoulder. As Josh fell, he managed to get off only one shot, but it found its mark.

Tom Barton wouldn't be robbing any more banks or killing any more bank tellers.

Josh lay on the ground, holding his bloodied shoulder. His mood was grim as he slowly struggled up. He knew he was lucky to still be alive, but he was beginning to wonder how much longer his luck was going to hold out.

Fortunately, Ned was still unconscious. Josh had to clean up his wound and stop the bleeding or he wouldn't be taking anybody in. Though the gunshot wound was painful, at least the bullet had passed on through, so he wouldn't have to dig it out. He took the outlaws' guns with him as he headed over to the campsite to see what he could use to dress the wound.

When Ned finally regained consciousness, he found himself lying facedown on the ground. His head was pounding and his wrists were tied tightly behind his back. He rolled over, all the while fighting to free himself, only to find a man sitting on a rock nearby holding a gun on him.

"So you've finally come around," Josh said coldly.

"Who are you? What's going on? Where's my brother?" Ned demanded angrily, still struggling to break free. He could see the blood on the man's shirt and wondered how he'd been shot.

"My name's Grady—Josh Grady."

"The bounty hunter . . ." Ned realized what big trouble he and his brother were in.

"That's right, and I'm taking you back to Big Rock."

"No, you're not! My brother will stop you!" he threatened.

"He already tried."

Confused, Ned lunged awkwardly to his feet. "What are you talking about?"

It was then that he saw his brother's body, and rage filled him. Knowing the bounty hunter had been wounded, Ned charged at him, wanting revenge, but Josh knocked him back down to the ground and stood over him. He stared down at the outlaw, his expression cold.

"It's over, Barton."

And it was.

Josh grimaced as the doctor in Big Rock stripped off his makeshift bandage and examined his wound.

"You're one lucky man, Mr. Grady," Doc Murray told him. "An inch or two the other way and you might not be here right now."

"That's what I figured," Josh agreed.

"The folks in town are going to be real grateful for what you did, bringing those killers back."

Josh didn't say anything. He just nodded. The trek to town had been grueling, but on the way he'd had time to realize just how close he'd come to dying. He was beginning to wonder if the offer his friend Hank Ryan had made some months back about taking a job on his ranch, the Rocking R, still held. He was seriously considering it, and decided to wire Hank as soon as he was done with the doc. Working on a ranch sounded real good right then.

# Chapter Two

*Shotgun, Texas*
*One year later*

Les Gallagher, Hank Ryan's attorney, stood up as Josh Grady came into his office. The two men solemnly shook hands. It was a sad day for both of them. They had just buried a good friend.

"Have a seat, Josh," Les invited.

Josh sat down in the chair facing the lawyer's desk and waited to hear what he had to say.

Les sat and spread out some papers before him. "This is Hank's will."

Josh only nodded. He had known when Les had asked him to come to the office that the lawyer wanted to discuss their friend's will.

"He went over it with me not too long ago, and he was serious about how he wanted things handled if anything happened to him."

"I still can't believe he's dead." Josh shook his head. The memory of his friend's death would be with him forever. He and some of the boys had been right there with Hank when the stampede happened.

"I know. He was a good man—a hard one, but good."

They shared a knowing smile as they thought of the rough-and-tumble way Hank ran things.

"Which brings me to the terms of his will. Since you're part owner of the Rocking R, he wanted me to go over everything with you first."

Josh just nodded, remembering the meeting he'd had with Hank when he'd sought him out for a job the year before. Hank had told him that the offer to work for him still stood, but explained that he'd been going through a hard time and was short on cash. Josh had been sitting pretty with the reward from bringing in the bank robbers, so he'd offered Hank a deal—he'd give Hank the money he needed to keep the ranch running in exchange for part ownership of the Rocking R. They'd agreed to a 70/30 partnership, had drawn up a contract, and had shaken on the deal. He'd come to the Rocking R, and when the older foreman moved on, Josh had taken the job.

"Hank has left everything to his daughter, Emmie—"

"Not his wife?"

The lawyer's expression was pained. "No. He didn't leave Sarah a thing."

"All right, then we'll have to figure out a way for me to buy the place from Hank's daughter." Josh was surprised by the terms of the will. Hank had never said much about his wife, but since he'd still been married to her at the time of his death, Josh had thought she would inherit.

"Well, it's not that easy. There's more. . . ."

Josh wondered why the lawyer paused, looking at him awkwardly.

"Emmie inherits the estate, but only if she comes out here and takes over running the ranch."

"What? He thought a female could run the Rocking R?" Josh was shocked. Hank had spoken of how much he'd missed his daughter, but because she'd been raised back East, Josh had never even considered that Emmie would be returning permanently.

"He did, because she is *his* daughter. He asked me to explain the situation to you in the event that something like this happened. I know you've never met Emmie, but I think you'll understand better once you do."

"What if she decides not to come back?"

"I seriously doubt that will happen. According to Hank's will, if Emmie chooses to stay back east, she and her mother will both be cut off. All funds will be denied them."

"Hank would leave them destitute?" Josh was shocked. The Hank he'd known always took care of his own.

"Those are the terms he set out," Les said grimly. "I tried to reason with him, but, stubborn man that he was, there was no changing his mind. So it looks like you're going to have a new partner to work with."

"There's no way I can just buy her out so she can stay back East?" Josh was frowning, his mood dark as he thought about trying to run the ranch with Hank's daughter—a girl who'd been brought up to be a society lady, not a ranch owner.

"No."

"What about the ranch hands? What should I tell them?"

"For now, just tell them Hank wanted to keep things going exactly as they are."

"And you think the ranch will remain unchanged when a female who's been raised back East takes over?"

"That's right." Les looked up at Josh. "He trusted you, Josh, and he admired you."

"I felt the same way about him, but this isn't going to be easy." Josh knew it was going to be a challenge.

"Nothing worth doing ever is," Les assured him. "But remember, Emmie has spent every summer with her father here on the ranch. She may surprise you."

"I've heard the boys talk about her occasionally, but there's a big difference between paying a visit every year and actually knowing the business and running things."

"You're right about that," the lawyer agreed. He paused and then added, "There is one other thing."

"What?"

"Hank never told his wife or daughter about taking you on as a partner. He was going to tell Emmie when he introduced you to her, but now that won't happen. I thought it would be best if we could let her know after she returns to the ranch."

"All right. Have you wired them about Hank yet?"

"No, I'm not going to send a wire. I want to be there with them when I break the news, and then I have to explain the terms of Hank's will. I'm leaving for Philadelphia tomorrow."

"What will happen if Emmie refuses to come back?"

Les held up a sealed envelope. "Hank's directions are here, and he gave strict instructions that this was to be opened only if Emmie didn't agree to the terms and she and her mother ended up being disinherited."

Josh stood, ready to ride back to the ranch. "How long do you think the trip will take you?"

"I'll be gone for at least three weeks, possibly longer, depending on the trains. I'll wire you from Philadelphia and let you know when I'll be returning—hopefully with Emmie."

"I'll be waiting to hear from you."

"I'll make arrangements with Fred Harris over at the bank so you can access Hank's money in case you need anything on the Rocking R."

They shook hands again, then Josh left the office.

After Josh walked through the door, he stood for a moment, just staring down the street at the saloon. He thought about stopping off for a drink, but decided to ride back to the ranch instead.

There was a lot of work to be done.

*Philadelphia*
*Ten days later*

The party at the Randolph mansion was well under way when the carriage carrying Sarah and Emmie Ryan arrived. They descended gracefully with the help of the doorman and were welcomed warmly by the Randolphs as they went inside to join the festivities.

Mother and daughter were both looking forward to enjoying themselves this evening, but Sarah, in particular, was eager to see how the evening progressed. Kenneth St. James, a sophisticated young man from a wealthy family, had recently been showing interest in Emmie, and Sarah thought he would be the perfect match for her daughter. He had prestige, and his family was well established here in the East. The last thing she wanted was for Emmie even to consider returning to live in Texas. Her yearly visits to the ranch were troubling enough for Sarah. She wanted her daughter's future to be safe and secure.

For her part, Emmie was well aware of her mother's interest in Kenneth as a possible suitor for her. She did enjoy his company, but at that particular moment she had only one thing on her mind: finding her best friend, Millie. Emmie immediately spotted her on the far side of the room.

"There's Millie, Mother," she announced.

"Go and have fun, dear," Sarah said.

"You, too," Emmie replied, knowing how much her mother enjoyed socializing.

Sarah watched proudly as Emmie made her way across the room to join her friend. Emmie had grown into a beautiful young woman, and tonight, in a new shimmering satin gown and with her dark hair styled up in a sophisticated arrangement, she looked absolutely lovely. It was Sarah's hope that Kenneth

St. James would be smitten and ultimately propose. The thought left Sarah smiling even more brightly as she moved off to join her own circle of friends.

Emmie was smiling, too, as she watched Millie openly flirting with the young men who were hovering around her. Her pale pink gown was elegant, and she was wearing her blond hair down around her shoulders in a tumble of fashionable curls. Millie might appear to be the perfect lady, but Emmie knew she had a wild side to her. In fact, the last time they were together, Millie had mentioned that she wanted to go to Texas with her when she went for her next visit. Emmie had been truly surprised by the notion, but the more she'd thought about it lately, the more she wanted her friend to go. Emmie loved being with her father, but there were times when she did get lonely, and Millie would certainly liven the ranch up.

"I was wondering when you were going to show up," Millie teased as she greeted Emmie. "Did you come late just so you could make a grand entrance?"

"Hardly, although I'm sure my mother enjoyed it." Emmie laughed. "The truth is, she insisted on styling my hair up this way, and it took longer than we expected."

Millie eyed her, smiling. "You look lovely."

"Why, thank you, and so do you," Emmie responded. "Are you enjoying yourself?"

"Yes, and soon you will be too," Millie said with confidence, adding, "Kenneth is here."

"Oh, good."

Millie didn't think Emmie sounded too excited, but she had no chance to say more as the music started up again and one of her own suitors claimed her for the next dance. As she was whisked away onto the dance floor, Millie spotted Kenneth on his way to join Emmie.

"Good evening, Emmie," Kenneth said, his gaze warm upon her.

"Hello, Kenneth." She smiled up at him. He was a handsome young man with his brown hair and blue eyes, and he was certainly a gentleman.

"May I have this dance?" he asked.

"Of course."

Kenneth took her into his arms to squire her about the room.

On the far side of the dance floor, Sarah was looking on with delight. The evening couldn't have been working out more perfectly. Perhaps Kenneth would even propose tonight.

The party passed in a whirlwind.

Kenneth spent most of the time with Emmie, and it was past midnight when he managed to slip out onto the balcony with her.

The night sky was a canopy of stars, and the moon was a mere sliver of light low on the horizon. The distant sound of the music indoors just added to the romantic feel of the evening.

"It's a beautiful night," Emmie said, enjoying being away from the crowd for a moment.

"Not as beautiful as you," Kenneth said in a deep, suggestive voice as he drew her over to a quiet corner, away from prying eyes. "I've been wanting to do this all evening."

"What?" She looked up at him questioningly. "Come outside?"

"No. This." He answered her with a kiss, pulling her into his arms and holding her close.

Kenneth had kissed her before, but never quite so boldly or so passionately. She was surprised by the heat of his ardor, and a little relieved when they heard someone coming and had to move apart.

"We'd better go back inside," she said, knowing how her mother would feel if someone started gossiping about her and Kenneth being out on the balcony unchaperoned.

"I'd like to call on you tomorrow, if that would be all right. Say around three in the afternoon?" he asked as they started indoors.

"I'll be looking forward to it," she answered as they went in to join the others who'd gathered near the refreshment table to partake of the punch that was being served.

"Millie tells me she's planning to travel to Texas with you," commented Charles Hill, one of the men who was courting Millie. "How soon will you be leaving?"

"I visit my father every summer, and I can't wait to go again."

"You really enjoy it there?" Kenneth asked, sounding a little surprised. "I can't imagine living so far from civilization."

"I love the ranch," Emmie answered. "I miss it when I'm away."

"But it's dangerous, isn't it? We've all heard the story of why your mother moved back," Charles put in.

Emmie looked at Charles and knew he wouldn't last long on the Rocking R. As she tried to imagine him spending the whole day in the saddle, working stock, she had to struggle to keep from smiling. "It's a different way of life, that's for sure, but I love it."

"And I can't wait to go. It's going to be such an adventure," Millie put in excitedly. "Emmie's told me so many fascinating stories. I can't wait to see the real Wild West for myself."

"And your parents are letting you go?" Charles asked incredulously. "I guess you're just too headstrong to keep at home."

Millie didn't mention that she hadn't told her parents of her adventurous plan yet. There would be time for that later.

The conversation turned to other things, and before long it was time to say their good-byes.

Sarah was quite pleased with the attention Kenneth had paid to her daughter. She'd kept an eye on Emmie and was eager to speak with her about her beau.

"Did you enjoy yourself tonight?" Sarah asked as they settled into their carriage for the short ride home. "I noticed Kenneth spent quite a bit of time with you."

"Yes, he did, and he's coming to the house tomorrow for a visit," Emmie told her.

"That's wonderful. We'll have to be ready for him. What time is he stopping by?"

"Midafternoon." Emmie glanced over at her mother and saw her delight at the news.

"Good. That gives me time to get everything prepared."

Emmie had to hide a smile, for her mother seemed to be more excited about Kenneth coming to call than she was. "Mother, Millie mentioned tonight that she'd like to travel with me when I go to visit Papa again."

"What?" Sarah was horrified by the thought. "Her parents will never allow her to do that."

"Well, we're hoping they will. She's very excited about visiting the ranch. I can't wait to show her around. It will be fun."

"I would hardly call ranch life fun," Sarah said bitterly, and her comment evoked a frown from Emmie.

"Some of us enjoy it, and I think Millie will be one."

Sarah had had this argument with her daughter many times and knew there was no point in trying to change her mind. Though she'd grown into a lady, underneath she was still a lot like Hank.

"We'll have to see. We still have a while before we have to make the plans for your trip." Sarah couldn't understand why anyone would want to go out west. Haunted by memories of the bloody Comanche raid she'd survived, Sarah still found it painful to let Emmie go every year.

# Chapter Three

The following afternoon Emmie was in her room getting ready for Kenneth's visit when she heard a carriage pull up in front of the house. She assumed it was Kenneth, arriving a bit early. So she quickly finished dressing, gave herself one last look in the mirror, and started from her room to go downstairs to greet him.

Emmie was surprised when she got halfway down the staircase and found it wasn't Kenneth at all, but an elderly gentleman who looked vaguely familiar, and was speaking in very serious tones to her mother in the foyer. Her mother's expression was most troubled as she listened to the man, and Emmie immediately grew worried.

"What is it, Mother?" Emmie asked, glancing between them as she approached.

Sarah looked over at her daughter. "Let's go into the sitting room, shall we?" She led the way into the elegantly appointed room. "Please, Mr. Gallagher, have a seat."

Les waited until both ladies were settled on the

sofa and then sat in the chair facing them. He hadn't seen Emmie in several years and couldn't help admiring what a lovely young woman she'd grown into.

"Emmie, this is Mr. Gallagher. He's from Shotgun—he's your father's attorney," Sarah explained.

Emmie realized then that she had met the attorney on one of her trips to the ranch and that was why he looked familiar. "It's good to see you again, Mr. Gallagher."

Les inwardly grimaced at her polite welcome. He doubted she would feel it was good to see him after he broke the news of her father's death. He'd known how close Hank had been to his daughter. "I'm glad to see you, too, Emmie. I just wish it were under different circumstances."

"I don't understand." Emmie tensed at his words, realizing something must be wrong for him to have traveled all this way to see her and her mother.

"Mr. Gallagher has brought us some news from your father," Sarah explained. Ever since she'd answered the door, she'd been feeling most uneasy about the attorney's reason for coming to Philadelphia. "What is it? Is Hank having some kind of trouble at the ranch?"

"There's no easy way for me to tell you this. . . ." He paused, looking pained. "Hank . . ." He looked at Emmie. "Your father . . . is dead."

Shock and horror radiated through Emmie. "What!"

"No!" Sarah stared at him in disbelief. "There must be some mistake. . . ."

"I'm sorry." He'd known it was going to be hard to witness their pain.

"Mother . . ." Emmie looked at her in complete devastation and then began to cry.

Sickened by the news, Sarah reached out to Emmie and took her in her arms. She held her daughter close as they wept, her fury with her husband nearly uncontrollable. He should have come back east with her when she'd left. If he had, he would still have been alive. Her hatred of the ranch grew even deeper.

Les waited in silence, for there was nothing he could say or do to make the loss of Hank any easier for them.

"What happened?" Sarah finally asked as Emmie regained some of her composure and they moved slightly apart.

"Hank was out working stock and there was a stampede," he explained.

"Oh, God . . ." Emmie sobbed, thinking of what her father must have suffered in his last minutes.

Sarah held her again as she looked at the lawyer. Her relationship with Hank had been distant, both emotionally and physically. She had no idea what was going to happen to them now. "What are we going to do?"

"That's why I came here to see you and explain everything," the lawyer continued.

"I don't understand—"

"Your husband did have a will. It was drawn up several years ago, and there are certain..." He paused, trying to find the right words to explain what Hank had done. "Certain requirements that need to be met, so we can take care of the estate."

"What kind of requirements?" Emmie asked, suddenly afraid of what else the lawyer might have to tell them.

Les looked at Sarah. "You know how much Hank loved the Rocking R. The ranch was his life."

"I know," Sarah said bitterly. She had never forgiven him for choosing to stay on the ranch rather than save their marriage.

"And because he worked so hard to make the Rocking R the successful ranch that it is, he was very clear about how he wanted things handled in the event of his passing."

"What is there to handle?" Sarah asked. "With Hank dead, we'll sell the ranch and be done with it." She wanted to sever any and all connections to the nightmare of the Rocking R.

Emmie's heart was breaking even more as she listened to her mother. She always looked forward to her annual trip to the ranch, and she loved the time she spent there with her father. The Rocking R was her second home, and now it was all lost to her.

Les remembered Hank's warning on the day they'd drawn up the will. He'd accurately predicted his wife's reaction. "I'm afraid selling the ranch is not a possibility."

"What?" Sarah was taken aback by his declaration. "I don't understand—"

"Hank had other plans for the Rocking R, and he made certain they were spelled out in detail."

Sarah watched as the lawyer carefully took an envelope out of his coat pocket and opened it to remove the will. As he unfolded the document, she grew cold inside, fearing what she was about to hear.

Les began to read her the terms her husband had set down. " 'I, Hank Ryan, being of sound mind and body, do hereby bequeath all my worldly belongings to my daughter, Emerson Ryan, on the one and only condition that she return to live at the Rocking R and take over running the ranch for a period of no less than two years.' "

Emmie had been quiet until that time, but she was completely caught off guard by the news.

"What?" She looked up at the lawyer in shock. "Papa wanted me to run the ranch?"

Les looked at her proudly. "He most certainly did. He believed you loved the Rocking R as much as he did."

"I do, but . . ." The thought of going to live on the ranch permanently was startling to her. Her life was mainly in Philadelphia. Her mother and all her friends lived in the city.

"I can't let this happen." Sarah was almost hysterical as she interrupted them. She knew her daughter was actually considering following the dictates of her father's will, and she had to stop it. She looked at Emmie. "You are not going back there to live. I don't know what your father was thinking." She turned a cold-eyed glare on the lawyer. "Did Hank do this deliberately to hurt me? Was he still trying to get back at me for leaving?"

The lawyer returned her icy glare, defending Hank's motives. "This has nothing to do with you. It is all about Emmie and her inheritance."

"What are you talking about?"

"You have no voice in this matter."

"I most certainly do!" she countered heatedly.

"No," he emphasized, "you do not. Hank made sure of that. According to the terms of his will, Emmie inherits everything as long as she agrees to return to the Rocking R and take over the ranch." He turned to speak directly to Emmie as he went on. "However, if you choose not to follow your father's wishes, you and your mother will no longer have any access to Hank's funds."

"Papa would do that to us?" Emmie was shocked.

"Yes."

"Hank really would leave us penniless?" Sarah had always known Hank was a hard man, but she'd never thought of him as cruel.

"That's right," Les affirmed. "Hank was very careful about how he set this up. He knew you would object to his plan, and for that reason, he made it perfectly clear that you both will lose everything if the will is not followed."

Emmie now understood what her father had done. She spoke up before her mother could say anything more. "Is my mother required to travel with me and live on the ranch?"

"No—only you."

She was relieved by that news. She looked the

lawyer straight in the eye as she told him, "All right, I'll do exactly what he asked of me."

"No! You can't!" Sarah couldn't let Emmie put herself in danger this way. It was troubling enough when Emmie went out west to visit every summer, but the thought of Emmie moving to Shotgun permanently tormented her. "I won't let you!"

Emmie knew there was no real choice. She had to do what was required of her. Even as she thought of how changed her life was going to be, she found she was honored that her father had believed she was capable of handling such a great responsibility. She looked at her mother. "I'm going. It's what Papa wanted."

"But, Emmie . . ." She was outraged that her daughter cared so much about Hank's wishes. What about her own? She had raised Emmie! She had protected her! She had kept her safe from harm!

Emmie could tell her mother was angry, and she didn't let her finish. She turned to the lawyer. "Who's been running things since Papa died?"

"Josh Grady."

Emmie nodded. Her father had written her and told her that Josh Grady was the new foreman on the ranch. "How soon do you have to head back?"

"I didn't make any plans. I was waiting to see what you decided to do."

"I'll need a few days." She was overwhelmed as she considered all that had to be done.

"Take as long as you like." Les stood up to go. "And if you need anything from me, just send word." He told them the hotel where he was staying.

"I will," Emmie assured him.

Sarah was devastated. She remained sitting on the sofa while Emmie saw the lawyer out. When Emmie came back into the sitting room, Sarah looked up at her, all the pain she was feeling mirrored in her expression.

"Are you sure you want to do this?" she asked in a tight voice.

"Yes."

"You don't have to. We can find some other way," Sarah insisted.

"There is no other way. You heard Mr. Gallagher. If I don't go back, we'll be left with nothing." Emmie went to sit beside her mother and took her hand reassuringly. "Papa believed I could do this. I have to prove he was right—for both our sakes."

Sarah lifted a gentle hand to touch her daughter's cheek. "I want you to be safe." Her words revealed the agony in her heart.

"I know." Emmie hugged her mother. Needing some time alone to deal with her own heartbreak, she said, "I'm going up to my room for a while."

"I understand. What about Kenneth?"

In her grief over losing her father, Emmie had momentarily forgotten Kenneth was due to arrive soon. "Have Mary tell him I can't see him today."

"I will."

Emmie disappeared upstairs as her mother sought out the maid to tell her they wouldn't be accepting any visitors for the rest of the day.

Emmie entered her bedroom and shut the door behind her. Alone at last, she fell across her bed and gave in to her sorrow. Heartrending sobs tore from the depths of her soul and racked her as she mourned the loss of her father. The pain of her grief was overwhelming as she realized she would never see him again.

He was lost to her forever.

And she had never even had a chance to tell him good-bye.

# Chapter Four

Kenneth was looking forward to seeing Emmie, and he was smiling as he climbed down from his carriage and made his way up the walk to her house. He was surprised when the maid answered the door.

"I'm here to see Emmie," he said, ready to step inside.

"I'm sorry, sir, but Mrs. Ryan and Emmie aren't seeing anyone today."

"She's expecting me." He wasn't accustomed to being denied or put off, especially not by a mere servant. Arrogantly, he demanded, "Tell her I'm here."

"I'm sorry," she repeated, "but Miss Emmie gave me instructions that she wasn't to be disturbed."

"I don't understand." Kenneth was growing even more irritated—with the maid and with Emmie.

"There's been a family emergency."

"What happened?"

"They just received word a short time ago that Mr. Ryan has passed away."

"Oh, that's terrible news." Kenneth was shocked

to hear of their loss and immediately changed his attitude. "Please offer them my condolences, and if there's anything I can do, let me know."

"I'll tell Emmie, sir."

"Thank you." Kenneth turned away and started back to his carriage, lost in thought. He knew how much Emmie loved spending time with her father, and he wondered what would happen to the ranch in Texas. Logic said the family would sell it, and he knew that would give Emmie a very nice inheritance.

That thought alone made him smile as he climbed back into his carriage.

It was late that afternoon when Emmie recovered enough to write a short note to Millie. She gave it to the maid to deliver to her friend, and it wasn't long after the girl returned from her errand that Emmie heard a soft knock at her bedroom door.

"Come in," Emmie called out.

The door opened and Millie rushed in. She went straight to Emmie and hugged her tight.

"Oh, Emmie, I got your note!"

"I'm so glad you came," Emmie said in an emotion-choked voice, struggling to keep from losing what little control she had.

They sat down together on the side of the bed while Emmie told her all that had happened.

"I don't believe it." Millie gasped when Emmie explained the terms of the will.

"I do." She looked at her friend. "The Rocking R meant everything to my father. He worked his whole life to make it the success that it is, and he wanted me to love it, too."

"But can you do this? Can you just move away and never come back?"

The look in Emmie's eyes was haunted as she answered, "I only have to live there full-time for two years, and I can still come back and visit, just like I did with my father."

"What did your mother say?"

"She's upset. She doesn't want me to go, but I told her I was going to do what Papa wanted me to do. The lawyer's staying in town to make the trip back with me. I'll probably be ready to leave by the end of the week."

As feisty as ever, Millie gave her friend a conspiratorial smile. "Well, you're not making this trip alone."

"No. I told you, the lawyer's going with me," Emmie repeated, frowning at her.

"And so am I," Millie declared. "I was planning to go with you for your regular visit this year, so we'll just move up the date. I'll be ready to leave when you are."

"But, Millie, are you sure?" Emmie's spirits brightened considerably at the thought of having her friend along. She was going to need all the moral support she could get once she arrived at the ranch. It wasn't going to be easy, living there without her father, and she wasn't sure just how the ranch hands were going to react to taking orders from a woman.

"I've never been more sure of anything in my life," Millie replied loyally. There was no way she would let her friend face this life-changing challenge alone.

"What will your parents say?"

"They'll say yes, of course," she said with a grin. "Have you ever known them to deny me anything? Of course, they might be concerned about a chaperone, but I'll think of something."

Emmie gave her friend a warm hug. "Thank you."

Millie returned her hug with heartfelt emotion, for she could well imagine just how sad and alone her friend was feeling.

It was early in the evening five days later when Kenneth arrived at the Ryan house. He hadn't seen Emmie since she'd learned of her father's death, and when he'd received a note from her letting him know that she was leaving for Texas the following day, he'd made arrangements to stop by.

"I'm glad you could come," Emmie told him as she welcomed him in the front hall.

"I couldn't let you leave without seeing you again. This has all been so sudden," Kenneth said.

"There are times when I don't believe what's happening either," she said sadly as she led the way into the sitting room.

Kenneth followed her and was disappointed to find her mother there. He'd hoped to have some time alone with Emmie. He'd wanted an opportunity to continue his courtship. "Hello, Mrs. Ryan."

"It's good to see you, Kenneth."

"I'm so sorry about your loss," he said. But even as he spoke his condolences, he couldn't help wondering if she really cared that her husband was dead. True, she was wearing mourning clothes, but from the talk he'd heard around town, she'd rarely spent any time with him after she'd moved back to Philadelphia so many years ago.

"Thank you. It's been a very difficult time for us, and now with Emmie leaving . . ." Sarah looked from him to her daughter.

"I know," he agreed.

"Well, I'll leave you two to visit," she announced as she stood up and started from the room.

She could tell just by the way Kenneth was gazing at Emmie that he cared about her, and she wanted to give them time alone, in the hope that he might propose. She knew Emmie liked him, and she prayed he would say something that would convince her to give up this wild notion of following the dictates of her father's will. She would do anything she could to keep her daughter in Philadelphia, with her. Certainly, if Kenneth proposed, he had sufficient funds to support them both in the style to which they'd become accustomed.

Kenneth remained standing until Mrs. Ryan had gone, then sat down on the sofa with Emmie. He didn't waste any time getting to the point. "I'm going to miss you," he declared fervently.

"I'm going to miss you, too," Emmie said.

"You know, you don't have to go," Kenneth suggested.

Emmie looked up at him and saw the ardor in his gaze. It only made the moment harder for her. "Yes, I do. It's what my father wanted."

"But what do *you* want?" he asked. Egotistically, he expected her to say she wanted to stay in Philadelphia, to be with him. Ever so gently, he took her in his arms and drew her to him. He kissed her, sweetly at first, and then more deeply.

Emmie accepted his kiss without protest, but she was glad when he finally released her.

"You could stay, Emmie," he said, his tone coaxing. He'd spent the last several days thinking about marrying her, and how much richer he would be after the ranch was sold.

"Kenneth, please don't make my leaving any harder than it already is. This is something I have to do."

"But—"

"You could always come to the ranch for a visit," she offered.

"Or you could say you'll marry me and stay here," he countered.

"Marry you?" She was surprised by his proposal. "Oh, Kenneth . . . I do care about you, but I can't even think about marriage now. Not after everything that's happened. My whole life has changed so quickly."

His frustration with her turned to anger. He had never proposed to a woman before, and to have her respond to him so halfheartedly was infuriating. She cared more about some stupid ranch than she did about him? Somehow, he managed to hide his anger. "So, there's no convincing you to stay?"

"No. The ranch meant too much to my father. I can't just let it go."

"I don't understand. Sell it and stay here."

She hadn't told anyone but Millie about the unusual stipulations her father had put in the will, but she knew she had to explain to Kenneth. "I can't."

"Of course you can. It's your inheritance."

"That's what you don't understand." She went on to tell him what her father had done.

"Why would he do that to you?" His anger with her eased as he recognized that she had no choice in the matter. One thing he did know: he certainly had no desire to marry her and go live in Texas for two years.

"Because he loved the Rocking R—and he knew I loved it, too."

Kenneth nodded, realizing there was nothing more he could say to change her mind. He stood up to go. "Just know that if I can ever help you in any way, all you have to do is ask."

"Thank you."

She rose to walk him to the door. They were alone in the foyer, and he bent to kiss her again.

"Good night, Kenneth," she murmured.

"Good night, Emmie." He gently touched her cheek, playing the role of ardent suitor perfectly. Then he turned and strode briskly out the door.

Emmie waited in the entrance, watching until his carriage had driven away. Only then did she turn back inside. She wasn't sure if she was sorry Kenneth was gone or relieved. She'd just started up the staircase when her mother appeared in the foyer.

"Well? How did your visit with Kenneth go?" Sarah asked, trying not to sound too eager to hear the details.

"It was very sweet of him to come over and say good-bye." Emmie didn't want to tell her mother that he'd proposed. She knew how Sarah felt about the possibility of her marrying Kenneth, and she dreaded the thought of getting into an argument on the night before she was to leave for Texas.

"Yes, it was," Sarah agreed. She wanted to ask more, but Emmie had already turned away.

Sarah was disappointed that there was no exciting news of a proposal, and she realized now that there was no way to keep Emmie from leaving her. She felt completely and utterly alone as she watched her daughter go up the stairs to her room. She was overwhelmed by a feeling of bitterness.

Hank had known exactly what he was doing when he'd set up his will.

It was obvious now that he'd never forgiven Sarah for leaving him, and he was taking his revenge from the grave.

# Chapter Five

"There's a rider coming!"

Josh was working in the stable when he heard one of the ranch hands call out. He quit what he was doing and went to see who was riding in. He recognized the man as Rick from the telegraph office and figured he was probably bringing news from the lawyer. Les Gallagher had been gone for more than two weeks, and Josh had been wondering how things were going back in Philadelphia.

"Rick, it's good to see you," Josh greeted him.

"I was hoping you'd be here," Rick said as he dismounted. "This just came for you." He handed over the telegram.

"Thanks."

Rick rode out again as Josh glanced down at the message in his hand. He wasn't quite sure he wanted to read it, but he knew he had no choice. Unfolding the telegram, he quickly read the lawyer's words.

"What's the news?" asked Burley Thompson, a longtime hand on the Rocking R whose name fit his size. The big man walked out of the stable to join Josh.

"Looks like things are going to turn out the way Hank wanted."

"Emmie's coming back?" Burley asked.

"They're on their way."

"I didn't think we'd ever see her again. I thought her mother would sell the place and be done with it. Is Sarah coming with her?"

"No." Josh didn't reveal any of the details of Hank's will.

"Figures." Burley had watched little Emmie with her father and knew how close they'd been. "So Emmie's planning to stay?"

"It looks that way."

"I'll let the boys know. It ain't going to be easy for her. That's for sure."

As Burley moved off, Josh stared down at the telegram one more time before stuffing it in his pocket and heading back to work. He wondered how a girl raised back East was going to handle the many challenges of ranch life.

Emmie was staring out the window of the stage at the vast Texas countryside on the final leg of her journey home. She realized as the thought formed in her mind that no matter how many years she'd spent in Philadelphia, the Rocking R was still home to her. She almost smiled thinking of the ranch, but then the memory of her father's death returned to haunt her, and sadness overwhelmed her again. She'd managed to keep her spirits up during the trip by telling herself it was just time for another visit, but the game she'd been playing with herself was over now.

This wasn't just another trip to the ranch.

This time her father wouldn't be there.

"Emmie, how close are we?" Millie asked. She'd seen the change in her friend's expression and wanted to distract her. Every passing mile brought them closer to the town of Shotgun—and to the Rocking R. Millie knew Emmie's sorrow was only going to deepen once she had to face the reality of her father's death.

"We should reach town within the hour," Emmie told her.

"Thank heaven," exclaimed Miss Harriet Adams, the very prim and proper chaperone, who'd been hired to accompany the two girls. The endless hours riding in the hot, dusty stagecoach had taken their toll on the older woman.

Emmie smiled at her, but cautioned, "Once we get to Shotgun, we're still not finished. From there, we have to make the trip out to the ranch."

"And just how do we do that?" Miss Harriet asked, looking a bit unsure about what was to come.

"Since we weren't certain how our stagecoach connections were going to work out, there probably won't be anyone from the ranch to meet us," Les said. "I'll have to see if Will down at the stable has a carriage we can use. If not, I'll send a rider out to let Josh know that we've arrived and we'll have to wait for him to send someone to get us."

"And Josh is the foreman, right?" Millie asked.

"Yes. He's been at the Rocking R for almost a year now," Les explained. "Emmie hasn't met him yet, but you all will today. He's done a fine job of running things."

Emmie wasn't sure whether she was glad to hear that or not. Her father should be the one running things at the Rocking R, not a stranger. Not a man she'd never met.

But even as she thought it, Emmie reasoned with herself that her father had hired Josh on, and that said a lot about what Hank had thought of him.

"This is exciting," Millie said, glancing out the window. "We're actually here . . . in Texas." She had been raised in the city, surrounded by people and buildings. This Western landscape was a far cry from what she was used to, but instead of feeling intimidated, she thought of the trip as a big adventure. She couldn't wait to get out and explore everything. "So, Emmie, tell me about Shotgun again. What's the town like? And how did it come to be named Shotgun?"

"Charlie Miller was one of the first settlers here, and he always carried a shotgun. He got elected the first sheriff and was real good at using his shotgun to keep things quiet. Some outlaw who was passing through ambushed him one night, and that's when the folks decided to name the town after him."

"Oh, dear." Miss Harriet gasped. "What happened to the outlaw?"

"From what my father told me, the townsfolk got up a posse and went after him."

"Did they catch him?" Millie asked.

Emmie wasn't sure her traveling companions were ready to hear the truth, but she told them anyway. "Yes. They tracked him down and strung him up."

"Strung him up?" Miss Harriet repeated, confused in her innocence.

"They hanged him," Les spoke up.

"Gracious me." Miss Harriet looked sorry she'd asked.

"But don't worry, Miss Harriet," Les assured her. "Things have been pretty peaceful in Shotgun for a while now."

"That's good news," the older woman said, relief apparent in her tone.

They fell silent again as the stage continued on its rough, jarring ride toward town.

"There's Shotgun," Emmie told them as she caught sight of the buildings in the distance some time later.

Miss Harriet took a quick look out the window. She wasn't sure what she'd expected, but it wasn't the forlorn grouping of run-down-looking buildings she saw about a mile off. She'd expected a town—a city. She sat back, troubled, but taking great care to keep her expression pleasant. From the looks of things, her job was going to be quite a challenge. After all, she supposed, they didn't call it the Wild West for nothing. She just hoped the Rocking R Ranch was a bit more civilized-looking.

Millie was glad the trip was over. It had been a long, hard one, but now the really difficult time was upon them. She looked over at her friend and gave her a reassuring smile. "I wish we were here under different circumstances," she said softly.

Emmie nodded, her eyes full of sorrow. "So do I."

The stagecoach rolled into town, leaving a trail of dust swirling behind it.

Les climbed out of the vehicle first, then turned to help the ladies descend. They stood in front of the stage office, looking most out of place in their fashionable traveling clothes. The coach driver threw their bags down, and Les quickly stacked them on the wooden sidewalk.

"Why don't you wait here at the office while I check with Will about getting us a carriage?"

"I need to send a telegram to my mother to let her know we've arrived safely."

"I'll take care of that for you," Les offered.

"Thanks."

He moved off as they started inside.

Millie stopped, though, fascinated by her first look at a real Western town. She wanted to see as much as she could before they left for the ranch. "Could we walk around a bit?"

"Sure. Mr. Gallagher will probably be a while."

Emmie led the way, showing them where the church was and the school. They'd just come up to the dry goods store when Paul Mason, the owner, stepped out.

"Why, Emmie! Carol!" he shouted back to his wife. "Emmie's here!"

Carol Mason came hurrying outside. "Oh, Emmie, we were hoping you'd come back. We're so sorry about your pa."

"Thank you. So am I."

"Are you doing all right?"

"As well as I can be," she answered a bit evasively, drawing a curious look from Millie.

Paul went back inside while Carol stayed out to talk.

"Who've you brought with you?" Carol asked, looking at the strikingly pretty blonde and the middle-aged woman with Emmie.

Emmie quickly introduced everyone.

"Well, nobody believed it at the time, but it looks like your pa did the right thing, making a partner out of that gunman Josh Grady," Carol said, turning the topic back to the reason for Emmie's return. "Just think where you'd be without him right now."

"Gunman? Partner? What are you talking about?"

"Your pa didn't write you about Josh?" Carol asked, giving Emmie a surprised look.

"I knew we had a new foreman."

"Dear me . . . I guess you'll be finding out soon enough now. Well, excuse me, I've got to get back to the store."

"What was all that about?" Miss Harriet asked as they started walking back to the stage office. "What was that woman suggesting?"

"And why don't you like her?" Millie asked perceptively.

"Mrs. Mason is the town gossip."

"Oh."

"She just has to know everybody's business—but I don't understand what she was saying about the new foreman." Emmie frowned. "I've got to talk to Mr. Gallagher about this—now."

Les drove the carriage up to the stage office just as they returned.

"Were you giving them the scenic tour?" he asked Emmie as he got down and started to load their bags.

"I thought they'd be interested in getting a look at our town," she said.

Les helped Millie and Miss Harriet climb up into the carriage. When they were seated, he turned to Emmie to give her a hand.

"I think we need to have a talk before we go anywhere," Emmie said.

"What is it?" Les asked, sounding concerned at her tone of voice.

She stepped away from the carriage and walked off to the side of the office, leaving him to follow. She wanted their conversation to be private. She turned and confronted him when she was certain they were alone.

"My father left the Rocking R to me, and I've come back here to run it."

"Yes. I know." He looked puzzled. "Those were the orders in his will."

"Then who is Josh Grady, really?" she demanded.

"What do you mean?" he asked in confusion.

"Carol Mason said—"

"Oh, Carol . . ."

"Yes, Carol," Emmie said heatedly. "She just told me this Josh is part owner of the Rocking R!"

Looking shamefaced, Les quickly explained what her father had done in offering Josh a partnership.

"And just when did you plan to tell me all this?"

Emmie demanded, surprised to learn about her father's shortage of cash and his decision to take on a partner.

"I was going to explain everything once we were out at the ranch and you'd already met Josh. I thought it would be better that way. Now I realize I was wrong. I should have told you up front."

"Why didn't my father tell me? He wrote to me and let me know we had a new foreman—"

"He probably didn't tell you the rest of it then for the same reason I waited. He wanted to introduce you to Josh first. Josh is a good man. He was a big help to your father, and he's been running things since—"

Emmie looked up at the lawyer, sorrow and pain deep in her eyes. "I think we'd better get out to the Rocking R."

# Chapter Six

*E*mmie remained quiet for most of the carriage ride to the Rocking R. What she'd just learned from Mr. Gallagher troubled her. The ranch was her inheritance. She'd traveled back to Texas planning to take over running it. She was deeply disturbed to learn that this man—this Josh Grady, a man she didn't even know—was part owner.

In a way, Emmie was a little bit glad for the distraction of her anger, for it kept her from facing the reality of what was to come next. As the miles passed and they drew closer to the Rocking R, Emmie could no longer ignore the heartache she was about to face. She was returning home—and for the first time ever, her father wouldn't be there.

She told herself she was strong.

She told herself she was her father's daughter.

But even as she girded herself emotionally, she knew it was going to be painful entering the house and not finding him there waiting for her with a smile and a big hug.

Millie sat across from Emmie in the carriage,

watching her. She could see the haunted look in her friend's eyes and understood why she was so silent. She didn't try to engage her in conversation, for she knew this was the most difficult part of the whole trip for Emmie, and there was nothing she could do to make it any easier.

It was Miss Harriet who, after riding in the carriage for nearly half an hour with no sign of civilization in sight, broke the silence. "When are we going to get to the ranch? Is it much farther?"

Emmie looked over at the elderly lady and managed a slight, ironic smile. "We've been on the Rocking R for the last fifteen minutes."

"Oh, my," Miss Harriet said, truly surprised. "Then where's the house?"

"Just a little farther on—a few more miles."

"The Rocking R is certainly a big ranch," the chaperone said in amazement. "I don't know quite what I was expecting. My experiences with country living back East were limited to visiting farms, and this is certainly nothing like a farm."

"Yes, it is big. It's over forty thousand acres," Emmie explained.

"Goodness." Miss Harriet looked around with more interest now.

It was only a short time later that Emmie told them, "We're here."

Emmie had described the house to Millie, but Millie was still impressed by the sight of the large two-story home in the distance, with all its outbuildings. Millie could see a group of ranch hands gathered around the corral near the stable.

"I wonder what's happening?" she asked.

Emmie saw them, too. "Hard to say from this far out, but someone could be breaking a horse."

"There's some kind of excitement going on," Les agreed when he heard a rousing cheer go up from the cowboys. "Let's go see what it is."

Josh got up slowly from where he'd been thrown yet another time. He picked up his hat and angrily knocked the dirt and dust from his clothes before jamming it back on. He knew he was going to be hurting tomorrow, but right now that didn't matter. All that mattered was breaking the defiant black stallion. The look in Josh's eyes was steely as he squared his shoulders and started after the horse, which had moved off to the far side of the corral and was standing there staring back at him.

"What are ya goin' to do now?" called out Steve, a young, smart-mouthed hand.

Josh didn't even glance his way as he answered, "I'm going to ride him."

The men watching heard the fierce determination in his voice and knew the stallion had thrown Josh for the last time. They watched as the foreman slowly picked up the reins and then, talking softly to the stallion in a low, calm voice, moved to mount up again.

Josh swung up into the saddle, ready for another rough ride. The stallion didn't disappoint him. Even though the horse was obviously tired, he put up another good fight. This time, though, Josh managed to hang on. It wasn't easy, but he stayed in the saddle.

The stallion charged toward the fence and then stopped quickly and bucked as hard as he could, spinning around in his effort to unseat the man who was trying to break him, but Josh was as hardheaded as the stallion.

The two battled on.

Les had intended to drive the ladies straight up to the house, but there was so much cheering going on out at the corral, he drove there first.

Burley saw the carriage coming and called out, "Hey, boys! Emmie's here!"

At his shout, the ranch hands glanced over to see the lawyer pulling up in the carriage with Emmie and two other ladies. They forgot all about Josh's fight with the stallion as they hurried over to welcome Emmie home.

Burley reached the carriage first.

"Burley!" Emmie greeted him with a warm smile. He had always been one of her favorite ranch hands. She knew the gentle giant had a tender heart.

At her greeting, the big man didn't hesitate, but went straight to her to lift her down from the carriage with ease.

"We heard you were coming," he told her. He looked back up at the carriage and asked, "Who'd you bring with you?"

"This is Miss Harriet, our chaperone, and my best friend, Millie," Emmie said, quickly introducing her companions. Then looking up at the ranch hand, she told them, "And this is Burley. He's worked here on the Rocking R for as long as I can remember."

"That's right, I have. I've known this pretty lady

since she was knee-high to a grasshopper. We used to call her 'Little' Emmie, but not anymore. It's nice to meet you," he returned.

Emmie smiled, remembering Burley's affectionate nickname for her when she was a little girl.

Les climbed down to help Millie and Miss Harriet descend from the carriage while Emmie went to greet the other ranch hands who'd come over to welcome her home.

"We're real sorry about your pa." Burley's mood turned solemn as he spoke up for all of them.

"Thank you," Emmie said sadly, looking at the men who'd been so loyal to her father. "I'm still having trouble believing he's gone."

"So are we," one of the other men offered in consolation.

"Is Josh around?" Les asked Burley. He knew this was going to be the hardest moment of her homecoming—going up to the house and finding her father not there—and he wanted to get the introductions over with so she could have time alone to adjust to all the changes in her life.

Burley gave him a wry grin. "Who do you think's riding that bronc?"

As he spoke, everyone looked back toward the corral. Josh was still in the saddle. While they were watching, the stallion gave one last weak buck and then gave up the fight.

Josh had been so caught up in breaking the horse that he hadn't realized the ranch hands were gone until that moment. Glancing around, he spotted the carriage. Les and the three women standing beside it were talking to Burley and the other boys. Josh reined in and dismounted.

"Here he comes now," Les said to Emmie.

Emmie looked over toward the corral. She didn't know what she'd been expecting of the partner her father had taken on—an older man, maybe, someone closer to Hank's own age, but the sight of the tall, lean, ruggedly handsome cowboy striding their way unsettled her. There was something about him—an air of confidence and control, and even an edge of danger—that said he was a man to be reckoned with. She remembered what Carol Mason had said about him in town. She'd called him a gunman. Emmie wondered if Josh really had made his living with a gun before he'd come to the Rocking R. She waited, more than a little tense, while he approached.

As Josh drew near, it took him only a moment to recognize Hank's daughter. Hank had a portrait of her in his office, and the young woman standing before him was as pretty as her picture. Josh had been worrying about what was going to happen when she showed up, and now that day had come. Hank had told him all about his wife's ultimatum and her decision to live in Philadelphia, and Josh figured Emmie was going to be just like her mother—a lady who couldn't handle the harshness of ranch life. If she was, she wouldn't last six months at the Rocking R, let alone the two years she needed to stay. Coming to visit her father once a year had been one thing. Actually living on the ranch day in and day out was another. As pretty and ladylike as she looked, he didn't think she'd last.

Les was the first to speak. "Josh, good to see you."

Josh went to him and shook his hand. "Les. I see you made it back in good time."

"Yes, we did. Let me introduce you." He quickly made the introductions.

"Hello, Miss Ryan," Josh said respectfully. He could see the wariness in her regard and realized that the lawyer must have already told her about the partnership.

"Mr. Grady," she returned. "I understand we have a lot to discuss."

"Yes, we do."

Burley looked from Josh to Emmie, wondering at the unspoken tension between them and why they were being so formal with each other. He knew that was going to have to change real quick; they had a ranch to run.

"Shall we go on up to the house and get out of this heat?" Les suggested, breaking the awkward moment.

Emmie girded herself for what was to come. "Yes. I think Miss Harriet could use a cool drink right now."

"It is a bit hot here in Texas," the chaperone agreed, busily fanning herself.

"You coming with us, Josh?" Les asked.

"I'll be along," Josh told him. He wanted to check on the stallion again and clean up a bit before meeting with Emmie.

The three women accompanied Les to the house

and went up the steps to the wide, shaded front porch.

Emmie hesitated at the top of the steps, her gaze fixed on the front door. In her heart, she expected her father to come rushing out and give her a big hug, as he always did when she came home, but she knew it wasn't going to happen. She drew a ragged, steadying breath as she led the way inside.

"Here we are," she announced, entering the front hall.

Millie and Miss Harriet followed her in and gazed around the spacious hall and up the wide staircase that led to the second floor. It was obvious her father had spared no expense on the house.

"Do you want me to show you around?" Emmie asked.

"Please," Millie said. "I've heard you talk about the Rocking R for years, and now I'm finally here."

"I'll wait for you in the sitting room," Les said, leaving them to their walk through the house.

Emmie was just starting toward the back of the house when Kate, her father's cook and house-keeper, came rushing from the kitchen to welcome her home. Kate was the wife of one of the ranch hands.

"I thought I heard you," Kate said, going straight to Emmie to embrace her. "How are you?"

Emmie fought back tears. "I'd be a lot better if Papa were here."

"We all would, honey," Kate said sympathetically as they moved apart.

Emmie quickly introduced everyone, and they chatted for a moment longer before Kate went back to the kitchen. Emmie continued showing Millie and Miss Harriet the rest of the house and let them pick which of the guest bedrooms they wanted to stay in. The only rooms she didn't take them into were her father's office and bedroom. Those doors were closed, and she was glad. She wasn't ready to go into either room yet. She would do that later, when she was alone.

They were on their way back to join Les in the sitting room when they saw two of the hands coming in with their trunks. Millie and Miss Harriet decided to go back upstairs with the men so they could show them where to put the trunks. Then the women would settle in for a while and unpack. Emmie went on into the sitting room to speak with the lawyer privately.

Les looked up from where he was sitting on the sofa when she came into the room. "Well, we're here," he said.

"Thank you for everything," she said earnestly, taking a seat across from him. "I really appreciate how you handled all this."

He was sympathetic as he looked at her. "I'm just sorry you're returning home under such sad conditions, but I know your being here meant a lot to your father."

"It means everything to me. The Rocking R . . . it's my life now." Her voice was hoarse with emotion.

"You are truly your father's daughter," Les told

her with a gentle, encouraging smile. "He always said the same thing about the ranch. You know, he was very proud of you, Emmie."

"I hope I can make him even prouder of me now." The tears she'd been fighting overwhelmed her, and she gave in to her grief.

Les had just gotten up to hand her his handkerchief when Josh appeared in the doorway.

"Sorry I took so long. I . . ." Josh began, but he went silent at the sight of her crying.

"Please join us, Josh," the lawyer said. When Emmie regained control, he returned to sit on the sofa. "This is a hard time."

"I understand," Josh said, coming into the room.

Emmie managed to look up at the man her father had taken on as a partner.

"You and I need to talk," she managed.

"I agree." Josh sat down on the sofa with the lawyer, facing her.

"I know my father thought highly of you. He wrote to me and told me you were the new foreman. However, I didn't find out until today that you actually became my father's partner."

"Les explained to me that your father wanted to tell you about our partnership when he introduced us, and I'm sorry it didn't happen that way."

"So am I," she agreed sadly. "I just find it hard to believe that he took on a partner."

"Your father and I had known each other for a time, and he had offered me a job a while back. I wasn't much interested in ranch work then, but I changed my mind this last year and decided to see if his offer was still good."

Wondering about his life as a gunman, Emmie watched him carefully as she asked, "What kind of work did you do before?"

Josh had known that his past would come up at some time, so he decided to tell her straight out and get it over with. "I was a bounty hunter."

"The gossip in town said you were a gunman," she challenged.

He managed a tight smile as he answered. "There were days when it was hard to tell the difference, and that's why ranching started to look good to me."

"So you're through with all that now?"

"That's right. When I came to see your father, we made the agreement that I could buy into the ranch thirty percent and stay here and work it with him."

"It was all handled legally. I took care of the paperwork," Les assured her. "Your father made a good choice in Josh. Then, when the old foreman quit, Josh took on the job."

Realizing there was no way out of the partnership, Emmie looked up at Josh and met his dark-eyed gaze straight-on. "It looks like we're going to be working together from now on, Mr. Grady."

"Since we are going to be working together, I'd appreciate it if you'd start calling me Josh," he told her.

"All right, Josh, and you can call me Emmie."

"We can meet later, if you'd like, and go over the books."

"That'll be fine." Now that the introductions were over with, she wanted some time alone.

"And if you need me for anything else, just send word into town," Les told them both.

Josh stood up to go, as did the lawyer. Emmie thanked the attorney again for all his help as she saw the two men from the house.

When she came back inside and closed the door behind her, she stood quietly in the front hall, just remembering all the laughter and love that had filled the house when her father had been alive. This was her first moment alone since they'd returned, and it was as painful as she'd feared it would be. Needing the sanctuary of her bedroom, Emmie hurried upstairs and locked herself in her room. She was glad Miss Harriet and Millie were in rooms at the other end of the hall. At that moment, she needed all the privacy she could get as she dealt with the harsh truth of her father's death.

# Chapter Seven

Josh left the house and headed back to the stable to check on the stallion. He found Burley there waiting for him.

"How'd things go up at the house?" Burley asked.

"Hank hadn't told her I was his partner yet, so she was upset when she learned about that."

"I'll bet she was," Burley sympathized. "She and her pa were real close. These next few days will be rough, but she loves this place as much as he did, so I think she'll make it all right."

"Let's hope so," Josh said, wondering how difficult it was going to be to get things done with Emmie around.

Emmie spent some time alone in her room, getting freshened up and changing out of her traveling clothes. She took out a shirt, a pair of pants, and her boots—the attire she always wore on the ranch—and managed to smile as she got dressed. Her father had never criticized her for dressing so practically.

He knew she wanted to work hard when she was there, and he encouraged her.

Emmie was always glad her mother hadn't been there to see her dressed this way. She would have been harsh in her criticism of her daughter's choices. She would never have permitted her to wear pants, for that was something a lady just didn't do. But Emmie had long known that deep down in her heart, she had no interest in being a lady. She loved ranch life and belonged here. Feeling a little more like herself now, she brushed out her hair and tied it back with a simple ribbon before going down the hall to her father's bedroom.

Emmie let herself in and stood just inside the door for a moment, looking around. She'd feared Kate might have cleaned his room out, and she was relieved to find that the housekeeper hadn't touched anything. Her father's gun and holster were on the dresser, along with his razor and other personal items.

Emmie moved farther into the room and closed the door behind her. Needing this time to accept what she could no longer hide from, she went to sit on his bed. It was then that she saw on the nightstand her father's favorite tintype, a picture of the two of them together. Tears welled up in her eyes, and she grabbed his pillow to have something to hug. Her father's scent surrounded her then, and thoughts of his horrible death assailed her. No longer able to control the sorrow she'd been struggling so hard to keep under control, she gave in to her grief.

It was some time later when she finally pulled herself together enough to leave his room. She went back to her own bedroom to bathe her face with cool water before going downstairs. She hadn't seen Millie or Miss Harriet and thought they were probably lying down. She found Kate in the kitchen.

"Did you get some rest?" Kate asked as Emmie joined her there.

"A little." She sighed. "Kate, I wanted to ask you . . . where is Papa buried? I need to see his grave."

Kate gave her a sympathetic look. "You know how much he liked the view from out back? Well, Josh and the boys thought that would be the best place for him."

Emmie smiled sadly, remembering all the times growing up when she'd sat with her father on the low rise, staring out across their endless acres, talking about the future of the ranch. "He did love it there."

"Yes, he did," Kate assured her.

"If Millie or Miss Harriet comes looking for me, tell them I'll be back in a little while."

She didn't say any more as she left the house and made her way to her father's final resting spot. The marker was a simple cross with his name on it, and she stood there in silence looking down at it, remembering what a wonderful, vibrant man he'd been.

"I'm here, Papa," she said softly. "I came home just like you wanted me to, and I'm going to do what you wanted me to do. I'm going to run the Rocking R."

She waited in silence, half expecting to hear an

answer from him, but there was only the faint sound of the warm breeze blowing across the land.

Emmie lifted her gaze to stare out across the endless miles of the Rocking R. It was a beautiful sight, and she was proud of what her father had accomplished. He'd made the ranch successful, and she was going to honor all his hard work and determination by keeping it that way.

After all, she told herself again, she was her father's daughter. She could do this. Wanting to spend time with her father, she sat down to savor the peace of the moment. Emmie knew she had much to be thankful for. His love and the faith he'd had in her were the best legacy of all.

Millie had taken her time unpacking and changing her clothes, and then had rested for a while. When she got up, she was eager to go exploring. She left her bedroom and stopped at the chaperone's room first to see if Miss Harriet wanted to go along, but the older woman didn't answer her knock. Curious, Millie peeked inside to find her sound asleep in bed. The arduous trip had obviously taken its toll on her, so Millie quietly closed the door and went downstairs by herself, hoping to find Emmie. She was surprised when she found no sign of her friend or Kate. Thinking Emmie might have gone out to the stable to speak with the ranch hands, she headed there to see if she could find her.

Steve had been working, shoeing a horse, when he saw her coming, and he stopped to enjoy the view. The blond-haired Millie was one sweet-looking woman, and he liked the way she moved. When she reached the stable, he was there to greet her, eyeing her with open interest. "Afternoon, Miss Millie."

"Hello," she returned, smiling a little uncertainly at the young cowboy who was so openly looking her over. "Have you seen Emmie? She's not up at the house, and I was hoping she could show me around."

"I saw her walking back toward her father's grave," he offered. "It's behind the house a ways."

"Thank you." She started off in the direction he'd indicated.

"And if she don't want to show you around, I'll be glad to," he called out, thinking there was a lot he'd like to show her.

Steve watched her until she'd moved out of sight before returning to his work.

As soon as Millie had reached the back of the house, she saw Emmie in the distance, sitting on the ground near the grave. She went to join her friend there.

"It's beautiful up here," Millie said quietly as she looked out across the vast Texas landscape.

Emmie smiled up at her friend. She'd seen Millie coming and was glad for her company. "My father and I used to come up here to just sit and talk. It was one of our favorite places."

"I can understand why," Millie said, glad to see Emmie was smiling a bit. She knew there was no easy or fast way to deal with grief, but Emmie seemed to have found some peace here.

"Sit down."

"I think I will, but it looks like you're better dressed for it," Millie said, taking care with her skirt as she sat beside her friend. "Do you always wear pants when you're on the ranch?"

"Yes, but I never let my mother know. She would be outraged. No lady would ever think of dressing this way."

Millie grinned at her. "Did you ever really want to be a lady?"

Emmie gave her a conspiratorial grin. "No."

"I thought so!"

They both laughed.

"Oh, that felt good."

"What?"

"Laughing," Emmie told her.

They both smiled and went quiet for a moment.

"So, what do you think of the Wild West?" Emmie asked, interested in Millie's first impression.

Millie looked around and grinned. "Everybody talks about how big Texas is—well, they're right. It is big. When you're used to city life, this is quite a change. Aren't you afraid you'll get bored after a while? I mean, a visit once a year is one thing, but to think about living here permanently . . ."

"The ranch hands appreciate days like these. It is quiet right now, but that won't last long. You'll see. There's always something happening on the ranch."

They stayed there for a while longer, and then Emmie offered, "Would you like to take a look around?"

"You're ready to give me the grand tour?"

"That's right, but it won't be anything like touring the Continent."

"You're right. It's going to be better."

They got up and started back. Emmie pointed out the bunkhouse and the small house near it that was the foreman's. They went to the stable next to look at some of the horses. The black stallion was still in the corral, and they stopped to get a look at him.

Steve saw them and came out to talk to them. "That's Buck."

"Buck?" Emmie asked, wondering at the horse's name.

"That's what Josh named him this afternoon. The stallion bucked Josh off a few times, and that don't usually happen," he explained.

Emmie could believe that. Josh didn't look like the kind of man who gave up easily. "Tomorrow we'll need two horses. I want to show Millie around the place."

"I don't reckon you want me to saddle up Buck for you?"

"No," Emmie said, and then she looked at Millie with a grin. "Not unless you'd like to ride him?"

"I think I need a less spirited mount," Millie said. "I wouldn't last very long on a horse like Buck."

"Not many of us would," Emmie agreed.

"Just let one of us know what time you want to ride out, and we'll have two all saddled up for you."

"Thanks, Steve. We'll see you in the morning."

"I get the feeling there's not much your foreman can't handle," Millie said as they made their way back up to the house. "What have you found out about him?"

"Not a lot, other than that everything was done legally regarding the partnership, and my father trusted him. Although . . ."

"Although what?"

"You remember how the storekeeper in town said he was a gunman?"

"Is he?" Millie's eyes widened at the thought.

"Well . . . Josh admitted he was a bounty hunter. You know, the kind of gunman who goes after wanted men and brings them in."

Millie was fascinated. "I wonder how he got involved in that?"

"I didn't ask, and I don't know that I want to find out. He's left that behind him, and that's fine with me. We've got to work together."

"You said 'we,'" Millie said softly. "So you're coming to accept that you have a partner now?"

Emmie sighed. "I don't really have a choice."

"You know, he might be your guardian angel, even though you don't realize it just yet."

"A bounty hunter/gunman is my guardian angel?" She looked at her friend as if she were crazy.

"I've heard all your stories about the Wild West. What if there really was some kind of trouble, and you were out here all alone?"

"I can use a gun," Emmie declared. "My father taught me."

"And so can your Josh," her friend said.

"He's not 'my' Josh."

"All right, let me put it this way: so can your partner, and I'll bet he's a better shot than you are."

Emmie always liked a challenge. She glanced over at her friend, a spark of defiance in her eyes. "Have you ever handled a gun?"

"No!" She shuddered visibly at the thought.

"Well, if you're going to be out here in the Wild West, I think you'd better learn how to use one."

"Are you serious?" Millie was shocked and intrigued at the same time.

"Tomorrow you're going to start learning how to shoot."

Millie was quiet for a moment as she considered the prospect of actually learning how to use a gun. "Do you think I can do it?"

"I guess we'll find out. We'll have to get you some different clothes to wear if I'm going to transform you into a cowgirl."

"I've never worn pants like you've got on," Millie said. "Are they comfortable?"

"Yes, but if you don't want to wear pants, I have a split riding skirt you can have."

"I'll try anything once," Millie declared. "Has Miss Harriet seen you dressed this way yet?"

"No, not yet."

"It'll be interesting to hear what she has to say."

"Maybe we can convince her to dress for ranch work, too," Emmie said with a grin, trying to imagine the older woman out working stock dressed like a ranch hand.

They both laughed at the idea.

"I don't think that will go over very well with her," Millie responded.

"You're probably right."

They lingered there a little longer before returning to the house for the evening.

# Chapter Eight

$\mathscr{I}$t was long after dark when Josh finally finished working in the stable and started up to the main house. He wanted to check the books and make sure all the paperwork was caught up. The house was dark, so he let himself in, not wanting to disturb anyone. He went straight to the study and closed the door. He lit the lamp and settled in at the desk. Tired as he was, he hoped he could finish quickly and call it a night.

For Emmie, the day had been long and exhausting, both emotionally and physically, but she was finding comfort in being home at the ranch. She had spent the evening at the house with Millie and Miss Harriet, enjoying the delicious dinner Kate had made for them, and then they had all retired early.

Emmie had fallen asleep as soon as she'd gone to bed, and it was much later that night when she was jarred awake by the sound of someone moving about downstairs. She got out of bed and quickly opened her bedroom door to check. She thought Millie or Miss Harriet might need something. She was surprised when she found the house was completely dark.

Uneasy, she quickly donned her robe and silently went into her father's bedroom to get his gun. She didn't know who was downstairs, but she intended to find out.

Gun in hand, Emmie carefully made her way down the steps and looked around. She was surprised to see light coming from beneath her father's closed office door, and her first thought was that someone was trying to steal the cash kept there. Her father had always locked what cash he had on hand in a small safe hidden in the office. She was frightened, but knew she had no time to go for help. Yelling would do her no good, since there was no one within earshot who could come to her aid in time.

Taking a deep breath, Emmie tightened her grip on the gun and in one smooth move threw the door open and rushed in to confront the thief.

"Hold it right where you are!" she ordered.

Josh had been hard at work when the door flew open. Startled, he looked up to find himself staring down the barrel of Hank's revolver—but Hank definitely wasn't the one holding it.

Shocked to find Josh sitting at her father's desk, Emmie just stood there staring at him.

Josh tried to stay calm, but, in truth, he was furious. He was usually on the other end of a loaded gun. "I hope you know how to use that gun."

"Oh!" Completely embarrassed, Emmie lowered the revolver. "It's you."

"And just who did you think it would be?" he demanded, glaring up at her. It was then that he noticed her robe had come untied and was gaping open, giving him a clear view of the pale blue silk nightgown clinging to her womanly curves. With her dark hair down and loose about her shoulders, she looked more like a seductress than Hank's little girl. Josh immediately grew irritated with himself over the direction of his thoughts.

Completely unaware of her state of undress, Emmie heard the anger in his voice and returned it, challenging, "I heard a noise down here and came to check on it. When I saw the light coming from under the door, I thought someone was robbing us."

Josh deliberately glanced down at the books spread out before him on the desktop before looking up at her again. It was then that he spotted Millie rushing down the steps out in the hall.

"The only thing anyone's getting robbed of tonight is sleep," he growled, nodding toward the door.

Emmie turned to see Millie hurrying toward her, wide-eyed with fear.

"What is it? What's wrong?" Millie demanded as she entered the study. She was shocked to find that Emmie was holding a gun.

"Nothing's wrong," Emmie quickly assured her. "I didn't know Josh was here working, so when a noise downstairs woke me up, I came down to see what was going on."

"Did you really need to carry a gun?" Millie asked, unnerved.

"You never know."

"Well, thank heaven it was only Josh," Millie said, relieved, giving him a quick smile. Then she realized Emmie's state of undress. "Emmie! Fasten your robe!"

Emmie glanced down at herself and was mortified. She quickly turned away, setting the gun aside so she could retie the belt to her robe.

"Ladies?" Miss Harriet's call from the top of the staircase drew their attention. "Is everything all right?"

Millie stepped out into the hallway to reassure her.

"Very well," the chaperone said, sounding calmer once she'd heard the explanation. "Good night, then." She turned away from the railing and went back to her room, murmuring, "I suppose this kind of thing goes on often around here."

"Well, now that I know you're all right, I'm going back to bed, too," Millie declared. "Good night, Josh."

"Good night," he told her.

"Are you coming?" she asked Emmie as she started from the study.

"I'll be along."

Millie could sense the tension between Josh and Emmie, but she said nothing more as she left them alone.

Once Millie had disappeared upstairs, Emmie glanced back at Josh to find him still watching her, his expression unreadable. She felt more than a little awkward. They hadn't gotten off to the best start. First she'd discovered he was the partner she never knew she had, and just now, in her haste to be vigilant, she could have taken a shot at him.

It was all very hard for her, and finding him at her father's desk—working on the books, a job that her father always spent so much time on—just made it that much more difficult. This room had always been Hank's sanctuary. His presence there reminded her once again that her father truly was gone.

"I'm sorry I came barging in on you the way I did," Emmie said, swallowing her pride.

For the first time, Josh managed a wry half smile at her. "You're definitely Hank's daughter."

"Why do you say that?"

"You're not afraid of a fight—and I'd say you know how to handle a gun."

"He thought it was important I learn how in case I needed to defend myself."

"He was right. You never know what you're going to run into in these parts."

"Yeah—like you in the study in the middle of the night," she said, finally relaxing a bit and managing a smile. "Do you do this often?"

"Work on the books this late?" he asked. At her nod, he explained, "I've been trying to get caught up, but it's been so busy, I haven't had a lot of time to devote to the paperwork. From now on, I'll let you know before I come up to the house. I didn't mean to scare you tonight." He was glad she'd covered herself again. He didn't need such a potent distraction.

"I know, and I appreciate what you're doing. When you get time, I want to learn how to handle the bookwork, too. I think it's important I learn everything there is to know about the ranch."

"Your father never went over any of this with you?"

"No. I'm sure he thought we had plenty of time to worry about that later." Pain flared within her. "And he did like to be in control of all the finances."

"I understand," he said sympathetically. "As soon as things calm down around here, I'll start showing you how he kept the books."

"That'll be good. We've got a ranch to run."

"Yes, we do."

"I'll see you in the morning." She started from the room.

"Good night."

Josh watched as she picked up her father's gun and left the study, closing the door behind her. He gave a shake of his head and pushed the image of her with her robe unfastened from his mind as he turned back to the books. It had been a very interesting day—and he wondered if Hank had known what he was doing when he'd insisted Emmie had to live at the ranch to gain her inheritance. Working together wasn't going to be easy.

Emmie was more than a little embarrassed as she went back to bed. She'd thought she was being brave when she'd grabbed the gun to confront the intruder. She'd thought she was protecting the ranch, but all she'd done was make a fool of herself. And then to have her robe fall open . . . She was so embarrassed. Closing her eyes, she sought sleep. If today was any example of what her life was going to be like on the Rocking R, she was going to need all the rest she could get.

Millie was up early, eagerly looking forward to the day to come. Emmie's promise to take her for a ride and teach her how to shoot excited her. She knew her parents would frown on such unladylike behavior, but she had no intention of telling them.

Adventurous spirit that she was, Millie couldn't wait to ride out and get a real look at the ranch. The carriage ride from town had given her an idea of just how big the Rocking R really was, but actually covering the miles on horseback would be even more exciting.

Last night had given her a whole new perspective on learning how to use a gun, too. When Emmie had first offered, she'd found the thought of learning to shoot entertaining, but after seeing Emmie in the study with a gun in her hand, she had changed her opinion. Her friend had thought someone was robbing them, and she had done what she'd needed to do to protect her home. That wasn't entertainment; that was survival.

Millie wondered if Emmie was up yet. She was just about to dress and go knock on her friend's bedroom door when a knock came at her own door.

"Who is it?"

"It's me," Emmie announced. "I've got something for you."

"What?" Millie hurried to open the door and found her friend standing there with an armload of clothes and a pair of riding boots.

"Here—see what fits and meet me downstairs. We'll have breakfast and go for our ride before it gets too hot."

"I'll be right down."

Millie took the clothes from her and quickly set about sorting through them. She found a pair of pants just like the ones Emmie had on and decided to wear them, along with one of the simple shirts. It didn't take her long to change, and after pulling on the boots, she turned to study herself in the mirror over the dresser.

Millie had to smile as she stared at her own reflection. She'd always considered herself a bit of a tomboy, and today she was going to be really adventurous. She grinned mischievously and grabbed a ribbon to tie her blond hair back out of the way before hurrying down to find Emmie.

"Don't you look like you belong here," Emmie teased when Millie entered the dining room.

"Do you really think so?" she asked, joining her friend at the table.

"Absolutely. How do you like wearing pants?"

"It's rather liberating, don't you think?"

"Very."

They grinned at each other, knowing how the

girls back East would talk if they ever saw them dressed this way.

"Well, eat your breakfast. We've got a lot to do today," Emmie told her.

Millie was surprised by the amount of food Kate had made for them. There were eggs and biscuits and bacon. "Is breakfast like this every day?"

"No, sometimes she makes hotcakes, and they're wonderful!"

"If she feeds us this way all the time, we're going to need bigger pants." Millie laughed.

"We're going to need all the breakfast we can eat to get us through the day. You'll see."

They dug in, enjoying every bite of the delicious, homemade fare.

"Emmie . . . I wanted to ask you . . . did you and Josh get everything settled last night?" Millie had recognized that there was tension between them when she'd left the study, and she'd been wondering how the confrontation had turned out.

Emmie looked over at her. "Yes. I don't think I'll be breaking down the study door in the middle of the night anymore."

"Is it safe for us to ride out alone?" Millie had heard the story of why Emmie's mother had gone back East to live.

"We'll be fine. There hasn't been any trouble around here for some time now."

"Good. Where are we going?"

"I want to take you out to one of my favorite places on the ranch."

"Where is it?"

"You'll see. I want to surprise you."

"I love surprises."

"I know."

They finished eating and went out to get their horses.

# Chapter Nine

Josh had been working hard out on the range checking stock since just after sunup. He rode back in to find Steve in the stable telling one of the other hands that Emmie and Millie had gone for a ride.

"How long ago did they leave?" Josh demanded, breaking into their conversation.

"A couple of hours," Steve answered.

"Did they say where they were going?"

"Emmie just wanted to show her friend around the ranch."

"And you haven't heard from them since?" Josh was growing worried.

"No. Emmie knows her way around."

Josh was irritated. When he'd become a partner in the ranch, he'd never dreamed he'd end up running it with Hank's young daughter. He had enough to worry about on the Rocking R without having to keep track of females from back East. Emmie might know her way around, but this was a hard country, and there was no telling what kind of trouble two women out there riding all alone might run into.

"I'll be back," he snarled, mounting up again.

"Where are you going?"

"I'm going hunting."

"Hunting?" Steve was confused and didn't understand why the boss seemed so angry. "What are you hunting?"

"Lost females," he growled, not the least bit happy about having to waste time looking for Emmie.

"You want some help?"

"No. Keep working. I'll find them."

With that, he rode out.

Steve watched Josh go and knew that the foreman would find the women, for Josh was one of the best trackers he'd ever known.

Emmie and Millie had been riding for quite a while as Emmie showed her friend around the Rocking R. When it neared midday and the sun was blazing down, Emmie could tell Millie was getting hot and tired.

"Warm enough for you?" Emmie asked.

"Yes," Millie answered without hesitation. "I'm glad you loaned me a hat." She definitely appreciated the Stetson she was wearing.

"Next trip into town, we'll get you one of your own."

"Good. I'm going to need it."

"Come on," Emmie encouraged, urging her horse forward. "There's one more place I want to show you—and I think you're really going to like it."

Millie followed her lead, wondering how sore she was going to be the following day after sitting in the saddle so long. They rode on for another mile or two before Emmie turned down an overgrown path. Millie followed after her, but wondered where in the world they were going.

And then she found out.

"This is my favorite place on the ranch."

"No wonder you wanted to come here!" Millie said excitedly as they reined in on the bank of a small lake. "It's heavenly!"

"I thought you might like it," Emmie said as they dismounted. "I used to swim here when I was little."

"It's so hot today, I wouldn't mind jumping in there right now," Millie said as she walked down to the water's edge.

Emmie shot her friend a mischievous look. "We are all alone."

Millie looked back at her, a twinkle in her eye. "Really? Are you sure? You think we could—"

"Come on! Let's cool off!"

Millie glanced around a bit nervously. She'd never undressed in such an open place before. "How much should I take off?"

"Nobody's going to see us. It's safe." Emmie set about removing her pants, shirt, and boots, and then she ran into the cool, welcoming water wearing only her underclothes.

Millie couldn't believe her friend was being so bold, but when Emmie started splashing around like a little child, she couldn't resist. She shed her riding clothes, too, and charged into the lake to join her, squealing in delight at the chill of the water.

\* \* \*

Josh hadn't had any idea where to look for Emmie and Millie as he'd started out. There was no telling where they might have gone, and that was what worried him.

He'd been riding, trying to track them down, for almost half an hour when he heard what he thought was the sound of a woman screaming off in the distance. It sounded like trouble, and he grew even more worried. Josh drew his gun as he urged his horse to a gallop, heading in that direction, fearing the worst. He charged through the brush as he heard more shouts coming from ahead of him, and then abruptly reined in as he reached the water's edge. It was Emmie and Millie, but they weren't in trouble. They were almost completely stripped of their clothing, and they were frolicking in the water.

"What do you think you're doing?" he demanded, unable to look away from the sight of the two women standing waist-deep in the water, completely soaked.

Their hair was unbound and down around their shoulders, and they were wearing only their dripping wet, clinging undergarments. If ever there were two women out looking for trouble, it was these two. He wasn't sure what he was going to do with them.

Emmie and Millie both shrieked as he came upon them so suddenly, his gun drawn. Then they realized just how exposed they were and quickly sank down in the water up to their chins to shield themselves from his view.

"What are you doing here?" Emmie countered, completely surprised by Josh's appearance.

Josh was swearing under his breath as he holstered his gun.

"I'm here looking for you!" he growled. He couldn't decide whether he was relieved to find them safe or aggravated to see them swimming practically nude. "Steve said you'd ridden out early and he hadn't heard from you since."

"There was no need for you to come after us," Emmie protested. "I know my way around the Rocking R."

"From now on, take someone with you, or at least let someone know where you're going," he ordered.

Emmie bristled at his arrogant, commanding tone. "I can take care of myself. I don't need you telling me what to do! You're not my father!"

"I'm well aware of that," Josh returned sarcastically as his gaze went over her.

Emmie blushed, embarrassed by his unexpected appearance and by the way he was looking at her. "And you're not my boss, either!"

"I am the foreman of this ranch," he reminded her, "and I don't have the time to waste searching for you every time you get lost."

Millie stared up at the darkly handsome foreman who looked so very attractive sitting on his horse. She thought it was thoughtful of him to care enough to come looking for them, but it was obvious her friend wasn't of the same opinion.

"We weren't lost," Emmie insisted heatedly.

"Good. Then you know how to find your way back to the ranch." Josh had had enough of arguing with her. Hank used to talk about how much Emmie was like him, and Josh recognized his friend's stubborn streak in her. Somehow he had to make Emmie see that they had to get along for the sake of the ranch.

"Yes, I know my way home."

"Ladies," Josh said sarcastically, tipping his hat to them.

Without another word, he wheeled his horse around and rode off. He tried to turn his thoughts back to ranch business, but the image of the two girls, Emmie in particular, frolicking in the water so scantily clad was burned into his mind.

Josh frowned, angry with himself for his reaction. He couldn't believe that Emmie had been there only two days and he'd already seen her in a revealing nightgown and now almost naked. She was one of the most beautiful women he'd ever known. There was no denying it, but she was also Hank's daughter, and now his partner. Somehow he was going to have to find a way to keep his mind on the ranch when they were together. It wasn't going to be easy, for he knew they were going to be together a lot. Josh tried once more to focus on work as he kept riding. He had a lot more to get done yet that day.

Millie had remained quiet through the whole conversation, and she looked over at Emmie now as Josh disappeared from sight. She wondered at her friend's reaction to his unexpected appearance. It was obvious to her that he'd been concerned about them, and she wondered why his concern had made Emmie so testy. She decided to bring the question up once Emmie had calmed down. "I guess it's safe for us to get out of the water now."

"I guess," Emmie said, still irritated

They waded out and quickly pulled their clothes on over their wet undergarments. It wasn't easy or comfortable.

"That was fun. It did cool me off," Millie said with a smile, wanting to lighten Emmie's mood. "But I'm not sure I'm going to like the ride home, still being wet this way."

Emmie grinned back at her. "Don't worry. We'll dry out real quick once we start moving."

They mounted up to return to the ranch.

"Emmie . . ." Millie began tentatively.

"What?" Emmie glanced at her friend as she rode along beside her at a leisurely pace.

"Why did you get so angry with Josh?"

"What do you mean?"

"You were really rough on him, telling him he wasn't your father or your boss."

"He isn't."

"I'm sure he's well aware of that. The only reason he came out here looking for us was because he was worried."

"But we weren't lost," Emmie declared.

"He knows that, too, now, but he might have thought we'd run into some kind of trouble when we were gone so long."

Emmie sighed, still trying to understand her own feelings about her new partner. "It's just that . . ."

"What?"

"Well, I understand he's the foreman, but learning he was my father's partner and all . . . it takes some getting used to."

"I thought you two were getting along all right after last night."

"I thought we were, too. He just surprised me today, checking up on me like that."

"Yes, but think about it. Josh was only trying to help."

"But I didn't need——"

"I know, I know." Millie smiled. "You didn't need any help, but be glad you've got it. What if we really had been in trouble and nobody even cared enough to notice we were missing until it was too late?"

Emmie begrudgingly had to admit to herself that Millie had a point. She halfheartedly conceded, "You're right."

"You know what you should have done?" Millie began, trying not to smile and let on what she was about to say.

"What?"

"You should have asked him to come swimming with us instead of sending him packing."

"Millie!" Emmie gasped, completely shocked by the idea.

"He's awfully handsome in a rugged sort of way, don't you think?" Millie teased, grinning at her friend's reaction.

"Well, yes."

"Maybe one of these days he *will* come swimming with us. Think how much fun that would be!"

"You are a wild woman!"

"Isn't that why you like me? Because we're so much alike?"

Millie started laughing, and finally Emmie did, too.

"All right. You win. I'll apologize to him," Emmie said.

"Good."

"But I don't know that I'll tell him about your idea."

They laughed again.

"You're going to have to find a way to make your partnership work. It was important to your father. He obviously trusted Josh and admired him, or he wouldn't have let him buy into the Rocking R."

Emmie knew her friend was right. "Maybe if I knew more about Josh and how they came to know each other . . . My Papa would never have taken on just anyone as a partner."

"You're right. He wouldn't have, knowing that you were going to inherit the ranch if anything happened to him. Talk to Josh. See what you can find out about him. It'll make things easier for the two of you if you understand each other, and you're going to have to do that to keep the Rocking R going."

"I am so glad you made the trip with me. Think how lonely I'd be if you weren't here."

"I'm glad I came, too," Millie said. This was a difficult time for Emmie. Everything had changed, and her life was never going to be the same again.

"This isn't going to be easy, you know," Emmie said with a tight smile as she prepared to humble herself. She had a good idea of what Josh thought of her right now, and it wasn't flattering.

"It'll be all right. You'll see," Millie countered. "I get the feeling he's a good man."

For the rest of the ride back, Emmie prepared

herself to seek Josh out and apologize. She would do it. It was time for her to grow up and take on her responsibilities.

Emmie found she was almost disappointed when, upon returning, they discovered Josh hadn't made it back to the ranch yet. Knowing she'd have to wait until later, Emmie led Millie up to the house to tell Miss Harriet about their adventure.

# Chapter Ten

*A*fter his encounter with Emmie earlier that day, the last thing Josh wanted to do was go up to the house and possibly see her again, but he had no choice. He had more work to do on the books and it couldn't wait. He ate dinner with the hands and then went up to the main house to get it over with.

He'd been thinking about Emmie most of the afternoon. He realized that although she had spent every summer with her father, there was still a lot she didn't know about ranch life, and it was going to be up to him to teach her. He grimaced at the thought. Judging from their encounter today, he had the feeling that she wasn't going to listen to anything he had to say.

Josh was relieved when Kate came to the door to let him in and he saw no sign of Emmie downstairs. He went straight into the study to get to work. His peace and quiet didn't last long, though, for a knock came at the door shortly after he'd settled in.

"Josh, it's me—Emmie."

"Come on in," he called out.

A moment later, she opened the door and stepped into the study, closing the door behind her.

Josh hadn't seen her dressed in pants and boots before, although he'd heard some of the hands talking about her. He found himself staring at Emmie openly now, his gaze going over the shapely curves of her hips and legs. Josh couldn't believe it. First Emmie had shown up in the study in a nightgown, then he'd found her swimming in the lake, and now here she was wearing pants. He hoped whatever she had to say, she would say fast and leave. He had work to do.

"You're not carrying your gun tonight?" he remarked. The truth was that she didn't need one to distract him.

Emmie saw the way Josh was staring at her and suddenly felt a little flustered and unsure of herself. "No. I didn't think it was necessary."

"Good."

"Josh, I wanted to talk to you for a moment," she announced.

"All right."

He was still watching her, and the look in his eyes sent a shiver of sensual awareness through her. Emmie had never felt that way before, and her reaction to him made her nervous.

Quickly, she explained, "My father didn't mind if I dressed this way. He understood that I wanted to work right alongside him. Skirts aren't very practical—they get in the way."

His gaze raked boldly over her again. "I see." He waited for her to go on.

"And in case you were wondering," she went on, "Millie and I did find our way back to the ranch."

She had hoped the last comment would make him smile. It didn't work. His expression remained serious as he stared up at her.

"What was it you wanted?" he asked, suddenly growing annoyed with himself. He forced his thoughts back to business.

"Well . . ." Emmie swallowed her pride as she sat down in the chair before the desk. "I want to apologize."

He frowned in surprise. "You do?"

"Yes, I'm sorry for the way I acted this afternoon. It was nice of you to be concerned about us."

Josh could tell it was hard for her to apologize to him, and he finally relaxed and grinned. She not only had her father's stubbornness, she had his pride, too. "That hurt, didn't it?"

She was surprised by Josh's unexpected show of humor, and she couldn't help smiling back at him. "You have no idea."

The tension went out of the moment as they finally both relaxed in each other's company.

Josh looked at her. "I know you've spent a lot of time here on the Rocking R and you do know your way around, but things aren't always as peaceful as they seem. Did you take your gun with you today?"

"Yes, but I left it up on the bank when we got in the water."

"What if someone else had ridden up on you? What would you have done?"

Emmie was suitably chastened. "I just wanted to show Millie around, and then it got so hot we decided to stop and cool off for a while. Papa used to take me swimming there when I was young."

"I understand, but in case you didn't realize it, you're not ten years old anymore."

"Oh . . ." This time she did blush at the knowing look he gave her.

"And," he added, "there's probably a lot that's gone on here at the ranch that your father didn't tell you about."

"Like what?"

"Lately there's been some rustling going on. That's why, when I heard what sounded like screaming up at the lake, I thought you were in some kind of trouble."

"We'll be more careful from now on."

"Good. I want you safe."

His words surprised her. "Thank you."

He nodded, then tried to focus on his work again. After a moment, he asked, "Do you have time to go over some of the paperwork with me tonight?"

"All right."

"And tomorrow I'd like to take you out and show you some of the changes your father was making."

Emmie genuinely appreciated his offer. "How early do you want to leave?"

"How early can you be ready?"

"Whenever you say."

"Let's plan on riding out right after sunup. The earlier we start, the earlier we'll get back."

With that he spread out the books on the desk.

"Now, you might as well move your chair over here by me, so you can see what I'm doing."

She did as she was told, and Josh immediately wondered if his suggestion had been a mistake. Still, he set about explaining the way her father had handled the finances. Though he was concentrating hard on the books, he was still completely aware of her sitting so close beside him.

It was almost an hour later that Emmie looked up at Josh and gave a slow shake of her head.

"I'm not sure which is harder—breaking a horse or keeping all these numbers straight." She sighed.

Josh thought about Buck and had to smile. "I'm not sure either. You're father told me you had a head for figures, and I have to agree with him. You catch on pretty quick. Between the two of us, we should be able to keep the books up-to-date now."

Emmie stood up to leave. "I'm going to call it a night, since I have to be ready early in the morning."

"Good night." He watched her leave the study and then finished off the last of the paperwork before quitting for the night, too.

Ned Barton was exhausted as he fled across the night-shrouded land, but he couldn't stop to rest.

He had to keep going.

He had to keep moving.

He couldn't let his guard down, not even for a moment, for the men who were tracking him would find him and drag him back to prison.

And he wasn't going back.

He would die before he'd ever let them take him

in again. The endless months of backbreaking labor had hardened him even more. He'd had only one thing on his mind as he'd made his escape. It was the one thing that had kept him going all this time.

Revenge.

He was going to find the bounty hunter who'd killed his brother and turned him in to the law, and he was going to make him pay for what he'd done.

Ned already had his plan made. He'd had a lot of time during the eighteen-hour days of hard labor to figure out just what he was going to do to Josh Grady, and now it was just a matter of time before he had his revenge. It might take a while, but that didn't matter. He was going to get even with the bounty hunter.

In spite of his exhaustion and weakness, Ned smiled to himself in the darkness and kept moving.

He was a driven man.

# Chapter Eleven

$\mathcal{E}$mmie didn't get a lot of rest that night, for she was afraid she would oversleep. As the eastern sky started to brighten, she was already up and dressed, ready to head out.

Emmie was looking forward to spending this time with Josh and getting to know him better. Right now he was still a mystery to her.

She left a note for Millie and Miss Harriet so they would know where she'd gone and then went out to meet Josh at the stable.

Josh had already saddled up the horses and fixed a lunch to take with them. He knew they were going to be gone for a large part of the day.

He was waiting for her when she left the house. As he watched her coming his way, he realized that from a distance she could pass for a young ranch hand. Wearing pants and a Stetson, with her hair tied up, she showed no outer sign of her femininity, but he knew better. She might act as tough as a hand, but she was all female—he had no doubt about that.

"Good morning," Emmie greeted him as she

walked up to where he was waiting for her with the horses. She noticed right away that he hadn't shaved that morning, but the shadow of the day's growth of beard only added to his rugged good looks.

"Yes, it is," he agreed.

There wasn't a cloud in the sky, and the air was cooler than it had been the last few days.

"Are you ready?" she asked.

"If you are."

"Let's go."

He handed her the reins to her horse and then quickly mounted up on his own.

Josh rode out slightly ahead of her, and Emmie found herself watching him. Broad-shouldered and lean, his gun resting easy on his hip, he rode as if born to the saddle, and she found it hard to look away. He was a handsome man. There was no denying it.

Josh intrigued her. During the night, when she'd lain awake in bed, he'd been in her thoughts. There was so much she didn't know about him. Today she hoped that she'd be able to learn where he'd come from and how he'd met her father. She wanted to find out, too, what had led him to become a bounty hunter. It was no doubt a very dangerous job and not for the faint of heart. She urged her horse to a quicker pace to catch up with him.

They rode across the Rocking R, passing vast herds of cattle surrounded by the seemingly endless plains. After several hours, Josh reined in on top of a low rise.

"This is what I wanted to show you," Josh said.

"Your father was worried after the drought we had last year, so he had the creek dammed up to make a new watering hole for the stock."

Emmie was impressed by the sight of their cattle grazing near the muddy water. "He was a smart man. Let's just hope we don't have any more dry spells like that anytime soon."

Josh looked over at her and tried not to laugh as he asked, "Are you ready for a swim? I don't think the stock will mind."

She had been getting hot as the morning went on, but this muddy watering hole was a far cry from her special lake. She laughed at him. "No, I think I'm through swimming for a while, but you can go on in if you want." She suddenly found herself wondering what he'd look like with his shirt off.

"No, I think I'll pass."

They rode on.

"Josh . . ." She looked over at him. So far, their conversation had been confined to ranch business, and she'd learned little about him. "Tell me, how did you meet my father? It's obvious he thought highly of you or he would never have taken you on as a partner. When did you two meet?"

"It was a few years back. I was on the trail of some rustlers and I tracked them to Shotgun. They were trying to steal some of the Rocking R's stock when I caught up with them. Your father was real grateful when I brought them in. That's when he offered me a job on the ranch, but at the time I wasn't ready to quit what I was doing. He told me the job would always be open if I ever changed my mind."

"How did you get started being a bounty hunter? It's such a dangerous job."

"I've always been fast with a gun, and tracking just came naturally to me. I figured I might as well make some money doing what I was good at."

"Why did you decide to quit?" As she asked the question, she glanced over at him and noticed how his expression hardened.

"I knew after bringing in the Barton brothers that it was time to give it up."

"Who were they?"

He told her how he'd tracked them down.

"No wonder you were ready to quit."

He nodded. "I was tired of living in the saddle and never knowing when someone was going to come gunning for me. I decided it was time to settle down. When your father mentioned the financial difficulties he was facing, I had enough money to buy into the ranch. I was real glad he made me his partner. He built the Rocking R into a fine spread, and I want to work it and keep it successful to honor all his hard work. He died too soon," Josh said sadly, missing the older man who'd been such a good friend.

"Yes, he did," Emmie agreed, an ache in her heart as she thought of her father. "Much too soon."

Josh saw her pain, and understood what she was feeling. "So, tell me about your life here on the ranch. I know that when you were young there was an Indian raid, and that was when your mother decided to take you back East to live, but that's about all I know."

Emmie nodded. "I don't remember a lot about that time—just my mother dragging me away, and the fact that I didn't want to leave. I wanted to stay here with Papa. I loved him so, and I cried a lot, but my mother had had all she could stand. She'd been raised back East and couldn't live this way. She told me about the attack a few years ago. It was so traumatic for her, I can't get her to come back for a visit even now."

Josh knew how bloody the Comanche could be when they were raiding. "But you visited every year."

"It was part of the agreement my parents came to, and I'm glad it was. I always felt this was where I belonged—with my father."

"So you don't like city living."

"It's a whole different way of life, and I believe— as you said—I'm my father's daughter. Even though I spent all that time in Philadelphia, this is home."

"You're lucky to have a home."

"You didn't?" She was surprised by his comment.

"My parents died when my brother and I were young, and we stayed with some relatives for a while before striking out on our own."

"You're so lucky to have a brother."

"George is younger than me by a few years, and wilder." Josh added the last sardonically, thinking of his brother and the life he'd chosen for himself.

"How does it get wilder than being a bounty hunter?"

"George took to gambling and found out he was real good at it."

"You were a gambler, too. You were gambling with your life," she said.

"I guess I was, but I think George enjoys his gambling more."

"Do you see much of him?"

"I haven't seen him for a while now."

"Do you have any idea where he is?"

"No. He just shows up for a visit every now and then. Before I came to the Rocking R, we hardly saw each other, because I was traveling around so much."

"The closest I've got to a sibling is Millie. We've been best friends ever since my mother first took me back East."

"She is a true friend to travel all the way out here with you. I doubt there are many Eastern ladies who'd want to make that trip."

"You're right. I tried to tell everyone how wonderful ranch life is, but they only remembered my mother's story about why she left."

"It can be a hard life, but there's nothing else like it." He gazed out over the land that was now his home.

"I know." She looked over at him and smiled.

"I packed some food. Are you ready to stop and eat?" Josh asked, glancing her way to find her smiling at him, her manner completely relaxed and at ease.

"That sounds wonderful. I am hungry. I didn't eat anything this morning."

"There's a shady spot up ahead. We'll stop there and rest for a while."

They reined in and dismounted at a small grove of trees. Emmie was stiff from being so long in the saddle, and it felt wonderful to stretch.

Josh had just come around from tying up the horses when he caught sight of her. He found he couldn't look away. Only when she started to turn toward him did he grab his canteen and saddlebags off his horse and move toward her. Together they walked over to sit down in the shade.

"Here," he said, handing her the canteen.

"Thanks." She took a deep drink and then set the canteen aside. "I'm glad you thought of this. What kind of delicacy did you bring along?"

"Some bacon and two apples," he said.

"I'm so hungry, that sounds like the best lunch I've had in a long time."

"Eat up," Josh encouraged as he unwrapped the cooked bacon and handed her an apple.

Emmie didn't need any more encouragement. They ate in companionable silence.

"You're a good cook," she told him jokingly when she'd finished her share of the meal. "If you get tired of being the foreman, you could give Kate a run for her money up at the house."

"Kate's job is safe. I wouldn't last long as a cook. The boys would run me off in no time."

"They're a rowdy bunch, are they?"

"When it comes to mealtime, they are."

They were laughing when suddenly Josh's expression turned grave.

"Don't move," he said in a low, hard-edged voice. The pleasant mood of the moment suddenly changed, and she tensed as she watched his hand move slowly toward his gun.

"What . . . ?" Emmie had no idea what was wrong, but the tone of his voice and the look in his eyes told her she would do well to obey him. She froze.

"Rattler . . ."

In one swift move, Josh drew his gun and fired.

The snake was already moving to strike, but Josh's aim was true.

Emmie had always considered herself a strong-willed woman, but in that moment she couldn't help letting out a scream as she threw herself toward Josh. She found herself enveloped in the safe haven of his arms as he shoved his gun back in his holster.

"Are you all right?" he asked. He could feel her trembling against him and feared the snake had bitten her before he'd killed it. As he held her close for the first time, he realized just how fragile she really was, and something stirred within him.

Emmie nodded, not speaking for a moment as she treasured the feeling of safety that enveloped her while she was held in his strong arms. Finally, she drew a strangled breath and drew back to look up at him, forcing a wry smile.

"I'm not only glad you can cook, I'm glad you can shoot, too."

Josh gazed down at her. He'd always thought she was pretty, but at that moment he found her downright beautiful. "Being quick on the draw does come in handy sometimes."

"I'll say." She was surprised by her reaction to him and shifted away.

Irritated by his body's reaction to Emmie's nearness, Josh told himself she was Hank's daughter, and that was the end of it. He got up, needing to put some distance between them.

"Have you had enough excitement for one afternoon?" he asked as he turned to look out across the land.

"I think so." Emmie found herself staring up at him as he stood with his back to her. A shiver of sensual awareness ran through her as she gazed up at his broad shoulders and remembered what it had felt like to be held in his arms. She realized she'd never felt anything like that when Kenneth held her.

"Let's head on back then," he said. "We've got a good ride ahead of us."

Josh turned to where she was sitting and offered her a hand up. He thought she still might be a little shaky after her close call with the rattlesnake.

Emmie didn't hesitate, but put her hand in his and let him help her up. "Thanks. That was a little scary."

"Keep a watch for them. They're all over this time of the year. You might want to warn Millie, too."

"I will—and you know what?" A dangerous twinkle appeared in her eyes.

"What?" He frowned, unsure what she was up to.

"I'm going to take the snake back and show Millie just what a rattler looks like."

Josh just shook his head as Emmie went to pick up what was left of the dead snake. She came walking back, holding the mangled rattler by its tail.

"Wrap it up in this." He handed her the cloth he'd brought the food in.

She did just that, and he put it in his saddlebag before mounting up.

"Ready?"

"Let's go home," Emmie said, mounting her own horse.

Josh liked the sound of that as they started off. Emmie kept up with him, riding by his side.

"Thanks for taking the time to show me what Papa was working on."

"He loved this place—snakes and all," he told her with a half grin.

"Yes, he did," she agreed, knowing just how much the ranch had meant to her father. It had been his whole life. "I love it, too, but I'm not so sure about the rattlesnakes."

They were both laughing as they urged their horses into a gallop.

# Chapter Twelve

Millie had been the first one up after Emmie had left that morning, and she was delighted when she found the note explaining that her friend would be spending the day with Josh.

It was late afternoon, and Millie had gone up to her room to rest for a while, when she heard riders coming. She got up quickly to look out her window and saw Emmie and Josh approaching. Though she was eager to find out how their day had gone, she stayed in her room until she heard her friend come upstairs and go into her own bedroom. She wanted to be able to speak to her privately.

"Emmie?" Millie called out softly as she knocked on her friend's door.

"Come in," Emmie said.

Millie went in. "How did it go? Tell me everything. Obviously things got better between you after you apologized. You did apologize last night, didn't you?"

Emmie had to smile at her friend. "Yes, I apologized, and, yes, things have gotten better."

"Good," Millie said happily.

"It's so annoying when you're right, and you know what? It's starting to look like you were right about another thing, too," Emmie began.

"I was? What?"

"Josh may really be my guardian angel."

"What are you talking about?"

"He saved me today."

Millie was suddenly frightened for her friend. "From what?"

"A rattlesnake."

"A snake?" Millie's eyes widened at the thought.

"Yes, we stopped for lunch, and while we were eating, one came up behind me and Josh shot it."

"Oh, my God." A shiver of horror went through Millie. "Thank heaven you're all right."

"I know. I don't know what would have happened to me if he hadn't seen it in time."

"I don't even want to think about it."

"Neither do I."

Millie shuddered again.

"We brought the snake back. Do you want to see it?"

"Maybe later," Millie said with a slight grimace. "So, tell me all about your day."

They sat down together on the side of the bed, and Emmie told her of her adventures with Josh.

"I'm glad the two of you are starting to get along."

"It is a relief, since we're going to be spending so much time together." Inwardly, Emmie found she was actually looking forward to the hours she'd be spending in Josh's company. "Now, tomorrow . . ."

"What have you got planned?"

"I'm going to teach you how to use a gun."

"Are you sure?"

"After our run-in with the snake today, I think you'd better know how to fire one, at least."

"All right. I'll be ready whenever you are," Millie agreed.

When Emmie had been gone for two weeks, Kenneth went to pay a visit to Mrs. Ryan. He hadn't heard from Emmie, and he was wondering how she was doing. He had to admit to himself that he was annoyed she hadn't contacted him in any way, but he fought the feeling down. He told himself she was probably overwhelmed, getting adjusted to her new life.

Kenneth had been considering the terms of her father's will and began to wonder if living on the ranch might not be worth it in the long run. The more he'd thought about the amount of money involved, the more he thought following Emmie to Texas would probably be a good idea. Though his family was wealthy, it would be a long time before he came into his inheritance, and his tastes were expensive. He knew he had to be careful and play the role of ardent, concerned suitor as he waited in the parlor for the maid to let Sarah Ryan know of his call.

"Kenneth?" Sarah came into the parlor, delighted to see the handsome young man standing there. "This is a pleasant surprise."

"Good afternoon, Mrs. Ryan."

"Please sit down," Sarah invited.

He sat in the chair opposite the sofa where she'd taken a seat.

"To what do I owe the honor of your visit?" she asked, smiling warmly at him.

"Well, I've been missing Emmie and worrying about her. I wondered if you've heard from her yet?"

"Oh, yes, I have. She sent me a telegram letting me know they'd arrived safely." She looked at him, delighted to know he was concerned about her daughter. "I'm sure you'll be hearing from her soon."

"I hope so," he said. "I don't know if she told you or not, but the last time we were together, I proposed. I didn't want her to leave. I wanted her to stay here and marry me."

Sarah was thrilled, but she was also annoyed that Emmie hadn't mentioned his proposal to her. "What did she say?"

"She said she was so upset by everything that had happened, she couldn't think about getting engaged."

"It's true," she told him sadly. "It was a shock to learn of her father's death, and then to find out the terms of the will . . ."

"I know. She told me."

"She had no choice. She had to go."

"And that's why I decided to come and speak with you today. I want to go to Texas and see her. I want to propose to her again, now that she's had time to think about my offer."

She was impressed. "Would you really be willing to live there on the ranch with her?"

"I love Emmie, Mrs. Ryan. I miss her. I'll do whatever I have to do to be with her."

Sarah's heartbeat quickened at his proclamation of love for her daughter. It thrilled her to learn that he cared so much about Emmie. She thought he would be the perfect husband for her. Sarah didn't mention that living on the ranch was hell on earth. She didn't mention to him that, as a man born and raised to city life, the adjustment wasn't going to be easy for him. She didn't say a word to discourage him. She wanted Kenneth to marry Emmie, stay the length of time required on the ranch with her, and then bring her daughter back home to Philadelphia.

They spoke for a while longer and then Kenneth departed.

As she watched him go, Sarah felt better than she had in all the days since Emmie had left her.

"All right," Emmie said seriously as she looked at her friend. They were standing together in a deserted area a good distance from the house. "Are you ready?"

Millie swallowed hard and met Emmie's gaze. "Yes. I'm ready—as ready as I can be, anyway."

"Here." Emmie handed her a loaded six-gun.

"It's heavy." Millie was surprised.

"Yes, it is, so you're going to have to work to control it."

Millie nodded and tightened her grip on the gun.

"I set up those tin cans for you there on the log. See what you can do."

"What do you mean?" Millie asked in confusion.

"I mean try to shoot one of those cans off the log."

"What do I do?" Millie stared down at the weapon. She'd watched Emmie handle one, but this was the first time she'd ever even held a gun.

"The most important thing is to be careful. You never want to accidentally shoot yourself or someone else. Take aim at your target and slowly pull the trigger."

"All right."

Millie was determined as she lifted the gun and pointed it toward the cans. Nervous as she was, it was hard for her to keep her hand steady, but she finally pulled the trigger and got off one shot. It wasn't even close.

"It's a good thing you brought me out here to do this," she said, embarrassed.

"I know. The first time is never easy. It just takes practice."

"How old were you when your father let you try?"

"I think I was six or seven."

"Then you've got a few years' head start on me."

"Just a few."

They were laughing.

"You know, judging by how far off target you were, you might do better with a shotgun," Emmie teased.

Millie laughed, too. "I'm not afraid to try."

"Let's keep working on the handgun for now. We'll worry about the other later."

They continued practicing for the better part of an hour as Millie worked on her aim.

"I think it's safe to say that I'm not going to be

the fastest gun on the Rocking R—or the straightest shooter."

"That's all right. You didn't come out west to make a name for yourself as a fast gun," Emmie reassured her with a grin.

"Are there many women like that?"

"A few."

"I feel sorry for them." Millie couldn't imagine living her life with a gun constantly by her side.

"Some girls don't have anyone to take care of them, so they have to take care of themselves."

"Well, thank heaven for Josh. If it weren't for him, that would be you."

Emmie was a little startled by her friend's observation. "Well, my father made sure I'd be able to take care of myself if I needed to, and now you know how to handle a gun safely, too."

"Though I doubt I could hit anything. Let's just hope we never get in a situation where we have to find out."

They started back to the house, unaware that Steve had been watching them from the stable.

Steve's gaze was hot on Millie. He had every intention of getting close to her as soon as he could. He hadn't seen a girl as pretty as she was in a long time. Why, just watching her walk by with Emmie left him wanting her real bad.

Ned rode slowly into the small town of Sundown and reined in before the saloon. It was quiet that afternoon, and Ned wasn't sure if that was good or bad. One way or the other, he knew he would find out soon. He dismounted and tied up his horse, then headed inside for a drink.

"What'll it be?" the barkeep asked the unshaven, mangy-looking stranger who'd just walked in.

"Whiskey."

The barkeep was quick to oblige, setting the glass on the bar before the newcomer and filling it with a healthy dose of the potent liquor.

"New around here, aren't you?"

"That's right." Ned's answer was terse.

"Planning to stay awhile?"

"You never know. Is Sheriff Dawson still running things in town?"

"He sure is."

Ned nodded, glad that things were finally starting to go his way again.

"Why? You know him?" the barkeep asked.

"Yep, we go back a real long way. Where's his office?"

"Down the street a bit on the right."

"Thanks." Ned shoved some stolen money across the bar to pay for his drink, then downed the rest of the whiskey. He needed to talk to his old friend right away. He needed his help. "I'll be back."

"I ain't going anywhere," the barkeep said.

Ned had no difficulty locating the sheriff's office and walked right in to find his longtime friend seated at the desk.

"Well, well, well, look who's hard at work," Ned mocked good-naturedly.

"Ned?" Rich Dawson couldn't believe his eyes. He stared up at Ned in shock. The last he'd heard,

Tom had been killed by a bounty hunter and Ned had been sent to the penitentiary. "How . . . ?"

"Don't ask," Ned told him. "It's better you don't know."

The two men shook hands.

"I won't. It's good to see you."

"It's good to be here, believe me."

"I'll bet it is."

"You have no idea."

"What do you need? What can I do for you?" Rich knew Ned must have escaped from prison, and he wasn't surprised to see the stark change in Ned's expression.

"You're right. I do need your help."

"I owe you." Rich had a secret in his past that he kept hidden from everyone. Some years back he'd ridden on the wrong side of the law with Ned and his brother. Since they'd parted ways, the brothers had never let on about his involvement in their days of bank robbing. Now that he was sheriff of this nice, crooked little town, Rich could help Ned out. "What can I do?"

"You got someplace quiet we can talk?" Ned looked around, wanting to make sure they could talk without anyone overhearing.

"Let's go back by the cells."

Rich led the way, then turned to face Ned. "All right. What do you have planned?"

"Revenge," he snarled, the fierceness of his barely controlled emotions finally showing.

"Who are you wanting to get even with? Someone at the penitentiary?"

"Oh, no. This is far more personal than that." There was a haunted, hate-filled look in his eyes as he went on. "I want Josh Grady."

"The bounty hunter?" Rich asked in surprise.

"That's right. That bastard killed Tom, and I want him dead. Have you heard anything about him lately? Has anyone seen him around? Has he brought anyone else in?"

"No. I haven't heard a thing for quite a while. Now that you mention it, it does seem strange that there hasn't been any talk about him. I wonder if he gave up bounty hunting?"

"If he's settled in one place, it will make it that much easier to track him down." Ned smiled viciously.

"What's your plan? What do you want me to do?"

Ned leaned closer, knowing he was going to enjoy the results of his plan. "I want Josh Grady to know what it feels like to be hunted."

"What are you talking about?"

"I want you to put out wanted posters on him. 'Josh Grady—Wanted: Dead or Alive.' I want every other bounty hunter to go after him. I want them tracking him. I want them hunting him. I want him to know what it feels like to be a wanted man—before he dies."

Rich smiled coldly at his friend. "How big a reward do you want to put on his head?"

"They were offering five hundred dollars on me. It's worth that much to see him dead."

"You got the money?" Rich knew the situation

could get real ugly if a hired killer brought Josh Grady in and there was no reward money.

"Me and my brother had some cash stashed away in a safe place. When the time comes, I'll have the reward. Don't you worry."

"Good," Rich said, satisfied they could pull this off. "I can get the posters ready for you right away."

"How long do you think it will take to hunt him down?"

"Could be weeks or it could take months. It just depends on what Grady's been doing lately."

"Find out."

"I'll do my best for you," Rich assured him. "And you make certain you keep real quiet around here."

"Don't worry. They won't be taking me in again." Ned knew he'd have to bide his time, and he also knew he had to watch his step. He didn't want the law to find out where he was. He was a free man again, and he intended to stay that way.

# Chapter Thirteen

Miss Harriet wasn't too pleased as she came down to breakfast. The days seemed endless, and she couldn't wait to return to Philadelphia. When they'd first arrived, she had hoped Millie would quickly weary of ranch life and elect to return home early, but that hadn't happened. If anything, Millie seemed to be growing even more enamored with the ranch. Miss Harriet understood that Emmie needed her friend's companionship right now, so she tried not to dwell too much on having to spend another miserable day in the heat and dust. She found Kate hard at work fixing breakfast as she entered the kitchen.

"Good morning, Miss Harriet," Kate greeted her. "How are you this fine morning?"

"I suppose I'm as well as can be expected," the chaperone admitted.

"Being here is different from big-city living, that's for sure."

"Yes, it certainly is. I'm still astonished at the way

Emmie and Millie have been acting since we've been here."

"What do you mean?" Kate didn't see anything unusual in the way they'd been behaving.

"Why, both of them wearing pants . . . and Emmie trying to teach Millie how to shoot . . ."

"Emmie's just being practical by wearing pants," Kate said, trying to explain Western customs.

"You're wearing a skirt," the chaperone pointed out.

"Yes, but I'm not running the ranch. Emmie is, and as far as the shooting lessons go . . . well, Hank always wanted his girl to be able to take care of herself, so Emmie is just teaching her friend the same as her father taught her. They don't call this the Wild West for nothing."

"Emmie has told me some frightening tales, not to mention what I heard from Sarah about her reason for leaving all those years ago. I'm glad things have been quiet since we've been here."

"Let's hope it stays that way. How soon will you and Millie be going back?"

"She planned to stay at least a month. It will depend on how Emmie's doing."

"Our Emmie is one strong girl, but I can't help being thankful Hank took Josh on as a partner when he did. He's a fine man."

"But what about his past? Isn't all that talk about his being a gunman and a bounty hunter a little frightening?"

"This is a big country—and it's a hard country. A

man's got to be able to defend himself. You never know what kind of trouble you might run into."

"Who's looking for trouble?" Emmie asked, smiling as she and Millie entered the kitchen together. "You, Miss Harriet?"

"Every day," the chaperone answered.

They all laughed.

"Miss Harriet was just telling me how concerned she is about Millie learning to handle a gun," Kate offered.

Millie understood her chaperone's feelings and hastened to reassure her. "Don't worry, Miss Harriet. I have no intention of carrying a gun with me."

"Good," the elderly woman said, sounding relieved.

"And Kate . . ." Millie looked at Kate. "There is a very good reason why I won't be carrying one."

"What's that?" Kate asked.

"I'm such a bad shot, Emmie says if I ever did need a gun, it would have to be a shotgun."

Again they laughed.

Miss Harriet enjoyed the lightheartedness, but she knew she would never be comfortable with the idea of a woman needing a gun. She was missing Philadelphia very much and couldn't wait to return.

After breakfast, Emmie went out to the stable to check on what the hands were doing that morning. She found Josh deep in conversation with Burley. She hadn't spent much time with her new partner since the ride they'd taken the other day, and he looked so serious, she feared something was wrong.

"I'm going to ride up there and take a look around," Josh was saying.

"I'll ride with you, and I'll get some of the boys."

"All right."

"What's wrong?" she asked as she joined them.

"The rustlers might be moving in on us again," Josh explained.

"Well, if you're riding out, I'm going with you."

Josh knew it could be dangerous. "There might be trouble."

Emmie looked up at him and met his gaze straight-on. "Those are my cattle, too."

He saw her determination in her gaze and knew there was no talking her out of joining them. The last thing Josh wanted was Emmie along to distract him. He needed to concentrate on looking for the rustlers.

He told her, "We're leaving now."

"I'll be right back," she said.

"I told you we were leaving. Where are you going?" he demanded.

Emmie turned on him. "I'm going to get my gun."

With that, she hurried away.

Burley didn't say anything until she was far enough off not to hear him. Then he went over to stand beside Josh, smiling broadly. "You got yourself one headstrong partner there. She's a wild one, just like her pa."

"I know." Josh was not smiling as he swung up into the saddle. He couldn't help worrying about what might happen if they actually did get in a shoot-out.

"Give Emmie a chance," Burley encouraged as he mounted his own horse to accompany Josh. "She's a hard worker, and she does care about this place."

"I know. I've been watching her."

"I know you have," Burley said, trying not to smile.

Josh fixed him with a hard look. "What's that supposed to mean?"

"She's easy on the eyes, boss, real easy. That's what I mean. She's grown into one fine-looking young lady, don't you think?"

"I hadn't noticed," Josh said uncomfortably.

"Then you must be losing your eyesight. You been in the sun too long?" Burley taunted him.

"Emmie's my partner. Just ask her. She'll tell you."

"And a fine partner she is, too." Burley chuckled. Looking toward the other hands, he yelled, "Let's go, boys—and one of you saddle a horse for Emmie."

The ranch hands did as they were told, and they were mounted up and waiting with Josh and Burley when Emmie came running back, wearing her holster. She quickly mounted her horse and was ready to ride.

Josh glanced at Steve, who was staying behind. "Keep an eye on things for me."

"How long do you think you'll be gone?" Steve asked.

"There's no telling. It all depends on what we find," Josh told him. "Hopefully we'll be back before nightfall."

"Good luck."

Josh nodded and then wheeled his horse around to lead the way in search of the rustlers.

Millie had been up at the house when Emmie had come rushing back in to get her gun and holster. Emmie had told her what was happening, and Millie hadn't bothered to try to discourage her from going. She knew Emmie far too well to even try. She'd been watching from the window as her friend had ridden off with Josh and the ranch hands.

Millie had spent some time reading and talking with Miss Harriet and Kate. As the day aged and there was still no sign of Emmie returning, Millie decided to go down to the stable for a while just to get out of the house. She was bored and needed to do something. Miss Harriet had gone up to her room for a nap, and Kate was busy with her household duties.

Steve was angry as he worked in the stable. He didn't like it that Josh had left him behind. He wanted to ride with the others to track down the rustlers. He was good with a gun and could follow a trail as well as any of the other men.

His mood was dark as he continued his work in the stable, but it definitely improved when he caught sight of Millie coming out of the house. He watched her as she stood on the porch for a moment just looking around; she was the finest-looking woman he'd seen in a long time. Emmie was pretty, too, but he had always had a hankering for blondes, and this one was gorgeous.

Steve's gaze was fixed upon Millie as she left the

porch and headed his way. Moments before he'd been cursing Josh for leaving him behind, but now he was real glad the boss hadn't ordered him to ride out with the other hands. He was thrilled that he was finally going to get the chance to be alone with this little beauty. It had been months since he'd had a woman, and Millie suited him just fine.

Millie saw Steve as he came out of the stable, and she smiled at him. "Have you seen any sign of Emmie and Josh returning yet?"

"No. I don't think we'll see them till close to dark." He went over to speak with her.

"Are you working hard?" she asked, just trying to make conversation as she looked past him into the stable. It was dark and shady in there, and definitely looked a bit cooler than the treeless ranch yard.

"I was until I saw you coming. Now I've got an excuse to stop for a while," he said with a smile.

"I don't want to get you in trouble," she told him.

"You won't. I'm just about done." Steve moved closer to her. "How are you enjoying your visit?"

"I think it's fascinating out here."

"Are you missing Philadelphia much?"

"There are moments—like when Emmie told me about that rattlesnake Josh shot." She couldn't suppress the shudder that went through her.

"You don't want to get bit by one of them, that's for sure."

"You're right. I don't! Other than that, I have been enjoying myself. I'd always read about Texas, and Emmie told me a lot of stories, but until you actually get to see it, you never really understand what it's like."

Steve's mind was racing. He had to get Millie inside the stable. "It's hot out here in the sun. Why don't you come on in the stable where it's shady?"

"All right."

Steve led the way back into the building, trying hard to contain his eagerness. Millie was obviously ready and willing to be with him, and he couldn't wait.

"So, what have you been working on?" Millie asked. In her innocence, she was oblivious to his lecherous thoughts. She was always interested in learning something new, and thought he might be able to teach her more about ranch work.

Once they were in the stable, though, ranch work was the last thing on Steve's mind. He knew they were out of sight of the two other women up at the main house, so he could do whatever he wanted to do with Millie. He grinned at the blond beauty as his gaze went over her. "Well, I've been working on trying to find a way to get to talk to you alone."

"Oh . . . Why?" His words caught her off guard, and she suddenly felt a little awkward in his company.

"Because," he began, closing the distance between them, "I think you are a real special lady."

"Thank you," she said a bit breathlessly as she instinctively took a step back.

"And I am awful glad you came out here with Emmie for a visit. Otherwise, I would never have gotten the chance to meet you."

"I've enjoyed meeting you, too, Steve," Millie said awkwardly.

"I think we ought to get to know each other better, don't you?"

"What do you mean by 'get to know each other'?" The look in his eyes left her leery.

"I mean this." Boldly, Steve reached out and grabbed her by the upper arms to drag her to him. He kissed her then, his mouth claiming hers in a dominating, wet, hungry kiss. He figured she knew what she was doing. After all, she'd come with him willingly into the stable, knowing no one else was around.

Millie was shocked and completely disgusted by his actions. She'd had her share of stolen kisses back in Philadelphia, but she'd never been manhandled this way. Steve rubbed himself hard against her as he continued to kiss her, and she felt almost violated. After her first shock wore off, she started to fight to get away from him.

"No!" She gasped. "What are you doing? Let me go!"

"I like women with spirit. I like it when my women fight," Steve said, leering at her as he kept her tight against him.

"I'm not 'your' woman! I said let me go!"

"You're the one who came out here to see me, darlin'." He laughed unpleasantly as he kissed her again. Strong from years of ranch work, he had no trouble keeping his grip on her. "You are one pretty woman."

"Steve! Stop it!" Millie managed to get her hands up between them and pushed as hard as she could against his chest.

He only laughed at her pitiful efforts. "When I want something, I get it, Millie, and I've been wanting you ever since the first time I saw you."

Steve managed to half drag her toward one of the clean empty stalls.

"What are you doing?" she cried, resisting with all her might.

"Come on, sweetheart. We're gonna have us some fun back here where nobody will see us."

Millie cried out in desperation as he pushed her down on the fresh bed of straw he'd put down not long before. He lay down beside her, and when she tried to scramble away, he yanked her back to him. He pulled her forcefully beneath him and pressed himself full length against her.

"No! Get off of me! What do you think you're doing?" she shrieked.

"Why, I'm just giving you what you want," Steve said with a grin, enjoying himself.

"Let me go!" Millie yelled again.

"That's it, sweetheart. It'll be even better if you put up a little fight."

He was starting to unbutton her blouse and grope her when a man's voice came from behind him.

"I believe the lady said to let her go." The tone was cold and deadly and commanding.

## Chapter Fourteen

"*What* the . . ." Steve froze, then looked over his shoulder to find himself staring at the barrel of a six-gun that was pointed straight at him.

"The lady said to let her go, and I suggest you do it—*now!*" the tall, dark-haired man standing over him ordered.

Steve threw himself off Millie and scrambled to his feet. He stood there staring at the man holding the gun on him. "Who are you to order me around?"

"Someone who doesn't like to see a lady disrespected. Now, get off this ranch before I decide to shoot you where it will really hurt—for a long, long time," the stranger ground out, smiling savagely at the weasel who stood shaking before him.

Coward that he was, Steve ran from the stable.

The tall man went after him.

Gun still in hand, he waited and watched from the door of the stable until Steve had ridden out. Only then did he turn back to Millie. Holstering his sidearm, he made his way back to the stall, where she was standing in the back corner, clutching the edges of her torn blouse together and watching him suspiciously.

"Are you all right?" the dark-haired stranger asked in a calming tone.

Millie stood there, trembling, as she stared at the man who'd just saved her: tall and lean, clean-shaven and darkly handsome. She knew she'd never seen him before, for she certainly would have remembered him. "I . . . I think so. Who are you? Where did you come from?"

"My name's George—George Grady. I'm Josh's brother," he quickly explained.

"Oh." Now that she knew who he was, she did see a little resemblance to Josh, and a great sense of relief flooded through her.

He saw the change in her expression, and he went to her.

"Here, let me help you." He gently slipped a supportive arm around her shoulders to guide her from the stall. "Let's get you up to the main house."

Millie nodded, still too unsettled to say much more right then. She had always considered herself a strong, independent female—until now. The ugly physical encounter with Steve had left her reeling, and she was grateful for George's support as he led her from the stable.

"Thank you," she finally managed, struggling to regain her self-control as she looked up at him. "Steve's not coming back, is he?" Millie looked around quickly as they moved outside.

"No. He won't be back, if he knows what's good for him," George assured her.

"Thank heaven."

"Where is everybody?" George asked. "Where's Josh?"

"They rode out this morning—Josh thought there were rustlers around."

Kate came rushing out of the house at that moment, a stricken look on her face. She'd been passing by a window when she'd seen George and Millie coming her way. She recognized Josh's brother right away and was surprised to see him. She wondered why Millie looked so pale, and then realized from the state of her clothes that something must have happened. She feared Millie might have been thrown while trying to ride. "Millie! George! What's wrong?"

"We'll tell you once we're in the house," George said.

"All right." Kate looked between the two of them and then turned back to hold the front door open for them. "I didn't hear you ride in, George."

"I went down to the stable first and then everything happened fast," George answered as he ushered Millie inside and took her to the sitting room.

Millie sat down heavily on the sofa, and George remained close by. Kate went to sit with her, wanting to find out what had happened.

"Were you thrown?" Kate asked.

Millie looked up at her and shook her head. "No. It was Steve."

"Steve? What about him?"

George spoke up, wanting to save the young woman from the horror of having to relive Steve's manhandling again by speaking of it. "When I rode in I found Steve attacking her out in the stable."

"Dear Lord, no!" Kate reached out and took Millie's hand.

"I ran him off," George went on, "but if he ever comes back—"

"I can't believe Steve would do such a thing!" Kate was horrified. She'd known the ranch hand for some time.

"Neither could I," Millie said.

"He always seemed like a good man."

"He's not," George put in tersely.

"You're right," Millie agreed. "He's not. It was so scary—I tried to fight him off, but he wouldn't stop. If it hadn't been for George . . ." She looked up at him, the depth of her emotion showing in her eyes. "There's no telling what would have happened."

Kate hugged Millie, horrified by what the ranch hand had done to her. "He'd better not come back here—ever!" Kate declared heatedly. "I can just imagine what Josh will do to him if he sets foot on the Rocking R again."

"I know," Millie said, starting to feel a little more like herself. "I'm seriously thinking about taking more shooting lessons from Emmie."

"And I wouldn't blame you a bit," Kate agreed. "Are you sure you're all right?" She could tell Millie was still trembling a little.

"Yes—it just all happened so fast. I was bored, so I went out to the stable to take a look around. Steve and I started talking, and before I knew it, he grabbed me and threw me down in one of the stalls."

Kate looked up at George with even greater respect. "I'm glad you arrived when you did."

"So am I," Millie added, managing to smile at him for the first time.

"So am I," George agreed. He'd thought she was a remarkably pretty girl, but when she smiled, he decided she was downright beautiful.

Millie was feeling uncomfortable after being manhandled by Steve, and she was longing to take a bath. "I'm going to go upstairs. I want to get cleaned up."

"Do you need anything?" Kate offered.

"If you could bring me up some bathwater, I'd appreciate it."

"Right away." Kate hurried from the room to start heating some bathwater.

Millie looked over at George again. "Are you going to stay on here at the ranch for a while?"

"If my brother will have me," George said, smiling at her.

"He'll have you," Millie told him. "And if he won't have you, I will."

They both relaxed enough then to laugh together.

Millie got up and started to leave the room. She paused in the doorway to look back at him and found that he was watching her. "George . . . thank you."

With that, she disappeared into the hall to go upstairs, leaving George alone in the sitting room.

He stared after Millie for a moment, impressed by what a strong woman she was. He didn't know many women who would have recovered their composure so quickly, after what she'd just gone through. He thought, too, about the fact that she was wearing pants. It wasn't often that he saw a female dressed that way, and he had to admit it intrigued him.

George hoped Josh made it back to the ranch house relatively early that day. He had a lot to discuss with his brother, and he wanted to find out more about Millie. He didn't know anything except her name. He wondered, too, where Hank was.

George thought about asking Kate, but didn't see her again on his way from the house. He went to tend to his horse while he awaited Josh's return. He hadn't seen his brother in a while, and he had a big favor to ask of him. He had lost all his money in a poker game the week before, and now he needed work. He didn't like asking outright for money, but he figured Josh could always use an extra hand on the ranch.

Millie was grateful when Kate came upstairs with the hot water for her bath.

"This should help make you feel better," Kate said as she met Millie in the small room off the hall that was used for bathing.

"It will," she agreed, standing back while Kate poured the water into the tub. "How much do you know about George? It was so amazing to look up from struggling with Steve and find him just standing there like that."

"I've met him a few times since Josh has been here. He's younger than Josh, but not by much."

"What does he do? Is he a rancher somewhere nearby?"

Kate couldn't help laughing a little. "No, I've never known George to try his hand at ranching. He's more . . ."

At her hesitation, Millie was curious. "He's more what?"

"Well, let's say he's wilder than Josh."

"How could anyone be wilder than Josh?" She was stunned. "Josh was a bounty hunter and—"

"George is a gambler," Kate hastened to explain.

"Like a cardsharp?" Millie had heard the tales of gamblers who made their living cheating at cards, but there had seemed nothing dishonest about the man she'd just met.

"No. He doesn't cheat when he's playing cards. He's just real good at it."

"Oh, my. I wonder why he came here?"

"I'm sure he just stopped by for a visit with Josh. He does that occasionally."

"Whatever his reason for coming to the ranch, he couldn't have shown up at a better time."

"You are right about that, and I'm glad he's staying here right now, just in case Steve gets any foolish ideas about coming back."

"I almost know how to shoot," Millie said tentatively. She didn't know how close she would come to hitting Steve if he attacked her again, but she could at least try, thanks to Emmie.

"And I definitely know how to use a gun," Kate added, "but let's hope it doesn't come to that."

"Where does George stay when he's here?"

"When he's visited in the past, he's stayed with

Josh at the foreman's house. That's much easier for him than staying in town."

"Good. I want to get to know him better."

"He's a nice man, but remember—he is a professional gambler. He's smooth-talking, and he travels a lot."

"I'll remember," Millie said, but, in truth, she found the idea that George was a gambler intriguing.

Kate left her, giving her privacy to take her bath.

Millie quickly stripped off her clothes and got into the tub, eager to wash up. She wanted to erase all memories of the vileness of Steve's brutal touch. Bathing in the small tin tub at the ranch was a far cry from what she was accustomed to at home, but that didn't matter to her right then. She just needed to feel clean again.

It wasn't long before Millie was drying herself off and preparing to get dressed. She hoped to find George again and get to know him a bit now that she was feeling more like herself. She looked through the clothing she'd brought along and selected a modest day gown. After what had happened in the stable, she wasn't ready to wear pants and boots again just yet. Once she was dressed, with her hair brushed out and tied back in a simple ribbon, Millie was ready to go. She left her room and went downstairs, to find Miss Harriet in the kitchen with Kate.

Miss Harriet had been sitting at the table, but the moment she saw Millie, she got up and rushed to her to give her a big hug. She had been truly shaken when she'd found out what had happened while she'd been upstairs resting. "Oh, Millie, thank God you're all right! Kate was just telling me all that happened."

"Everything's fine, Miss Harriet," Millie said, hugging her back.

"Are you sure? You haven't been injured in any way?" she asked worriedly.

"No. George showed up just in time to save me."

"That's what Kate said. I have to meet this George and tell him how much I appreciate his valor. Men like him are very rare." She went on anxiously. "What was I thinking, leaving you unchaperoned that way? I should never have gone upstairs to rest."

"Miss Harriet, none of this was your fault. I'm fine. Really." Millie could just imagine that if she didn't convince Miss Harriet of her blamelessness, the chaperone would be by her side every minute of every day for the rest of their visit at the ranch.

The chaperone looked her over critically and then nodded. "If you're certain."

"I am."

"I would like to meet this young man. Kate was telling me he's Josh's brother."

"That's right, and after all that's happened, I want to get to know him better, too. I don't even want to think about what would have happened if he hadn't saved me from Steve."

"He's a hero. That's for sure," Miss Harriet declared.

Millie knew that was high praise, coming from her. "We'll have to tell him when we see him again."

"Do you think he'll be staying here at the ranch for very long?" Miss Harriet asked Kate.

"With George, you never know," Kate told them.

"Have you seen him since I've been upstairs?"

"No. He hasn't come back."

"I think I'll go find him and bring him up here to the house, so Miss Harriet can meet him."

"Is it safe for you to go outside?" Miss Harriet worried. "What if that Steve is still around somewhere?"

"George ran him off, but I'll go with her, just to be sure," Kate said, knowing Miss Harriet could offer little in the way of protection if Steve were lurking around out there.

Kate and Millie left the house together after Kate paused to find her pistol.

"George may be down at the stable taking care of his horse, or he could be at Josh's cabin," Kate said.

"I'll go check at Josh's. I don't want to go down to the stable," Millie said.

Kate understood. "All right. I'll go look down there. Just yell if you need me. I won't be long."

Millie moved off toward the small house where Josh lived.

George had stabled his horse and then walked all around the outbuildings. He wanted to make sure there was no sign of Steve anywhere. Once he was confident the other man was gone, he'd made his way over to Josh's house and let himself in.

George had been riding long and hard for days now, and after hearing Millie mention a bath, he decided he could use some cleaning up, too. He didn't have the luxury of hot water, or a tub like the one up at the main house, but he didn't care. He just needed to scrub off the trail dirt. George tossed his hat, saddlebags, and gear aside and stripped off his shirt as he went over to the washstand. He was glad to find there was water in a bucket, and he poured some into the bowl and started to wash.

George was just finishing up when he heard a knock at the door.

"Come on in," he called out.

Millie didn't hesitate to enter. She opened the door and walked in to find George standing across the room from her with his shirt off, drying himself with a towel.

"Oh!" she said, blushing a little at finding him partially unclothed.

When George had heard the knock, he'd thought it was probably just a ranch hand looking for Josh. He was surprised to find Millie standing there, and he couldn't help smiling at her. He'd known she was a beauty, but seeing her attired in a dress made him even more aware of her as a woman. "Hello, Millie. You look real pretty in that dress."

"Thank you," she said.

He reached for his clean shirt, not wanting to stand there before her only half-dressed. "Is there something you need?"

"Yes, there is," she told him. "I'd like you to come up to the house with me."

"Is Josh back?"

"No, not yet, but Miss Harriet is awake now, and she wants to meet you."

"Miss Harriet?" He'd never heard that name before.

"She's my chaperone. She came to Texas with me and Emmie."

"So you live back East with Emmie?" He had heard talk around the ranch about Hank's daughter on his last visit to see Josh.

"Yes. I didn't want her to make the trip alone after all that's happened."

"What's happened?" George was at a loss.

"You haven't heard about Mr. Ryan?"

"Hank? What about him?"

Millie realized then that she would have to be the one to tell George of Hank Ryan's death. "Let's go up to the main house. We can talk up there."

George finished buttoning his shirt and followed her outside to find Kate walking toward them from the stable.

"I see you found him," Kate said.

"Yes, I did. George hasn't heard about Mr. Ryan yet, so I thought we could tell him up at the house."

George had a bad feeling as he accompanied them to the ranch house. After introducing him to the elderly chaperone, Millie told him all about Hank's death and how Emmie now had to live on the Rocking R and run the ranch with Josh.

"How did my brother take the news?"

"I think he was worried at first," Kate offered, "but our Emmie's a strong woman. Hank would never have entrusted the Rocking R to her if he hadn't thought she could work it."

"I'm looking forward to meeting her," George said, just trying to imagine his brother working side by side with a woman. Wondering whether Emmie was as pretty as Millie, he smiled. Some jobs were better than others.

# Chapter Fifteen

As the afternoon wore on, Emmie grew saddle weary, but she would never admit it. She'd insisted on riding with Josh and the other hands, and she wasn't about to let on that she couldn't keep up. She was going to do it no matter what. As she'd said to Josh earlier, the missing cattle were her responsibility, too.

They had split up into two groups earlier in the day to follow diverging trails that seemed suspicious. Emmie had stayed with Josh and Burley, and she kept pace with them as they covered endless miles without finding anything.

"How much longer do you want to keep going?" Burley asked Josh as he reined in and looked up at the dark clouds that were looming on the horizon. They could tell it was already pouring rain in the distance. "That sky ain't lookin' too good."

The terrain had grown rocky and harsh, making tracking almost impossible, and if they got caught in a gully washer, the sudden onslaught of rushing water could be dangerous.

Josh reined in. He was frustrated that they hadn't had more luck, but he'd known it wasn't going to be easy when they'd ridden out that morning. He wasn't one to give up easily, but, with the storm threatening, he knew it was time to quit. "You're right. We'd better head back."

"What about the rustlers?" Emmie asked.

"What little was left of the trail is going to be washed clean away once that storm breaks," Josh told her. "Let's go."

"But we've come too far to just quit," she countered.

Josh wasn't willing to risk their safety. "Have you ever been caught out in one of these storms with your father?"

Emmie looked up at the dark sky. "No."

"You've been lucky, and I'd like to keep it that way. Let's ride."

She knew by his tone that there was no point in arguing with him. So as Josh led the way, she kept pace with him and Burley.

They rode hard, but the powerful storm moved faster. The deep, echoing rumble of thunder across the land gave fair warning of what was to come.

"We'd better start looking for some shelter," Burley said.

Emmie could sense the two men's concern as they sought a safe place to wait it out.

The storm struck then, and lightning crashed around them as torrential rain began to pour down.

Emmie had always thought she was a good rider. She'd certainly managed to keep up all day, but her confidence was shattered when lightning stuck close by and her horse panicked and reared, unseating her.

Josh saw the whole thing and went quickly to Emmie's aid, throwing himself from his horse and rushing to her. He knelt down beside her as she lay unmoving, and he feared she'd been seriously hurt.

"Emmie! Are you all right?"

Emmie had landed hard. She stirred and opened her eyes to see Josh hovering over her in the rain, his expression dark and worried. "I think so."

"Josh! How is she?" Burley asked as he rode up.

"She's moving," he said, trying to shield her from the downpour that was drenching them.

"Do you need help?"

"No, I've got her."

"I'll see if I can catch her horse," Burley said.

"If you do, just keep on going. I'll bring Emmie in with me."

As Burley rode off in the rain, Josh was silently cursing himself for not realizing the danger Emmie would be in trying to ride in such bad weather. He blamed himself as he started to pick her up and carry her to his horse. He hoped she'd just had the wind knocked out of her, but he couldn't be sure.

Ever the independent young woman, Emmie started to protest as he scooped her up in his arms. "No, Josh. I can walk. You don't have to—"

One stern look from Josh silenced her as he carried her to his horse. He didn't bother to say a word as he helped her up into the saddle before quickly mounting behind her. He brought her back against his chest to protect and shield her from the rain as best he could. He kept his arms around her as they rode off. Josh knew there was an old line shack not too far off. He figured they could wait out the storm there, and he could make sure Emmie wasn't seriously hurt in any way.

Emmie was drenched and sore and miserable, but she had never felt so safe in her whole life as she did right then in the haven of Josh's arms.

Josh saw no sign of the storm letting up or of Burley as they continued on, and he knew the storm was only going to get worse before it got better. He hoped Burley would make it back to the ranch house safely.

When at last Josh spotted the run-down shack ahead, he was relieved. He reined in before the one-room building and quickly dismounted.

Emmie was thrilled to see the old line shack. As Josh reached up to help her off the horse, she put her hands on his shoulders, believing he would set her on her feet. Instead, he swept her up into his arms again and cradled her against him as he hurried to the entrance. He kicked the door open and carried Emmie inside; only then did he put her down.

"Stay here," he ordered.

"Trust me. I'm not going anywhere," she returned, grateful to be out of the torrent.

"Good."

Without another word, he went back outside to take care of his horse.

Emmie stood there for a moment, smiling after him as he shut the door behind him on his way out.

She'd often dreamed of the moment when she'd be carried over the threshold by a strong, handsome man, but the fantasy had never ended like this—being left all alone in the middle of a shack with only an old table, two chairs, and some bunks that didn't look very comfortable or particularly clean. She just shook her head at the irony of it, and at the same time she breathed a sigh of relief. Run-down as the shack was, it still offered the shelter they needed to weather the storm, and for that she was grateful.

Emmie tossed her soaked hat aside and went looking for something she could use to dry herself. She had little luck and gave up. She had to smile again as she sat down at the table to await Josh's return. This wasn't going to be the first time he'd seen her soaked to the skin.

Josh led his horse to the one-stall lean-to and tied it inside. He grabbed up his bedroll and the rifle he carried with him, and made the run back up to the line shack. Dripping wet by the time he reached the shelter, he quickly shut the door behind him. He put his gear and hat aside and turned to Emmie.

"I think it's raining out there," he said as he entered the room.

"Just a little," she agreed, smiling at the sight of him with his wet shirt plastered against the broad width of his chest. "I looked around, but I couldn't find any towels."

"The boys don't usually worry too much about bathing when they stay up here," he remarked.

"I can tell. Do you want to get out of your shirt?"

"Yeah. I've got my bedroll. We can use that for a towel."

"Is it dry?" she asked, surprised.

"Drier than we are. I always wrap it in canvas for times just like this. My years of tracking taught me that."

Josh wasted no time stripping off his shirt. He hung it on the back of the other chair and then shook out his bedroll.

"Do you want to use it first?" he offered.

"Go ahead."

He made short order of drying off. Emmie could only sit and watch him, enjoying the sight of his darkly tanned, hard-muscled chest and arms. There could be no doubt he was a strong man. When he looked back at her, she quickly averted her gaze.

"I'll turn my back if you want to take off your shirt and wrap up in the blanket. I'll start a fire in the stove and we can dry things out while we're waiting."

"All right, but you'd better keep your word about turning your back," she said, grinning. "I'd hate for Miss Harriet to find out we were undressing around each other while we were unchaperoned."

"I think we'd be in trouble with her under those circumstances, even if we were chaperoned," he teased.

They were both chuckling as he gave her the blanket and then moved away to start the fire while she shed her wet blouse.

"Is it safe for me to turn around yet?" Josh asked once he had the fire going.

"Yes. It's safe," she told him.

He turned back to find her sitting at the table again, wrapped modestly in the blanket.

"Miss Harriet would be proud of you."

He took both their shirts and hung them on the end of the bed nearest the stove, then joined her at the table.

"So, how are you feeling?" He was still concerned after the fall she'd taken.

"I think I feel about like you felt when you finished breaking Buck," Emmie countered, grinning at him.

He found himself smiling back at her. "That bad?"

"Yes, but at least you had something to show for it after you were thrown. You tamed Buck. I just ended up stuck here in a line shack, all wet and real sore."

"It could be worse. We could still be riding, looking for cover."

"You're right," she conceded. "I should count my blessings. If you hadn't been with me, I'd be on foot, walking back to the house right now."

Josh was still grinning. "I never thought of myself as a blessing before."

"Then you don't know what Millie thinks of you."

"Millie?" he asked in a surprised tone.

"That's right. From the first day she met you, she's been telling me you're my 'guardian angel.' "

"I may have to have a talk with your friend and set her straight."

"Don't even try. It won't do any good. Once Millie makes up her mind, there's no changing it."

They were both laughing.

"Well, if Millie thinks I'm your guardian angel,

who do *you* think I am?" Josh asked, his gaze meeting hers across the table.

Emmie's breath caught in her throat at the look in his eyes.

"I know who you are," she began, a shiver of sensual awareness trembling through her. "You're my partner."

"You're right," he said. "We're in this together."

"The ranch or the line shack?"

"Both."

Again they were laughing, and Emmie was glad. For a moment there, she'd been caught off guard by the way he'd looked at her, and she wasn't quite sure what to make of it.

"How long do you think we'll have to stay here?" Emmie asked, wanting to change the direction of the conversation.

"The storm doesn't look like it's showing any signs of letting up, so we may have to spend the night."

"Here?" Emmie looked around the shack again.

"It'll be safer that way." Even as he spoke, a bolt of lightning split the sky, and thunder rumbled across the land.

"Miss Harriet won't think so," Emmie said, looking mischievous. "Not for my reputation, anyway."

"Then she should have ridden with us so she could keep an eye on you."

They both smiled at the thought.

"She probably would have slowed us down a little."

"There's no 'probably' about it," he agreed.

As the sound of the rain on the roof grew even

louder, Emmie left the table to go to the window and watch the downpour, keeping the blanket around her shoulders.

"It is ugly out there." Emmie couldn't suppress the shiver that went through her as she imagined them trying to ride through the storm. "What would we have done if we hadn't been close to the line shack?"

Josh got up to go stand beside her. "From the looks of things right now, I'd say we would have been swimming back."

Emmie couldn't help it. she laughed again, and then went quiet. Heartfelt emotion shone in her eyes as she looked up at him. "Thank you."

"For what?" Josh frowned, confused. They had been riding all day, trying to track down rustlers with no success, she'd been thrown from her horse, and now they were being forced to spend the night in a run-down line shack. It hadn't been one of his better days, that was for sure.

"For making me laugh. There hasn't been much laughter in my life lately," she said softly. "Not since . . ."

Their gazes met, and Josh could no more stop himself from taking her in his arms than he could have stopped the rain from coming down. Ever so gently, he reached out to her and drew her to him. He didn't say a word as he bent to kiss her.

Emmie was surprised by his move, but as his lips claimed hers she offered no resistance. She had been in Josh's arms before, but those times had been nothing like this. Logic told her to move away, but at that moment, being logical was the last thing on her mind. She wanted to be near him. She surrendered to his embrace, returning his kiss in full measure.

Josh felt her response and drew her even closer, deepening the exchange. As his mouth moved over hers, she lifted her arms to link them around his neck, and when she did, the blanket dropped to the floor. Emmie didn't notice, though. She was too caught up in the wonder of his kiss.

The feel of her pressed so intimately against him aroused Josh even more. He broke off the kiss for a moment to grab the blanket, then took her hand to draw her with him to a bunk. Emmie watched as he spread the blanket on the bed, and when he turned back to her to kiss her again, she didn't resist but responded eagerly.

A fleeting memory of Kenneth's kisses played in her mind, and she knew that what she'd felt when he'd kissed her was nothing like what she felt for Josh. She wanted Josh. She needed him. The realization surprised her, but she pushed all thoughts aside, giving herself over to the passion of the moment.

Josh felt her surrender and swept her up in his arms to lay her on the bunk. He joined her there and kissed her again.

Emmie lifted her arms to him, caressing his back and shoulders as he moved over her. Suddenly, their wet clothes didn't matter. Al that mattered was being close to him. It was just her and Josh, alone. The intimacy of their embrace was both startling and arousing for her. She had never lain with a man before, had never been this close, and the hard heat of him seared her, igniting a searing passion deep within her body. When he began to caress her, his touch stoked the flame of her desire. Innocent that she was, she had never known a man's caress could be so exciting.

Josh kissed her again, and then his lips left her mouth to trail heated caresses down the side of her neck and lower, across the exposed tops of her breasts. He heard her gasp at the touch of his lips against that sensitive flesh, and she arched against him in love's age-old invitation.

Josh knew she was his for the taking, and it was that very thought that stopped him.

Oh, he wanted her.

There was no doubt about his desire for her. He'd wanted her since that first night in the study, when she'd stood there holding a gun on him with her robe hanging open, but . . .

This was Emmie.

This was Hank's daughter.

She was his partner.

Josh stifled a groan as he ended their embrace and sat up on the side of the bunk, his elbows on his knees, his head in his hands.

"Josh? What is it?" Emmie was at a loss as to why he'd moved away. She'd been caught up in the power of his passion and wanted to be back in his arms again, kissing him.

Josh was still fighting to bring his desire for her under control as he looked over at Emmie and smiled wryly. "I thought I heard Miss Harriet coming."

"Oh." Emmie was suddenly forced back to reality,

and felt embarrassed when she realized just how caught up she'd been in his embrace. She blushed and quickly shifted to grab the blanket from beneath her. Hastily she covered herself, a bit ashamed at being so brazen with him. She'd never felt this way before.

Josh got up and moved over to the window, deliberately looking out so he wouldn't be tempted by the sight of Emmie anymore. He had always prided himself on being a man in control, but Emmie was turning out to be the one temptation that could threaten that control. And he wasn't sure if her effect on him was good or bad.

Emmie managed to gather her wits about her and sit up. She sensed the tension between them and wanted to ease it. Wrapping the blanket demurely around herself again, she got up and went to Josh. "Do you see her?"

"Who?" Josh glanced down at Emmie, wondering what she was talking about and wishing she'd stayed over by the bed, away from him, so he wouldn't be tempted to kiss her again.

Emmie smiled. "Miss Harriet. Is she out there? You said you heard her coming. I was hoping she was bringing me some dry clothes."

Josh couldn't help laughing. "No, Miss Harriet's not here."

"Good, because I wanted to kiss you one more time." She rose up on tiptoe to kiss him sweetly.

"Just once more?" he asked.

"We never know when Miss Harriet will show up."

"You're right, and I wouldn't want to disappoint Millie."

"Millie?"

"You told me she thinks I'm your guardian angel. That means I'm supposed to keep you out of trouble."

"And you're doing a fine job. Miss Harriet would be proud of you—and Millie, too."

They settled in to pass the time as the rain continued into the night.

# Chapter Sixteen

George had stayed up at the house talking with the ladies for the rest of the afternoon, and when Miss Harriet invited him to join them for dinner, he'd gladly accepted. It was late afternoon, and they were just getting ready to sit down and eat when they heard riders come in. Thinking Emmie and Josh were back, George and Millie hurried down to the stable. The ranch hands greeted George, remembering him from his last visit to the Rocking R.

"Where are Josh and Emmie?" Millie asked them.

"They aren't back yet?" asked a cowboy named Mike.

"No. We haven't seen them since you rode out this morning," Millie said.

"We found what we thought were two different trails, so we split up. They rode with Burley."

"Did you find any sign of the rustlers?" George asked.

"We didn't turn up anything. I hope they have better luck than we did, but I doubt it."

"Why's that?" Millie asked.

"There's a bad storm rolling in," Mike told them, pointing to the northwest.

They looked that way to see ominous black clouds on the horizon.

"And that's the direction they were riding. From the look of things, I'd say whatever trail they were following got washed out."

"So they should be back soon," Millie said hopefully, worrying about her friend.

"Not if they got caught in the bad weather," he explained. "They'll have to hole up somewhere until it passes, and if the storm lasts until dark where they are, we won't see them until morning."

"They won't be in any danger, will they?" Millie asked worriedly.

"This kind of storm can be dangerous, but Josh and Burley know what they're doing. They'll make it back all right."

Millie felt a little relieved at Mike's confidence in the two men, and she told herself Emmie was in good hands with Josh. "Thanks."

"Have you seen Steve?" Mike asked, puzzled that the other man wasn't there.

George looked down at Millie. "Go on up to the house. I'll be there in a minute."

Millie looked a little stricken and quickly hurried off, leaving George to explain to the other hands what had happened.

A short time later, George returned to the house and joined Millie and Miss Harriet for dinner. When the chaperone heard the news about Emmie being caught in a storm, she immediately began to worry—about Emmie's safety and her reputation.

"Don't worry," George assured her. "Your Emmie will be safe with Josh."

"She will, Miss Harriet. I know it," Millie agreed.

Millie's quick defense of Josh surprised George, for he knew she'd known his brother only a short time.

As sunset approached, they heard the distant rumble of thunder, and those gathered at the ranch house accepted that they probably wouldn't see Emmie, Josh, or Burley anytime that night. George and Millie decided to go outside on the porch to watch the storm move in, while Miss Harriet chose to observe it safely from a sitting room window.

"Thank you for inviting me to dinner tonight," George said as he and Millie stood together at the top of the steps. His gaze was upon her, and he knew he'd never seen a prettier woman than the lovely blonde. "Kate's cooking is some of the best around. After all these days of riding and eating my own cooking, this meal was definitely special."

"An invitation to dinner is hardly thanks enough for what you did to help me today." She looked up at him, seeing a hero and wondering if they grew heroes here in Texas or if George and his brother were unique.

"I'm glad I was there to deal with Steve. I'm just sorry it happened at all, and I'm sorry about Hank. Your friend Emmie must be going through a difficult time right now," he sympathized.

"She is, but she's strong. It's not easy for her, but she's handling it." Millie was about to say more when she caught sight of a single rider in the distance. It looked like he was leading a saddled but riderless horse. "George! Look! Something must have happened!"

They both rushed from the porch and ran down to the stable. They were waiting for Burley there when he reined in. Burley recognized George and greeted him as he dismounted.

"Isn't that the horse Emmie was riding? Where is she? Why isn't she with you?" Millie demanded.

"We ran into bad weather and Emmie was thrown."

"What? Is she all right?" Millie asked.

He quickly told them what had happened.

"You mean you just rode off and left them with only one horse, not knowing whether Emmie was hurt?" she asked incredulously.

George put an arm around her to reassure her, for he knew his brother. "I'm sure they're all right."

Millie looked up at him. "How can you be certain?"

"Josh is my foreman, Millie," Burley told her. "I do what the man tells me to do, and he told me to get Emmie's horse and not to come back for them. He said he would bring her in."

"Any idea where they might have gone?" George asked, knowing Burley had done what any good ranch hand would have done—he had followed the boss's orders. He understood Millie's concern, though, and had already made up his mind to ride out in the morning and look for Josh and Emmie, just in case.

"There's an old line shack up that way. Knowing Josh, he headed there."

"A line shack?" Millie asked, looking from one man to the other.

George quickly explained what it was.

"I hope they made it there all right," Millie said.

"If anybody could make it there in this storm, it'd be Josh," Burley said reassuringly. "He knows his way around."

They bade him good night and returned to the house to tell Miss Harriet what had happened, just as the rain started to fall. After George had left them, Millie went into the parlor and sat with Miss Harriet on the sofa. Both women were too upset to even think about going to bed yet.

"What makes this so hard," Millie was saying, "is that there is nothing I can do to help her right now. I know Emmie is more accustomed to ranch life than I am, but she might have been hurt being thrown that way."

"There's only one thing we can do right now," the chaperone advised.

"What's that?"

"Pray that they come back home safely."

They shared a look of understanding, knowing they would both do just that, and Millie gave Miss Harriet a hug.

The bounty hunter was sitting by his campfire, staring down at a wanted poster.

**Wanted!**
**Dead or Alive**
**Josh Grady**
**$500**
**For Murder**
**Sundown, Texas**

The bounty hunter had been surprised when he'd heard that Josh Grady was a wanted man. He'd never met the other bounty hunter, but he'd heard stories about the number of outlaws he'd tracked down and brought in over the years. He knew Grady was a dangerous man, but up until now he'd always been on the side of the law. He wondered why the other bounty hunter had turned to killing.

He told himself it didn't really matter. All that mattered was the reward, and the reward for bringing Grady in was a big one—five hundred dollars. He fully intended to claim it.

He had heard talk that Grady had quit bounty hunting and just disappeared, but he knew better. Some cattlemen he'd been drinking with a few months back had mentioned how Hank Ryan of the Rocking R had taken on a partner a year or so ago. They'd told him they'd thought the man's name was Grady. The bounty hunter was riding for the Rocking R now to check the story out.

If Josh Grady did turn out to be the man at the ranch, it wouldn't be easy to corner him and get the upper hand on him. The bounty hunter wondered, too, if Grady even knew about the wanted posters the lawman had put out on him. Sheriff Dawson was not the most upright lawman, but that didn't much matter. To the bounty hunter, only the money mattered. Nothing else.

He glanced at the picture again, then folded the wanted poster back up and put it in his saddlebag before bedding down for the night. He needed to get some rest. He had a lot of miles to cover over the next weeks.

"Good night, Josh," Emmie said softly as she lay in bed, wrapped in Josh's blanket.

"Good night." Josh was stretched out on the upper bunk, staring at the ceiling of the line shack, listening to the pounding of the rain and wondering if he would ever get to sleep. Though it had been a long day, the night promised to be even longer with Emmie bedded down so close to him—especially after the kisses they'd shared. And in the morning, when the weather cleared up, they would be riding double back to the ranch. He wasn't sure which would be harder on him—holding her in front of him as they rode or having her ride behind him. Either way the feel of her was going to be torturous for him—enjoyable, but torturous.

Josh found himself smiling into the night. Of all the difficult situations he'd found himself in over the years, this was one of the most complicated. As he'd told himself earlier when he'd forced himself to move away from Emmie, she was Hank's daughter.

She was not some casual acquaintance who would move on out of his life after a time.

She was his partner.

No matter what happened between them, they were going to be working side by side on the Rocking R from now on, and he had to figure out how to make their relationship one of trust. He just hoped he was smart enough to do it.

Emmie rolled over and closed her eyes. She tried to sleep, but she couldn't put the memory of being in Josh's embrace from her. In her mind, she was reliving the thrill of his kisses again and again. She couldn't forget the excitement that had filled her when he'd trailed kisses down her throat. A shiver of sensual awareness went through her, and she wondered if she was going to get any rest at all that night.

Josh awoke just as the eastern horizon began to brighten. He was glad to see that the rain had moved on. They could head out early, and he was more than ready to get back to the ranch. The thought of some of Kate's cooking was definitely appealing to him after missing dinner last night.

Josh swung his long legs over the side of the bunk and dropped down as quietly as he could so as not to wake Emmie. He figured he'd let her sleep while he went to check on the horse. He was surprised to find her bed empty, and Emmie nowhere in sight. Concerned about her, Josh put on his shirt and boots and went to search for her. He didn't have to look far. He found Emmie fully dressed, sitting on the step that led into the line shack.

"What are you doing out here?" Josh asked.

Emmie looked up at him and smiled. "I woke up a while ago, and you were sleeping so soundly, I didn't want to disturb you. I decided to just come outside and watch the sunrise."

"It is a glorious sight, especially after yesterday," he said, staring off toward the brightening sky.

"That's for sure. You won't hear me complaining about dry weather for a while."

"How are you feeling this morning?"

"Not as bad as I thought I was going to feel. I'm still sore, and I've got some bruises, but other than that I'm all right."

"You're tough, just like your father," he complimented her, impressed.

"Thank you." His approval meant a lot to Emmie.

"How soon can you be ready to ride?" Josh asked.

"I'm ready whenever you are. I know Millie and Miss Harriet are probably worried about us, so the sooner we get back, the better."

"All right. Let me take care of things inside and we'll go."

"How long will the ride take us?"

"We're a good two hours out, but we should make it back in time to get some breakfast."

"So you like Kate's cooking, do you?"

"Oh, yeah," he said with a grin.

Josh went back in to make sure the fire in the stove was completely out and to get his bedroll ready and gather up the rest of his gear. Then he went down to the shed to saddle his horse. Emmie was waiting for him when he rode up to the line shack.

"Do you want to ride in front of me or behind me?"

"It'll be easier for you if I ride behind you, won't it?"

"Yes," he answered, but he knew that either way, having her so close was going to test his self-control.

"Then I'll ride there."

"Let's go home," Josh said, offering a hand up.

Emmie took his hand and swung up behind him. She put her arms around him and held on tight as they headed out. She smiled to herself, enjoying being so close to Josh.

Josh concentrated on riding, but he was fully aware of Emmie pressed so tightly against him as they covered the long miles home.

# Chapter Seventeen

George was up before dawn and riding out just as everyone else was starting to stir. He'd gotten the general directions to the line shack from Burley the night before and headed that way now, taking another saddled horse with him. He'd asked Burley which horse to take along for Hank's daughter, and Burley had shown him the smoothest-gaited one in the stable. They both knew she would probably be hesitant to get back on her regular mount right away, after being thrown. George hoped there had been no further trouble, and that he would find Josh already on his way back to the ranch with Emmie.

George had been riding for over an hour when he came to the top of a low hill and reined in. He spotted a rider in the distance and immediately recognized his brother's horse. Putting his heels to his mount's sides, he hurried forward.

"Someone's coming," Josh told Emmie when he saw a rider heading their way leading a saddled horse.

"Is it one of the hands?"

"I'm not sure."

It took Josh a moment to recognize the other rider, and once he did he started smiling.

"I know who it is." He glanced over his shoulder at her. "It's my brother, George."

"Your brother is here?" Emmie asked, surprised. "The gambler?"

"He must have come to the ranch for a visit." Josh kneed his horse to a trot and rode to meet his brother.

George could see Josh riding along with a beautiful girl hanging on to him tightly, and he thought, *My brother sure has a rough life here on the Rocking R.* He was chuckling to himself as he reined in.

"You like riding double these days, Josh?" His gaze was warm upon the pretty, dark-haired girl who had her arms around his brother.

"Some days," Josh answered. "George, this is Emmie Ryan. Emmie, this is my brother, George."

Emmie looked up at the other man and thought there was no mistaking the resemblance between them. They both had the Grady good looks, with thick, dark hair and deep-set eyes. Looking at George, though, and seeing the glint in his eyes, she quickly decided he could be trouble—fun, but trouble. It didn't surprise her a bit that he was a professional gambler. "It's nice to meet you, George. Josh has told me all about you."

"Is that good or bad?" he asked, giving her a smile.

She couldn't help it; she laughed out loud. "It was all good."

"It's nice to meet you, too, Emmie. Do you often

go out looking for rustlers riding double with Josh this way?"

Josh wanted to groan. He knew George's sense of humor and guessed he wouldn't be hearing the end of this for some time.

Emmie appreciated George's humor and laughed. "You didn't hear the talk? I'm an Eastern girl, and I have trouble staying in the saddle. So we thought it was safer for me to hang on to him."

George immediately decided he liked this woman. Not only was she gorgeous, she was smart and quick with a comeback, too. "So you trust my brother?"

Emmie considered that question seriously. She did trust Josh, especially when she thought of the way he'd treated her with such respect last night. "Yes. My father trusted him, and I do, too. He's my partner, you know."

"So I heard. Emmie, I was sorry to learn about your father. He was a good man, and I'm sure he's missed."

"Very much," she managed.

Josh decided to put a word in. "Did Burley and the rest of the men get back to the ranch safely?"

"Yes. Burley rode in last. He told us that you were thrown." George looked at Emmie. "That's why I rode out this morning with a horse for you. I take it you're all right?"

"Thanks to Josh I am, and thank you for bringing another horse." Even as she spoke, though, Emmie felt disappointed that she was going to have to ride the rest of the way on her own.

"Burley said this one would be easy on you."

Josh helped Emmie down, and then dismounted to help her onto the other horse. He knew he was going to miss having her riding with him. Once he was certain she was comfortable in the saddle, he remounted his own horse.

"Let's get on back," Josh said.

"I take it you met Millie and Miss Harriet?" Emmie asked as they covered the miles back to the ranch at an easy pace.

"Yes, I did. They were very worried about you. Yesterday was a pretty rough day for them."

"Why?" Josh asked, glancing his way.

"Your not showing up last night wasn't the only trouble. There was a problem with one of the ranch hands, a man named Steve," George began, knowing that his brother needed to be told about the incident.

"Steve?" Emmie asked quickly. "What did he do?"

George explained what had happened.

"Poor Millie!" Emmie was horrified, but grateful for George's timely arrival and quick action.

"I chased Steve off, but that doesn't mean he's not still around somewhere."

"I'll take care of it when we get back," Josh said angrily. "I left Steve behind to keep an eye on things and to protect the women, not to harm them."

"Millie wasn't hurt, was she?" Emmie asked.

"No. She's fine," George reassured her.

Emmie sighed in relief at the news. She wished they were back at the house already so she could be with her friend.

"It was a good thing you showed up when you did," Josh said, glancing over at his brother as he rode beside them.

"Yes, it was," George agreed.

"So, what brings you to the Rocking R?" Josh asked. He sensed that George's visit was more than just social.

"I was missing you," his brother answered.

"You think I believe that?"

They both were chuckling.

"Actually, I was wondering if you're hiring any hands at the Rocking R. I'm looking for work," he admitted.

Josh was surprised. "What happened?"

"I ran into some bad luck. Can you use another hand around here? Or should I talk to your partner?" George grinned at Emmie.

"What do you think, Emmie? Should we hire him on?" Josh asked her good-naturedly.

Emmie didn't hesitate. She was impressed by how George had handled Steve and helped Millie in her time of need. "Yes. We can always use another good man around here, and since Steve won't be coming back, we are shorthanded right now."

Just then the ranch house came into sight, and a call went up as some of the men saw them returning.

Millie and Miss Harriet were waiting on the porch as they rode up.

Millie had been wondering where George was that morning, and now she knew. The fact that he cared enough to go looking for Emmie and Josh impressed her.

"Emmie!" Millie ran down the steps to welcome her friend home.

Josh swung out of the saddle and quickly went to help Emmie dismount. George dismounted and came to stand with them.

"We were so worried about you!" Millie said, giving her a big hug.

"There was no need to be. I was with Josh." Emmie looked up at Josh and smiled.

Miss Harriet was in a quandary as she watched the scene unfold before her. She wasn't quite sure what to say or how to react. By society's standards, it was unfitting for an unmarried young woman to spend the night alone with a man, but then again, this was the Wild West and not Philadelphia. She was coming to understand that life here was more about survival than high society, more about staying alive than impressing anyone with genteel manners. She knew Emmie and Josh might have gotten into serious trouble if they'd tried to make it back to the house in that horrible storm last night. Her mind made up, she left the porch to welcome them.

"I'm so glad you're safe," she told them both.

Josh looked down at Emmie. For an instant they both thought of the moment the night before, when Josh had said he'd heard Miss Harriet coming. It was hard for Emmie not to laugh.

"He took good care of me, Miss Harriet."

The chaperone looked up at the tall, handsome rancher and nodded her approval. "I knew he would."

The men moved off to tend to the horses and to let

the other hands know that George had been hired on. They also wanted to warn them about Steve, just in case he showed up and tried to cause trouble.

Emmie went inside with Millie and Miss Harriet. Kate was there to welcome her back, and then the cook set about fixing Emmie, Josh, and George a quick meal.

"Here you are," Kate said, setting the plate of fried eggs, biscuits, and bacon in front of Emmie, who was sitting at the kitchen table with Millie and Miss Harriet.

Emmie thanked her and wasted no time digging in, while Kate prepared plates of food to take to Josh and George.

"This is delicious."

"Thanks. I'm glad you like it." Kate was on her way from the kitchen with the plates of food when she remembered she had something to remind Emmie about. "Emmie, before I forget, this Saturday is the annual social in town."

"Oh, we'll have to go," Emmie said excitedly. She had attended the social several times over the years during her visits to her father, and she had always enjoyed herself.

"What goes on at one of your socials?" Millie asked.

"There's dancing and a big dinner. We'll have fun, and the social will give you a chance to meet more people. You'll go with us, won't you, Miss Harriet?"

"Of course, it sounds like a wonderful time."

"It is," Emmie assured them. She had been wondering when she would get the chance to spend some time with Josh away from the ranch, and the social would help with that. At least there she would be able to dance with him. The thought of being back in his arms thrilled her, but she couldn't let on. Not in front of Miss Harriet. She would talk to Millie later about everything that had happened.

"You can move in here with me," Josh told George as he finished off the breakfast Kate had brought to him.

"I was hoping you'd offer," George said. "How soon do you want me to start working?"

"I'll take you out this afternoon and show you around. I need to check with the other hands and find out if any of them has seen or heard from Steve. I want to make sure Steve knows he's been fired. I do owe him some back pay, and I'll see that he gets it, but I don't want him anywhere on the Rocking R near Millie again. If he'd try something like that with her, he might go after Emmie, too. We don't have time to ride herd on both of them."

"Oh, I don't know. That could be my new job—tending to your fillies. Millie is one fine-looking woman, and so is your Emmie."

"She's not 'my' Emmie," Josh denied a little too quickly.

"Well, you do have to admit she is beautiful," George insisted. He knew his brother well, and realized he was keeping his cards close to his chest.

"Yes, she is," Josh agreed. He'd been trying to remain focused on running the ranch since they'd gotten back. He'd been trying not to dwell on the time they'd spent alone together at the shack. He'd also been finding out that it wasn't easy to forget what had happened between them. The ride back had been rough, having her pressed so tightly against him the whole way, and memories of how it had felt tormented him. He'd always prided himself on being a man with good self-control, but there was something about Emmie that challenged his restraint.

"How's it working out having her for your boss? I mean, you get to see her every day and occasionally spend the night alone with her at a line shack. . . ."

"Emmie's not my boss. We're partners," Josh said quickly. "And nothing happened up at the line shack."

"Emmie can be my boss any day," George said. Then he added thoughtfully, "Come to think of it, now that you've hired me on, she is my boss."

"And I'm your boss, too—so remember that."

"Yes, boss." George was grinning at his brother.

"As soon as I get cleaned up and change my clothes, I need to go find Steve and settle things with him."

"Do you want me to ride with you?"

"No. I'll handle it. You can stay here and go to work."

Emmie had just finished bathing and washing her hair when a knock came at her bedroom door. "Who is it?"

"It's me, silly. Who else would it be?" Millie said. "Can I come in?"

"Of course."

Millie went into the room to find her friend sitting at the dressing table in her bathrobe combing out her freshly washed hair.

"Do you feel better now?"

"Much, although it's going to take a few days for the soreness to go away and the bruises to fade." Emmie dropped her robe off one shoulder to show Millie the large, nasty-looking bruise on her back.

"That must have been horrible," Millie sympathized.

"It was, but you know, I really was lucky. I didn't break anything. It could have been a whole lot worse."

"Can you imagine if you'd been out riding alone and something like this happened? Thank goodness Josh was with you."

"I don't know what I would have done without him. He knew right where the line shack was, and he knew it wasn't safe to try to make it back to the house."

"That's why he's the foreman around here. He knows what he's doing." Millie sat down on the side of the bed as Emmie shrugged back into her robe. "All right . . . I have to know. . . ."

Her friend sounded so excited, Emmie wasn't quite sure what to think. "You have to know what?"

"What was it like spending the night all alone in the middle of nowhere with Josh? That must have been so exciting!"

"It was," she admitted.

"I know you like him—a lot! I can tell just by watching you when you're around him. I've never seen that look in your eyes before, not even when you were with Kenneth. Are you in love with Josh?"

Emmie had always known that Millie understood her better than anyone else, and her friend had just proven it again. "I think I am."

"What happened?" Hopeless romantic that she was, Millie was dying to hear Emmie's story.

"Well, he kissed me."

"And . . . ?" Millie was breathless as she waited for the details.

"It was wonderful." Emmie sighed dreamily.

"So, what are you going to do now?"

"I don't know, but I can't wait for the social in town this weekend. Then I'll get to dance with him."

Millie gave her a smile as she pointed out, "You know, the two of you are already partners. Getting married would just make it an even closer partnership."

"Just because I think I'm in love with him, that doesn't mean he's in love with me."

"He hasn't said anything?"

"No."

"He will. Actions speak louder than words. You'll see," Millie said confidently.

Emmie looked up at her friend, excitement shining in her eyes. "I hope you're right."

The rest of the day passed quietly for Emmie. She stayed up at the house, resting after her ordeal, and didn't get the chance to see Josh again. As she went to bed that night, she found it hard to believe that only twenty-four hours before she had been alone with him at the line shack. The memory of his kiss and touch stayed with her, and left her restless as she lay in her solitary bed.

Emmie knew sleep wasn't coming anytime soon, so she got up and went to stand at the window. The moon was bright that night and cast its glow upon the miles of Rocking R land. Emmie stared out across the moon-kissed landscape. It was dark and peaceful, and she knew deep down in her heart that there was nowhere else she would rather be. She belonged here.

Emmie let her gaze drift toward Josh's place. There was a lamp burning in the cabin window, which meant he was still awake, and she wondered if he missed her as much as she missed him. She sighed and turned away.

She had to get some rest.

She had to get back to work tomorrow.

This was her ranch.

Josh sat at the small table in his house, trying to relax. He'd just returned from his trip into town to find Steve, and he was ready to call it a day.

"How did it go?" George asked, going to sit with his brother. He was worried about Steve causing more trouble on the ranch, and he wanted to make sure the man wouldn't be coming back.

"Luckily, Steve was real easy to find. He was down at the saloon, having a good old time."

"What did he have to say for himself?"

"He wasn't happy about being fired, but I think he knew it was coming. I paid him what he was due. Hopefully he'll move on now."

"Hopefully," George agreed.

They went to bed then.

George fell asleep right away, but it took Josh longer. He'd hoped to get back from town early enough to see Emmie. He'd wanted to tell her and Millie how his conversation with Steve had gone. When he'd ridden in, though, the main house had been dark, and he'd known it would have to wait until morning.

# Chapter Eighteen

The rest of the week passed quickly, and Emmie was glad. They'd been working hard, and she was ready to relax and have some fun—and spend some time with Josh. They hadn't had a minute alone together since the night at the line shack, and she found herself regretting that.

Saturday morning dawned clear and bright, and Emmie and Millie were eagerly anticipating the day ahead as they went downstairs for breakfast.

"If you can be ready to leave by eleven, we'll go into town then. That will give us time to get settled at the hotel before everything gets started," Emmie said.

"Do you always spend the night in town after the social?"

"The dance doesn't end until late, so it's easier that way."

"I'll be ready, and I'll make sure Miss Harriet is, too."

Miss Harriet was already at the table when they entered the kitchen. They found she was talking with Kate about the day's activities and was as excited as they were about the upcoming social.

"Why wait until eleven?" Miss Harriet asked. "I'm ready now."

"Josh and some of the men are going to ride in with us, so we have to wait until they finish their chores," Emmie explained.

"They should work faster," Millie teased.

"They're working plenty fast," Kate joined in. "They like the idea of a night in town, too."

"Are you wearing a dress on the ride in?" Millie asked her friend.

"Yes. I can get away with wearing my pants when I'm working, but not today."

"I guess I'd better wear a dress, too," Miss Harriet put in, laughing.

They all laughed with her and finished eating breakfast.

"What are you making to take to the dinner?" Emmie asked Kate. She knew the cook always prided herself on the desserts she brought to the social.

"Pecan pies," Kate said.

"Sounds delicious," Millie said.

"They are, trust me," Emmie assured her friend. "Most everybody at the social will be watching for Kate to come in. They all want to see what she's bringing for the dinner."

"I'm making four of them, so hopefully you'll all get a piece."

"I don't know. Some of those cowboys stake out the table and pounce on whatever dessert you bring."

"Yes, I know," Kate said, smiling. "Burley's already been up to the house this morning to check on me."

As soon as they were finished with the meal, they went up to pack what they would need for an overnight stay in town.

It was right at eleven o'clock when George drove the carriage up to the house. The women were ready and waiting for him.

"You ladies look lovely today," he told them, his gaze lingering on Millie.

"Why, thank you," Miss Harriet said.

He began loading their bags and then helped them up into the carriage. Soon they were on their way. When they drove past the stable, Josh, Burley, and the other ranch hands who were going to town rode out to accompany them into Shotgun.

It was a warm day, and the streets of the town were dusty as they rode in. George stopped in front of the hotel to let the ladies out before taking the carriage to the stable. Miss Harriet and Emmie got down first, and then George reached up to take Millie's hand to help her.

"Will you save me a dance tonight?" he asked, his dark eyes challenging hers. He was looking forward to the evening. Over the last few days he'd managed to spend more time with Millie, and he knew she was a very special woman. He wanted to get to know her better—a lot better.

Millie gave him a teasing grin as she asked, "Just one?"

Right then and there, in the middle of Shotgun, with lots of folks around, George wanted to take her in his arms and kiss her. It took a lot of willpower, but he managed to control the impulse. He grinned up at her. "I thought there might be a long line, and I wanted to be first."

Millie's heartbeat quickened at his romantic words. "You can have all the dances you want."

"I'll see you tonight."

"Don't be late," she told him, looking over her shoulder flirtatiously as she went to join Emmie and Miss Harriet where they were waiting on the sidewalk.

Josh tied up his horse, got the ladies' bags for them, and went to speak with George. "Take the carriage on over to the stable. I'll meet you down at the saloon."

"Sounds good to me," his brother agreed. He cast one last quick look Millie's way and then drove off.

Josh went to talk to Emmie, Millie, and Miss Harriet for a moment.

"It's going to get a little wild here in town tonight," he cautioned.

"It is? Why?" Millie asked.

Josh quickly explained, "It isn't often the boys get to come into town and party this way. They're going to be enjoying themselves, so be careful and stay together if you can."

He had managed to speak to Emmie earlier that day when Millie hadn't been around to warn her to keep a lookout for Steve while they were in town. He was reasonably certain the troublemaker had moved on, but there was no way to know for sure. He knew George would be spending as much time with Millie as he could, but he wanted the girls to remember they weren't back East anymore.

"We will," Emmie promised.

"But we don't have to worry," Millie protested. "You're here, and so is George." Then, giving him a teasing smile, she added, "That is, unless you're the ones we're supposed to be looking out for."

Josh laughed.

"You never know," he said as he opened the door to the hotel for them.

"I'll meet you here in the lobby just before four, and we can go over to the dinner together."

"We'll be ready and waiting for you," Emmie promised.

A short time later Emmie and Millie were busy unpacking in the room they were sharing. Emmie finished first and sat down on the bed to wait for her friend.

"So, you're looking forward to dancing with George tonight, are you?"

"Did you have any doubt? I can't wait. I wanted to spend more time with him this week and get to know him better, but he was working so much, I never got the chance."

"You will tonight," Emmie assured her.

"And you're going to get to dance with Josh. I think we've got an exciting evening coming up."

"We definitely do."

The dust was thick and the heat nearly unbearable as the stagecoach traveled the seemingly endless miles to Shotgun. The driver was pushing the team hard, for they were running late, and he was trying to make up time. It was obvious to the driver that the area had suffered a bad storm recently, for the roads were far worse than usual and almost washed out in some places. It made the ride rough, and he was certain his three passengers were feeling every bump, but there was nothing he could do about their discomfort except get the trip over with as soon as possible.

Inside the stagecoach, Kenneth sat staring out the window, trying hard to keep his seat. He could not remember another time when he'd been so hot and miserable, and he couldn't imagine why Emmie liked it out West. True, he hadn't reached Shotgun or the Rocking R yet, but judging from what he'd seen so far, he had little hope his surroundings would improve.

*Two years . . .*

*Two years!*

The realization that he would have to live out here in the middle of nowhere on Emmie's ranch for two years gnawed at him, but he kept telling himself the end result would be worth it. And there was still the hope that Shotgun would be a better town than its name indicated. Kenneth wiped the sweat from his brow with his handkerchief and looked over at the older couple, Victor and Margaret Turner, who were riding with him.

"What time will we reach Shotgun?" Kenneth asked.

"We've still got quite a ways to go," Victor informed him, trying not to smile. The Easterner had said little during their hours together on the stage, and he could tell the man was not enjoying himself at all.

"We will make it before dark, won't we?" Kenneth was hoping to reach the ranch and Emmie tonight.

"We should."

"Is someone meeting you in Shotgun?" Margaret asked cordially.

"No, I'm going to have to make arrangements to get out to the Rocking R once I reach town."

"The Rocking R is one of the biggest and most successful ranches in these parts."

"Yes, it is," he agreed, although he really knew very little about the matter. He didn't offer any more information. He had no interest in making casual conversation with his companions.

Margaret and Victor fell silent as the man turned his attention out the window again. They couldn't help wondering how he was going to like Shotgun. At that moment, though, the stagecoach gave a violent lurch, and they were thrown around the inside of the vehicle.

Kenneth was caught off guard and thrown from his seat. The stagecoach rocked wildly, and he could hear the driver cursing as he fought for control. When at last the driver brought the coach to a stop, it leaned awkwardly to one side, and Kenneth was hard-pressed to climb out. He finally managed to open the door and jump down.

"What happened?" he demanded of the driver.

Jack, the driver, had already gotten down to check what had happened, and he was swearing under his breath when he saw the damage to the front wheel. When he looked up and saw Mrs. Turner stick her head out the window, he quickly caught himself. "Oh, sorry, ma'am."

Margaret gave him an affronted look. "Are we stranded here?"

"I don't know yet. I have to take a look at the wheel."

Victor climbed out and went to stand with Kenneth as the driver quickly assessed how badly the wheel had been broken.

"I can mend it good enough to get us to town, but I'm going to need your help," Jack advised the two men.

"What do we need to do?" Victor asked, rolling up his shirtsleeves, ready to go to work.

Kenneth was disgusted for a moment. This would never have happened to him back home—but he wasn't back home. He was in Texas, and he had no choice but to help. He took off his suit coat and put it inside the stagecoach and then rolled up his sleeves. He had a feeling that they weren't going to make it to town anytime soon. He took a look around at the deserted countryside, remembering Mrs. Ryan's story about the Indian raid, and then got to work with the other two men.

"You look positively gorgeous. That shade of blue is lovely on you," Millie told Emmie as she stood back and stared at her friend. Her gown was simple yet elegant, and she had arranged her hair up in a sophisticated style.

"Thanks. You look beautiful yourself," Emmie replied. Millie's gown was pale green and enhanced her blond hair.

"Do you think I should wear my hair up like yours?" Millie asked, turning to glance at her own reflection in the mirror. She'd chosen to wear her hair down around her shoulders in a mass of soft curls.

"No, it's perfect just as it is."

"All right. If you say so. Are you ready?" She was eager to go downstairs.

"I'm ready."

They were both smiling as they left the hotel room to meet Miss Harriet.

The chaperone was waiting for them.

"Look at you!" she said in delight. "You're both stunning. I wonder if this town has ever seen two girls as pretty as you."

Millie gave her a quick hug. "You are so sweet!"

"Come on," Miss Harriet encouraged. "Let's go show those boys what real ladies look like."

"You don't think I should go back and change back into my pants?" Emmie teased.

"Not tonight, my dear. Not tonight."

They left her room and started down to the lobby to meet Josh.

Josh and George had taken a room at the hotel, too. After getting cleaned up, Josh had left his brother and gone out to take a look around town. He'd wanted to check on Steve and make sure he really had left town for good. He didn't want any fights erupting tonight at the dance. And that was sure to happen if Steve showed up unexpectedly and tried to cause more trouble for Millie and George. He'd been satisfied that things were quiet in Shotgun—or at least as quiet as they could be with everyone in town for the social that night. Now he and George were waiting in the lobby for the ladies, ready to enjoy the evening ahead.

Josh heard them coming first. He looked up just as Emmie appeared at the top of the stairs, and he could only stare at her as she started down the steps to the lobby. She was moving with a supple grace that held him mesmerized until George spoke up from behind him.

"I think your partner's ready to go to the social," George told him, a hint of mischief in his voice.

"Sometimes it pays to have a partner," Josh countered, going forward to meet her at the foot of the stairs.

Emmie knew the men were watching her, and she smiled. Josh looked even handsomer than usual, clean shaven and dressed up as he was. She met his gaze as she reached the bottom of the steps. "We're ready."

"So are we. Let's go have some fun," he replied.

"You boys behave yourselves tonight," Miss Harriet told them with a smile. "I'll be keeping an eye on you with my girls."

"Yes, ma'am." Josh and George had lost their

mother early in life, but they knew a true lady when they saw one.

"Of course, I might go a little easier on you if you both decided to save a dance for me."

"I was hoping *you'd* save a dance for *me*." George spoke up first, charming her even more.

They were all laughing in delight as they left the hotel to join the festivities.

# Chapter Nineteen

It was easy to tell that the social was the biggest event of the year in Shotgun. Excitement was the rule of the day as folks made their way down the main street of town to the church hall, where the dance was being held.

Josh and George escorted Emmie, Millie, and Miss Harriet inside, where they were welcomed warmly by Reverend Hunt. The hall was already getting quite crowded, so they went looking for a table and found one on the far side of the room. Emmie knew most everyone, so she took Millie and Miss Harriet around to introduce them. Many offered her their condolences over the loss of her father, and she thanked them for their thoughtfulness. Josh and George, meanwhile, decided just to stay at the table and wait for word that the food was being served.

"So, we're getting a real good meal tonight, are we?" George asked, looking around the room.

"Oh, yeah. All the ladies bring their favorite dishes. No one leaves here hungry, that's for sure."

"If the rest of the women are half as good cooks as Kate, this is going to be one fine dinner."

Miss Harriet decided to join a few older ladies at their table for a while, so Emmie and Millie started back to sit with Josh and George. Just then Carol Mason spotted them and made her way quickly over to speak to the two friends.

"Well, Emmie, Millie, it's good to see you," Carol said as she looked them over with a critical eye. She couldn't help being envious of the beautiful gowns Emmie and Millie were wearing. They were more elegant than anything that could be bought in Shotgun.

"Good evening, Carol." Emmie didn't particularly want to engage the town gossip in any lengthy conversation, but she knew she had to be cordial.

"Are you enjoying your visit?" Carol asked, turning to Millie. She'd been curious about how the young woman from the big city was adapting to ranch life.

"Oh, yes. It's been a true adventure," Millie told her.

"Will you be staying much longer?"

"I don't know. I haven't even thought about going back home yet."

Carol smiled at Emmie. "And how are things working out for you with your new partner?"

"Everything has been fine." Emmie knew the other woman was hoping to hear juicy tidbits about conflict between the two owners of the Rocking R, so she added, "I miss my father dearly. It's hard some days not having him there with me, but Josh has been a big help."

"I'll just bet he has," Carol said, thinking how much she would have enjoyed having Josh for a partner. He was one handsome man. She glanced over to the table where Josh was sitting with another man. "Who's the new fellow? I haven't seen him around before."

Carol knew the other ladies in town would be curious about the newcomer, and she always liked to have information first. The stranger was as good-looking as Josh, and she was certain some of the unmarried women in town would be interested in learning everything they could about him. She knew there were already quite a few who were enamored with Josh and would be setting their sights on him tonight.

"That's Josh's brother, George. He just hired on with us."

"Oh, my goodness. I didn't know Josh had a brother. How interesting. Well, I'll be speaking to you later." Carol hurried off to spread the news to the eagerly waiting ladies.

Emmie could only shake her head as she watched the gossip leave. "Soon everyone in the hall is going to know exactly who George is."

"From what you've told me, I don't think you need a newspaper in Shotgun—you've got Carol."

They shared a knowing look, for they both had dealt with nosy women before and knew how much trouble they could cause.

"I can't wait for the music and dancing to start," Millie confided as they went back to their table.

Emmie glanced over at her and smiled. "I feel the same way."

They were both looking forward to spending the evening with Josh and George.

They had just taken their seats when Reverend Hunt walked to the front of the room to get everyone's attention. Once the crowd had quieted down, he announced that the meal was about to be served and that it was time to say grace. All bowed their heads and said the prayer. Once everyone had murmured, "Amen," the social was officially under way.

"How does this work?" George asked, as he saw those seated on the far side of the room get up to go to the serving tables. He'd been watching as the ladies who'd volunteered to help brought out the bowls and platters piled high with delicious fare.

"We go up table by table, and everybody takes as much as they want," Emmie explained.

"We're sitting so far back, there might not be anything left by the time we get up there," George said anxiously. After hearing the talk of the other ranch hands, he'd been looking forward to this dinner for a few days now.

"You don't have to worry, George," Emmie reassured him. "There will still be plenty of food left when it's our turn. There always is."

As she remembered attending the social the previous year, Emmie thought of her father and the good time they'd had together that night. A pang of sorrow stabbed her, and she tried to fight it down. She wanted to enjoy the evening.

"Emmie? Are you all right?" Millie noticed that her friend had suddenly gone quiet, and she had seen the shadow of pain mirrored in her eyes.

She nodded. "I was just thinking of my father again. He would definitely be enjoying himself if he were here."

"Yes, he would," Josh put in. He'd noticed the change in Emmie, too, and he wanted to make sure she had a good time tonight. This was the first opportunity they'd had to be together away from the ranch, and he wanted to take advantage of it.

"When are the rest of the ranch hands going to show up?" Millie asked. She hadn't seen Burley or the other boys come in yet.

"They're probably over at the saloon right now, but they'll be here soon. They know Kate brought her famous pecan pies, and they won't dare miss the chance to get some," Josh said.

"And then once they're through serving the meal and everyone's finished eating, we go outside and the dancing starts," Emmie added.

"I can't wait," Millie said, casting a quick glance George's way to find his dark-eyed gaze warm upon her.

"There is one thing I need to warn you about," Emmie began.

"What's that?" Millie asked.

"Some of the ranch hands can get a little wild as the night goes on, and they aren't the most light-footed when it comes to dancing, so be careful when you're out on the dance floor."

"I will."

The time came for them to get their food, and they went up to the serving tables, more than ready to enjoy the feast.

And it *was* a feast.

The crispy fried chicken, steaks, mashed potatoes, corn, and biscuits looked delicious, and then they came to the dessert table. Fresh cut watermelon, chocolate cake, apple pies, and Kate's pecan pies were all there.

"Can I have one of everything?" Millie asked in delight as she looked over the vast array of rich desserts.

"I was thinking two of everything," George said.

"I just want Kate's pecan pie," Josh put in.

"It's that good, is it?" George asked.

"No, you won't like it," Josh told him, trying not to smile.

"I know you too well, brother. You're only saying that so I won't take a piece and that leaves more for you when you come back for seconds."

"You used to fall for it," Josh complained.

"That was a long time ago. I've caught on to your ways now." George laughed at him. He followed his brother's lead and chose a piece of Kate's pie.

With plates heaped high, they returned to their table to enjoy the meal.

Across the room, Mary Anne Watson and Linda Stewart had been watching Josh and George with open interest after talking with Carol Mason.

"I can't wait until the dancing starts," Mary Anne said, giving her friend a conspiratorial look.

"What are you planning?" Linda knew Mary Anne very well and could tell she was up to something.

"I'm going to dance with Josh Grady tonight if it's the last thing I do," Mary Anne declared.

"Even after Carol told you he used to be a bounty hunter?"

"That just makes him more intriguing," Mary Anne replied.

"I guess that leaves his brother, George, for me," Linda said with a slight grin, thinking the brother was just as good-looking as Josh. "How are we going to do this? Emmie and that friend of hers look like they've already staked their claims on the fellas."

"Hardly," Mary Anne said. "Josh is the foreman and part owner of the Rocking R, so I guess he thinks he has to stay with Emmie here at the social. You just watch. Once things liven up around here, he's going to be mine."

"Are you planning on branding him?" Linda teased.

"If I have to . . ."

"Or . . ." Linda's eyes lit up as she had an even better idea.

"Or what?" Mary Anne asked.

"Or . . . since he was a bounty hunter, we could put up a wanted poster with a big reward and have him go after you."

"Ooh, I like the way you think!"

"I thought you might enjoy having him chase you."

"I would. And I wouldn't run very fast. Then once he captures me and takes me in . . ."

"You'd give him that big reward, wouldn't you?" Linda was snickering. "What reward would you give him, Mary Anne?"

Mary Anne gave her a wicked look. "I'll have to think about that."

Both girls were laughing as they finished their meal and began to fantasize about the night to come.

"That was delicious." Millie sighed as she took the last bite of the pecan pie. "Kate's pie is wonderful."

"Yes, it is," George agreed. "That's the best pecan pie I've ever had."

"It was my father's favorite, too," Emmie added.

George looked at Josh and asked, grinning, "Is this why you decided to settle down at the Rocking R? You knew how good the cooking was?"

"Absolutely," Josh answered.

"Did you all enjoy your dinners?" Miss Harriet asked as she returned from visiting with the other ladies to take up her role as chaperone again. She'd been keeping an eye on Millie and Emmie from across the room and was glad to see that Emmie seemed to be enjoying herself. She'd been a bit worried that the evening might prove painful for her, but her young charge seemed all right.

"Dinner was wonderful," George said, looking up

at her. "And, since the dancing is about to begin, I was wondering . . ."

"What?" she asked, curious.

"I was wondering if you'd do me the honor of giving me the first dance, Miss Harriet?"

Miss Harriet smiled at George, a twinkle of mischief in her eyes. "Why, George Grady, you are such a charmer."

"It comes to me natural-like when I'm dealing with a lady like you." He smiled at her.

"So you think if you dance with me first, I won't mind if you spend a whole lot of time with my girls tonight?"

George never wavered. "Yes, ma'am."

"You're absolutely right. Let's go, young man."

As George rose from the table, Miss Harriet stepped brazenly forward to take the arm he offered to escort her outside, where the dance floor had been set up.

Miss Harriet was truly enjoying herself tonight, and she looked over her shoulder at Josh as they started to walk away. "I expect to be dancing with you very soon, too." Then she turned all her attention back to George, smiling delightedly up at him.

Josh, Emmie, and Millie got up to follow them from the hall. They were all enjoying the chaperone's sense of humor tonight.

"I don't know, Millie . . ." Emmie said, sounding a bit thoughtful.

"What?" Millie glanced over questioningly.

"The way Miss Harriet is acting, she may be having second thoughts about going back East. She seems to be enjoying herself out here in the Wild West."

"You're right," Millie said, laughing. "She is, but then, who wouldn't be with so many handsome men wanting to dance? We don't even have dance cards, and she's already got George and Josh lined up."

Emmie looked up at Josh as Millie walked on ahead of them. "I wonder if I'll ever get to dance with you tonight. It looks like I've got some serious competition."

"Yes, you do, but I think Miss Harriet likes my brother better." Josh was smiling.

"Well, I can try to make that up to you," she said in a soft, tenderly seductive voice.

"In that case, I think I might not mind being slighted by Miss Harriet," Josh returned, looking down at her.

For a moment their gazes met, and they were both caught up in the memory of that night in the line shack, when Josh had jokingly said the chaperone might show up at any minute. The music began then and brought them back to reality.

"I believe this is our dance," Josh said, taking her hand.

Emmie grinned up at him. "And I think we'll be safe, because George is going to keep Miss Harriet real busy."

"Let's go."

They joined the dancers on the floor.

Millie found a place at the side of the dance floor,

but she wasn't alone there for long. Burley and the other boys spotted her and wasted no time hurrying over.

"Would you like to dance, Millie?" Burley invited.

"Yes, I'd love to," she said.

Burley whisked her out onto the dance floor to join the others.

# Chapter Twenty

As far as Miss Harriet was concerned, the dance ended far too soon. She had enjoyed feeling young again, at least for a little while. The good news was, Josh owed her a dance, too. She was smiling as she looked up at George.

"Thank you, George," she told him.

"No, thank you, Miss Harriet," George said gallantly as he escorted her to the side of the dance floor, where Burley was standing with Millie.

"He's all yours, Millie," Miss Harriet said. "Now, where's Josh?"

They laughed as she went to find Josh and Emmie.

"So, Burley, how good a dancer is she?" George asked. "Is it safe for me to take her out on the floor?"

"None better, except maybe Miss Harriet," the ranch hand replied. "I'm going to have to get me a dance with that little lady."

"You'll have to get in line. Josh has the next dance with her."

"I'll see about doing just that." Burley chuckled, moving away.

Millie looked up at George. "And I've got the next dance with you. Miss Harriet trained me right—go after what you want and don't stop until you get it."

"Don't worry," he assured her. "I'm not going anywhere."

"Good."

George looked down at Millie just then and knew he'd never seen a lovelier woman. He didn't know how he'd come to this moment, watching her gaze up at him with such trust and innocence, but he didn't want it to end. He'd led a hard life. He'd spent a lot of time on the wild side, and yet the look in Millie's eyes made him feel like a totally different man. George grew a bit uncomfortable with himself and hoped he could live up to her expectations. Taking her hand to lead her out to dance, he knew he had to try.

Miss Harriet wasted no time finding Josh and Emmie. She claimed the ranch foreman as the music started up again. Les, the lawyer, was in attendance, too, and he left his wife with her friends as he went to ask Emmie to dance.

"How have you been doing? Are things working out well with Josh?" Les asked as he moved with her around the dance floor.

"Yes, he's been wonderful to work with."

"I was hoping the two of you would get along. It looks like Millie and Miss Harriet are enjoying themselves."

"I have to admit I've been a little surprised by how well Miss Harriet is taking to ranch life."

"And your friend Millie?"

"Being at the Rocking R has turned into a real adventure for Millie. I've even been teaching her how to shoot."

Les looked a bit shocked for a moment, because he knew what a lady Millie was, but then he nodded his head in understanding. "Let's just hope she never gets caught in a situation where she might have to use a gun."

"I know, but I don't want her to be defenseless either."

The lawyer knew she was right about that.

When the dance ended, he escorted her back to where Millie was standing with Josh, George, and Miss Harriet.

"It's nice to see you all tonight," he greeted them, and they chatted for a short while before he returned to his wife.

The dancing continued, and Emmie was thrilled when Josh claimed her again. It was a slower tune this time, and she willingly went into his arms. They moved together about the dance floor.

Millie and Miss Harriet were watching them.

"You know, Millie, they make a very nice-looking couple," the chaperone said with a smile of approval.

"Yes, they do."

"So, we could say they're dancin' partners and ranchin' partners?"

They were laughing as George glanced over at them, wondering what was so funny. "You're not making fun of my dancing, are you?"

"Not at all," Miss Harriet said quickly. "In fact, I was just trying to discourage Millie from grabbing you and hauling you out on the dance floor again—since you hadn't asked her to dance yet."

George didn't mind indulging Miss Harriet. "I was resting up a bit before asking you to dance again."

"I'm finished for the night," the chaperone told him, and then she added, "Millie is all yours, as long as you behave yourself. I'll be keeping an eye on you two."

"Yes, ma'am," he replied respectfully, enjoying her motherly dictates. That type of influence had been missing from his life for a long time, and he found he appreciated it. "May I have the pleasure of this dance, Millie?"

"Absolutely," she answered.

They moved out to the dance floor and joined the other couples.

Linda and Mary Anne were annoyed as they stood near the refreshment table, sipping their punch.

"I don't believe this! Josh is dancing with Emmie again!" Mary Anne hissed under her breath.

"I know, and his brother is dancing with that Eastern girl again, but we'll get our chance. We just have to be closer to them when they announce the ladies' choice dance, so we can claim those brothers before anyone else does. The switch dance is coming up, too."

"I know, but I'd like Josh to notice me and ask me to dance himself."

"Oh, he will, once you've managed to get him out on the dance floor," Linda assured her. She knew how determined her friend could be when she set her mind on doing something, and Mary Anne wanted Josh Grady.

"What about you? That other Eastern girl looks like she's got Josh's brother all to herself."

"I'll have my turn at him; you just wait and see. Come on. Let's work our way in their direction so we'll be ready when the time comes."

They quickly finished their punch and started off on their mission to get a dance with Josh and George.

Emmie found she was greatly disappointed when the music ended and she had to move out of Josh's arms.

"Want to get some punch?" she asked, hoping for some more time alone with him.

"Sounds good," he replied.

Emmie led the way toward the refreshment table.

Though Emmie was only a few steps ahead of Josh, it was all the distance Mary Anne needed to make her move.

"Ladies, it's your turn!" one of the musicians announced. "It's time for the ladies' choice dance! You gals go grab yourself a dancing partner!"

Mary Anne was thrilled. She had timed her approach perfectly. She stepped up to Josh just as he was walking past her and reached out to take his arm.

"It's the ladies' choice, Josh!"

"Mary Anne . . ." Josh glanced toward Emmie to find her watching him, but he knew there was no way out of dancing with Mary Anne.

"You're mine!"

"Let's dance," he agreed.

Emmie was surprised by the stab of jealousy she felt as she watched them go. She'd known Mary Anne for many years and had never liked the girl. The fact that Mary Anne had come after Josh angered her, and she decided she wasn't going to miss the ladies' choice. She quickly forgot about getting some punch and sought out Michael Collins, the local banker, to be her partner.

Mary Anne felt as if she'd won a major victory by getting to dance with Josh. She smiled up at him coyly. "How are things going out at the Rocking R?"

"Just fine," he answered, looking down at her.

"Are you having a good time tonight?"

"Yes, what about you?"

"Now that I'm dancing with you, I am," she answered, giving him a suggestive smile.

Josh thought Mary Anne was pretty, and he knew a lot of the men were after her, but there was really only one female he was interested in tonight. "I'm glad to oblige," he told her, but even as he spoke he took a quick look around the room and spotted Emmie dancing with the banker. He was surprised how irritated he was to see her in the other man's arms.

Mary Anne noticed Josh looking the other girl's way, and she frowned, wanting his full attention. "Josh, do you like having your brother working with you now?"

Josh had known everyone in town would be interested in hearing about George, so her question didn't surprise him. "It's good having him around."

Mary Anne gave up her attempt at conversation and just concentrated on enjoying the dance. When it ended, Josh thanked her and walked away, leaving her staring after him, more than a little disappointed. Mary Anne went to join Linda, and found her friend was frustrated, too. She'd had no luck wangling a dance with George, and the two girls were beginning to wonder if it was going to be a long night.

Emmie was on her way back to the refreshment table when Josh caught up with her.

"I'm ready for that punch now; what about you?" she asked just as the music started up again.

"No, it's time for the foreman's choice dance," Josh said, taking her hand.

Emmie was expecting him to go with the other couples back out onto the dance floor, but he surprised her. Josh drew her away from the refreshment area, off to a secluded spot behind the hall.

Emmie's heartbeat quickened as she looked up at him in the shadows of the night. "It's going to be less crowded for dancing out here," she said a little breathlessly.

"I wasn't planning on dancing," Josh answered.

Certain that they were alone, Josh didn't waste any time. He took her in his arms and drew her to him, claiming her lips in a passionate exchange. Emmie responded eagerly to his kiss. She'd been dreaming of kissing him again ever since the night of the storm, and she linked her arms around his neck to draw him even closer to her.

Above them, the night sky was a canopy of stars. It was a heavenly moment.

Josh deepened the kiss even more and crushed

her against him. Caught up in the heat of his need for her, he forgot everything except the excitement of Emmie's embrace. He realized then for the first time that he was falling in love with her. He wanted her—

His thoughts got no further as the sound of Miss Harriet's voice jarred him back to reality.

"I thought I might find the two of you out here."

Emmie had been lost in the heaven of Josh's kiss, and she gave a startled gasp. "Oh, Miss Harriet . . ."

"It's a beautiful evening, isn't it?" Josh said, grinning down at Emmie as he remembered their time in the line shack.

"Yes, it is. I take it you're enjoying yourselves?" Miss Harriet asked.

"Oh, yes," Emmie answered.

"I thought so." Miss Harriet turned away and headed back to the dance, leaving them to follow.

"Why didn't you hear her sneaking up on us?" Emmie asked.

"I was busy," Josh said, drawing her aside for one final, sweet stolen kiss. "And a little distracted."

Hand in hand, they returned to the festivities.

Kenneth couldn't believe how long it had taken to repair the stagecoach. It had been close to sundown when they'd finally gotten on the road again, and they'd still had miles to go. The driver had told them how lucky they were that it was going to be a clear night and the moon was nearly full. Otherwise they would have had to camp out and wait until morning to finish the run into Shotgun.

As it was, Kenneth was not the least bit happy about arriving in town so late. He had wanted to go straight out to the Rocking R—and Emmie. Now he was going to be forced to spend the night in Shotgun, and he wasn't looking forward to it.

"Well, your trip is turning out to be a little more exciting than you expected, isn't it?" Margaret asked Kenneth.

"I don't know that I would call it exciting," Kenneth said disparagingly.

Victor heard the irritation in the Easterner's voice and spoke up. "You might as well get used to it. Out here in these parts, you never know what kind of trouble you're going to run into."

"I'll remember that," Kenneth said, not doubting for a moment that the other man was right. He just hoped the misery of this trip wasn't any indication of what was to come. He knew living on the Rocking R with Emmie was going to be a challenge, but he believed that once they were married, he could tough it out for the necessary two years. When the required time was up, he didn't think it would be too difficult to persuade her to sell the Rocking R and return to Philadelphia—and to civilization. He knew he could always use the lure of being with her mother to help convince her that it was the right thing to do.

The hours passed, and Kenneth was staring out his window at the night-shrouded landscape when he caught sight of some lights in the distance.

"Is that Shotgun?" Kenneth asked the couple.

Victor took a quick look. "Yes, I'd say we're almost there."

"Good."

A short time later the stagecoach pulled up to the stage office. Because it was so late, there was only one lone clerk still there working. He'd been waiting for the stage to show up and had grown increasingly worried as the hours passed.

"I was wondering what happened to you," Ben Clark said as he went outside to speak to Jack. He watched as the woman and two men climbed out of the stagecoach.

"We had some trouble, but I managed to put things back together again," Jack explained as he tossed down the passengers' bags.

"I'm glad you made it to town."

"So are we," Margaret said, her tone reflecting her exhaustion.

"Well, welcome to Shotgun," Ben said, putting their bags on the sidewalk for them. He eyed the Eastern dude openly, wondering at his business in town.

"What's going on tonight?" Jack asked.

"It's the big social. Lots of folks are in town to celebrate and have a good time."

The last thing Kenneth was interested in was socializing with the people of Shotgun. He just wanted to get out to the Ryan ranch as quickly as possible.

"I need to get transportation to the Rocking R Ranch," Kenneth announced. "Can you arrange that for me?"

Ben looked at him strangely. "You're going to have to wait until morning. There's no way to get you out there tonight, and besides, most everybody from the ranch is probably here in town for the social."

"Do you know Emmie Ryan?"

"Sure, I know Emmie. I would imagine she's here, although I haven't seen her around today."

Kenneth grabbed his bags. "Where can I get a room for the night? Is there a hotel?"

"We got one, but I doubt they got any rooms left. Shotgun is always crowded on the night of the social."

"Where can I spend the night then?" Kenneth asked, annoyed. Emmie might be right there in town, and he wanted to find her as quickly as he could—but first he needed to wash up a bit.

Ben looked at the couple who'd arrived with him. "Do you folks have a place to stay tonight?"

"No. We're just passing through."

"All right, go on into the office while I see what arrangements I can make for you."

They went inside to wait as Jack drove off in the stage.

A short time later Ben returned.

"I managed to find you a room," he told the Turners.

"What about me?" Kenneth demanded. He wasn't accustomed to being ignored.

"For tonight, I can let you sleep in the back room here at the office. There's a cot back there."

"There's no room at the hotel?"

"No. This is the best you're going to get tonight. Go on back while I take these folks over to the house where they'll be staying."

"Thanks," was all Kenneth could manage as the clerk left him alone there.

Picking up his bags, Kenneth made his way into the small room, which contained a stripped-down cot and a washstand. He had hoped for far more comfortable accommodations after all his days of travel, but at least he knew this was better than bedding down in the stable with the horses. He found that thought completely repulsive.

Kenneth turned his thoughts to finding Emmie over at the dance. He stripped off his jacket and shirt and started to wash up. It excited him to know that she was so near.

# Chapter Twenty-one

Millie was having a wonderful time. She'd danced with several men and had been stepped on only a few times. George stayed close by, and she was glad. He had just handed her a cup of punch and she'd taken a deep drink when she heard the voice behind her.

"Hello, Millie," Kenneth said. He'd been a bit worried about finding Emmie in the crowd, but his worries had disappeared the moment he'd spotted Millie at the refreshment table.

Millie recognized his voice right away and spun around to face him. She was wide-eyed with amazement and shock as she found herself face-to-face with Kenneth. She choked on the punch she was drinking, but managed to swallow it down as she gasped. "Oh, my heavens, Kenneth!"

George was looking on, and he was startled by Millie's reaction to the stranger. He stared at the man, who was obviously from back East, and wondered at his connection to her.

"Yes, it's me," Kenneth, forcing himself to smile

though he was not the least bit amused by the look on her face.

"What are you doing here?" She was still all but gaping at him.

"I came for Emmie. Have you seen her? Is she here?" he asked.

"She's dancing—with Josh," she answered quickly.

Kenneth turned his attention to the couples on the dance floor, and it was then that he saw Emmie in the arms of another man, gazing up at him most adoringly.

A shot of pure possessiveness shot through him.

Emmie was his. She had no business dancing with anyone else, let alone looking at another man like that.

"Nice to see you, Millie," Kenneth said as he started off, making his way toward Emmie.

Millie could only watch as Kenneth moved through the crowd toward Emmie.

"Who is that?" George asked.

"His name is Kenneth St. James—he's a friend from Philadelphia," she explained awkwardly.

"'A friend'?" George asked.

Millie looked up at him. "Emmie's friend."

George glanced toward his brother to see what was going to happen.

Kenneth was not the least bit happy about seeing Emmie dancing with another man, but he was about to put an end to all that. He had their future all planned. He'd certainly had enough time to think it out during the endless hours on the filthy stagecoach. He knew that within the next few days she would become his wife. He was certain there was a reverend or at least a justice of the peace somewhere in town who could marry them, and now that he was willing to stay on the Rocking R with Emmie for the necessary two years, there was no reason for her not to accept his proposal. Eager to have her in his arms, he tapped the stranger on the shoulder.

"Mind if I cut in?" Kenneth asked smoothly.

Josh was surprised by the interruption. He turned to find a man he'd never seen before standing there, looking down at Emmie with open affection.

"Kenneth?" Emmie gasped.

"Hello, love," Kenneth said in an affectionate tone. He smoothly stepped in and, keeping his back to the other man, danced Emmie away.

Josh moved off to the side of the dance floor, but he kept an eye on Emmie as the other man squired her expertly about. He couldn't believe the way Emmie had reacted to seeing the stranger, and he couldn't help wondering just who he was and what he meant to her.

"What are you doing here?" Emmie asked as she looked up at Kenneth. She was still in shock over his unexpected appearance.

"I came after you, darling," Kenneth told her. "I was missing you so much, I just had to come here and tell you how much I love you."

"Oh, Kenneth . . ." Emmie's expression was guarded as she listened to his profession of love.

"Don't say anything now. We'll have plenty of time to talk later. Right now I just want to enjoy dancing with you again." He went silent as he played his role of ardent suitor to perfection.

Emmie pretended to be happy, but in her heart it was Josh she wanted to be dancing with.

Millie had watched Kenneth cut in on Josh, so she went with George to speak to him.

"His name is Kenneth St. James," Millie offered before Josh could say a word. "He and Emmie were seeing each other in Philadelphia."

Josh said nothing, but he wondered why Emmie had never mentioned the other man. Josh turned away and went to see what Burley and the other hands were up to.

When the dance ended, Emmie and Kenneth left the dance floor and went to stand with Millie and George. Emmie quickly made the introductions.

"It's nice to meet you, George. So, you're one of the ranch hands?"

"That's right."

"How do you like the Rocking R?" Kenneth knew little about the ranch except what Emmie had told him after her annual trips.

"It's one of the finest spreads around," George bragged.

"That's good to know," he said, thinking the ranch was obviously worth a lot of money if it was considered a "fine spread."

Josh saw them gathered together talking and he went over to join them.

Kenneth didn't waste any time when he saw the other man coming. He arrogantly stepped forward, and, assuming his role as future owner of the Rocking R, he put his hand out to shake the other man's hand. "I'm Kenneth St. James. I take it you're one of the hired hands, too?"

Josh couldn't help smiling at the fool standing beside Emmie. He shook his hand as he answered, "Nice to meet you, Kenneth. I'm Josh Grady. I'm Emmie's partner, and the foreman at the Rocking R."

"Partner? I thought your father was the owner." Kenneth turned to Emmie for an explanation. He'd always been led to believe the ranch was her inheritance.

"My father and Josh became partners about a year ago. We're running the ranch together now," Emmie explained.

"And from what George was telling me, the Rocking R is doing fine."

"We like to think so," Josh said.

"Why, Kenneth, is that you?" Miss Harriet exclaimed, appearing out of nowhere to greet him.

"Hello, Miss Harriet."

"What are you doing here?"

"I came for Emmie. I've been missing her."

"You certainly must have, to travel all this way." Miss Harriet knew her job had just become even more difficult with Kenneth in Texas.

There was little chance to say anything else as someone called out, "Ladies and gentlemen, it's time for the last dance of the night."

Emmie knew she shouldn't have been surprised when Kenneth took her arm in a possessive grip and drew her out onto the dance floor. She caught only one glimpse of Josh walking away as they began to dance, and she wondered if she would have a chance to see him any more that night. This certainly wasn't the way she'd hoped the evening would end.

"I can't believe I'm actually here, dancing with you," Kenneth told her.

"Neither can I," Emmie said, and that was the truth.

"Are you going back to the ranch tonight?" he asked.

"No, we've taken rooms at the hotel. We'll go home in the morning. Where did you take a room?"

"The stagecoach was very late getting in, because we broke down. There weren't any rooms left here in town, but the clerk said I could spend the night at the stage office. What time should I meet you in the morning?" As far as he was concerned, it was understood that he would be a guest at the ranch for the rest of his visit.

"We'll be attending church services first. If you'd like to go with us, why don't you come to the hotel a little before eight."

"I will."

Emmie was grateful for Miss Harriet's presence and Millie's and George's company as Kenneth walked her back to the hotel, but she missed Josh and didn't know where he'd gone.

As Kenneth parted from Emmie at the hotel, he was angry that they'd had no time alone. He'd wanted to kiss her, to claim her for his own. He felt the whole day had been a disaster—and the night to come promised no better. He was dreading the prospect of bedding down on the cot in the back room of the stage office.

Millie and George lingered downstairs in the lobby for a few moments after Kenneth had gone and Miss Harriet and Emmie had retired to their rooms.

"Let's go outside so we can talk," she said.

She took George's hand and they left the building, moving to a quiet spot near a small grove of trees.

"What's troubling you?" George asked. He'd known she'd been unsettled by Kenneth's sudden appearance.

"What makes you think something's troubling me?" she asked, looking up at him in the moonlight. "I just wanted to be alone with you."

"I like the way you think, Millie," he said, slipping an arm around her to draw her near.

Millie lifted her arms, linked them around his neck, and drew him down to her for a kiss. It was a sweet kiss, but the gentle exchange served only to light the fire of their desire for each other.

George had wanted her from the first time he'd seen her, but after the distress caused by her encounter with Steve, he'd been hesitant to move too fast. Now he knew hesitation was behind them. It seemed she wanted him as much as he wanted her.

Deepening the kiss, George held her close. Millie returned his kiss, thrilled at his nearness. When at last they broke apart, she gazed up at him, all the adoration she was feeling for him showing in her eyes.

"I love you, George," she whispered, lifting one hand to caress his cheek.

"You do?" George stared down at her, reveling in her beauty and innocence, and he knew in that moment that he loved her, too.

"Oh, yes." Millie sighed. "I know we haven't known each other very long, but it was love at first sight for me."

George slowly bent down to claim her lips in another passionate kiss. "It was for me, too."

"Oh, George."

They clung together in the sweetness of the night until the sound of someone coming down the street forced them to break apart.

"We'd better get inside before Miss Harriet comes looking for me."

"And she will, too," he said with a smile.

"I know. She takes her duties very seriously."

George walked her back to the lobby. He had a room in the hotel, too, but he wanted to see if he could find Josh before he called it a night.

"Good night."

"Good night," she returned. "I'll see you in the morning."

George waited until Millie had gone up the staircase, then he left the hotel in search of his brother. It didn't take him long to find Josh at the saloon.

"I wondered where you went," George said as he joined his brother at the bar. After ordering a whiskey for himself and a refill for Josh, he said, "Let's go sit at a table."

"Sure, why not?"

They settled in at a table near the back of the crowded room.

"Why did you leave the dance early?" George asked.

"I figured Miss Harriet wasn't going to dance with me again, so there was no reason to stick around," Josh quipped, managing a wry smile.

"She likes me best," George bragged.

"It seems that way."

"What did you find out about this Kenneth?"

"Millie told me he'd been courting Emmie for some time now, but she was real surprised that he'd come all the way to Texas to see her."

"He must be serious about Emmie."

"What about you? Are you serious about her?"

Josh looked uncomfortable for a moment.

"Well?" George pressed him.

"I think I am," Josh finally admitted. "I sure didn't like seeing her dancing with Kenneth."

"You're jealous."

"I am not!"

"You're jealous of a city slicker!" George was laughing at him. "Do you love her?"

"I don't know." Josh paused and then finally said, "Yes."

"Then do something about it."

Josh looked up at him, an expression of determination in his eyes. "I will."

"Good."

"What about you and Millie?"

"I love her, but . . ."

"But what?"

"I never thought about marrying and settling down before, but that little lady could make me want to stay in one place for a long, long time—if she were there with me. The trouble is . . ."

"What?"

"She's a lady, and I'm a man who's spent the last years doing nothing but gambling for a living. I'm not good enough for her."

"But how does she feel about you?"

"She says she loves me."

"Have you told her about your past?"

"Yes. She knows."

"Then ask her to marry you. You'll find out real quick if she's a gambler, too. You might be made for each other."

"I think we are."

"Then don't let her get away."

George took a deep drink of his whiskey. "You're right."

They shared a companionable silence as they finished their drinks and headed back to the hotel.

# Chapter Twenty-two

Emmie was waiting anxiously for Millie to come up to the hotel room.

"What took you so long?" Emmie asked as her friend came through the door.

Millie blushed. "Oh, Emmie, George told me he loves me!"

Emmie jumped up from where she'd been sitting on the bed to give her friend an excited hug. "That's wonderful!"

"I know! I love him, too, but it's all happened so fast!"

"That is so romantic! Did he propose or anything?"

"No, not yet. It's enough just knowing that he loves me." She sat down on the bed with Emmie. "But what about you? I couldn't believe my eyes when I turned around and found Kenneth standing there."

"I was shocked, too. I never dreamed he would come out here."

"He must care a lot about you to make the trip."

Emmie looked uncomfortable. "He did propose before I left, but I couldn't marry him, not with the terms of my father's will. I have to stay here and run the ranch for at least two years. I just couldn't see how he would fit in on the Rocking R."

"How do you feel about him?"

Emmie was silent for a long moment and then looked up at her friend. "I don't love Kenneth. I don't think I ever have. I know now that Josh is the man I love."

"He is wonderful."

"I know."

"Have you told Josh yet?"

"No."

"Don't you think you'd better tell him?"

"I will, but first I have to deal with Kenneth, and, knowing him, he's not going to make this easy for me."

Millie gave her a reassuring hug. "What really matters is that you end up happy with Josh. You know, if Josh and George really do propose to us, we wouldn't just be friends; we'd be related."

"I guess I could stand having you for an in-law," Emmie teased.

"I would think here in Shotgun that would be a whole lot better than an outlaw!"

They were laughing as they got ready for bed. The morning was not far off, and they had to be up and ready to meet the men for church.

Emmie and Millie both rose early the following morning. Emmie hadn't slept well, troubled as she was by Kenneth's unexpected arrival. She wasn't looking forward to the confrontation she had to have with him.

They went down to the lobby to find Miss Harriet there with the men, waiting for them. Without stopping for breakfast, they made their way to the church for the Sunday-morning service.

It was nearly noon by the time they managed to get a bite to eat and pack. George brought the carriage around to pick them up, and then they were on their way to the Rocking R, with Josh riding along beside them. Millie and Miss Harriet were sitting together, while Kenneth sat beside Emmie. The heat was intense, and Emmie could tell that Kenneth was suffering in his suit.

"You're going to have to get used to the weather," Emmie told him.

"Is it going to be this hot every day?"

"It is," Emmie said. "It's summertime."

Kenneth could only imagine how hot the late-summer months would get if the temperature was this high already. He studied the lay of the land as they drove along, and as they traveled mile after mile, he came to understand just how far from town the Rocking R was.

"How soon will we get to the ranch?" he asked.

Miss Harriet couldn't help laughing at his question. "I asked the same thing on my first trip to the ranch. I do believe we've been on the Rocking R for quite a while now, haven't we, Emmie?"

"You're right, Miss Harriet."

"This is a big ranch," Kenneth said, impressed.

"Yes, it is. My father and Josh worked hard to make it what it is today."

Kenneth fell silent at the mention of the other man. He went back to studying the landscape and wondering how he was going to like living there, once he married Emmie.

"There's the house," Emmie pointed out some time later.

Kenneth was impressed with the main house and the numerous outbuildings. The spread reflected the family's wealth and made him feel a little more at ease. For a while there he'd feared he was going to end up living in a one-room cabin.

George drove them up to the front of the house to let them out. He looked down at Emmie as he asked, "Do you want me to take Kenneth's bags on down to the bunkhouse?"

Miss Harriet, looking her most prim and proper, spoke up first, dictating, "Yes."

"The bunkhouse?" Kenneth repeated in confusion. He'd expected to stay at the main house.

"With Miss Harriet and Millie here, there aren't any extra bedrooms," Emmie explained.

"And," Miss Harriet added, "since you're not family, it wouldn't be proper for you to stay in the house with the ladies anyway."

Kenneth knew he had no recourse. "Which one's the bunkhouse?"

George pointed it out for him. "I'll leave your bags there, and the boys can tell you which bunk will be yours when they get back in."

"Thank you, George."

Kenneth followed the ladies indoors and was immediately impressed by the home's interior. Though he was going to have to tolerate sleeping in the bunkhouse for a time, as soon as he could get Emmie to say, "I do," all that would change. "Your house is very attractive."

"Thanks. My father believed in being comfortable when he came home after riding all day."

Millie and Miss Harriet retired to their rooms to freshen up a bit.

"Would you like to take a look around the ranch? We can ride out for a while, if you'd like," Emmie offered.

"Yes, I'd like that."

"All right, I'm going to go up and change my clothes. You'll need to change, too, and I'll get one of my father's Stetsons for you to wear. It's going to be hot this afternoon."

"Thanks."

"Why don't you go on down to the bunkhouse and take a look around, and I'll meet you at the stable shortly. George and Josh should be nearby if you need anything."

"I'll be ready and waiting for you."

Emmie started to move away to go upstairs, but Kenneth took her arm and drew her back to him. She had little time to protest as he kissed her.

"Kenneth!" Emmie broke away, startled by his move. "Someone might walk in on us."

He just smiled confidently down at her. "Hurry up and change."

Kenneth was feeling quite smug as he left the

house. He made his way toward the bunkhouse, but the closer he got, the more disgusted he became. The bunkhouse was located near the stable, and the smell in that area was nauseating.

*Two years,* he told himself. *Just two years . . .*

That was all he had to endure.

He could do it.

He went inside to change his clothes and get ready for the ride.

Millie knocked on Emmie's door a short time later.

"Come in," Emmie called out as she finished pulling on her riding boots.

Millie went into Emmie's bedroom to find that she'd changed into her work clothes and was obviously ready to get back to ranch life. "What are you planning to do this afternoon?"

"I'm going to take Kenneth out for a ride and show him around. Do you want to come?" she asked hopefully.

Millie could understand why Emmie didn't want to be alone with Kenneth for any length of time. "I'm a little tired," she fibbed. "Could you get Miss Harriet to ride with you?"

"Oh, you!" Emmie tossed the pillow from the bed at her friend, and they both broke out laughing. "If you won't go, I just *might* ask her."

"No, that's all right. I'll go, but I thought you might be taking him to your secret swimming hole this afternoon—it is a little hot out today."

"Millie!" The thought of swimming with Kenneth shocked her.

"All right, all right. Give me a minute and I'll change, too."

Emmie got her holster and checked her gun to make sure it was loaded. She knew Kenneth would question the need for it, but she didn't want to be caught unprepared.

It wasn't long before Millie returned, dressed in her pants and boots, too, and they started down to the stable. Kenneth wasn't there yet, so the two girls started to saddle up the horses, with Burley's help. Just as they finished and were leading the horses out of the stable, Kenneth came out of the bunkhouse.

"How do you think your dude is going to like being here?" Burley asked Emmie, eyeing Kenneth as he walked their way.

"I guess we're going to find out real soon," she replied noncommittally.

Kenneth was looking around for Emmie as he headed toward the stable. As he reached the open doors, he saw her for the first time dressed in her work clothes and wearing a cowboy hat, just like the ranch hands. If that sight wasn't shocking enough, Millie was with her, dressed the same way. He was mortified as he stared at the two women.

"Emmie . . . ?"

"There you are," she began, unaware that he was upset. She turned to face him. "We're all ready to go."

When Emmie turned his way, he realized she was wearing a gun and holster, too. "Emmie, what are you doing?"

"What do you mean?"

"I mean, you're dressed like a common ranch hand—and, my God, you're carrying a gun!"

She understood his shock and hastened to explain. "Kenneth, it's all right. Out here, there's work to be done, and I have to do it. As far as the gun goes, this isn't Philadelphia. There are times when there is no one else around, and we have to be able to take care of ourselves."

"I'll be with you today. You'll be safe," he insisted.

Emmie fought hard not to laugh at him. "Are you carrying a gun?"

"Well, no."

"Then you wouldn't be much help if we have a run-in with a rattlesnake or some rustlers. Come on. Let's go for our ride." She handed him the hat she'd found for him among her father's things.

Kenneth realized she had just made him look the fool in front of the ranch hand, and her response didn't sit well with him. She was a lady, and she was supposed to act like one. He let the matter go for then, but he knew he would have to speak with her about it later. He couldn't very well be a successful ranch owner if the hands didn't respect him. He jammed the hat on his head and walked to the horses.

They mounted up, and Emmie led the little group away from the ranch house. She was looking forward to showing Kenneth around the Rocking R. She knew he had his own ideas of what ranch life was like, and she hoped to show him what it was really like. She loved this place, and she wanted him to understand why.

The following three hours were among the longest Kenneth had ever spent in his life. He could tell that Emmie was enjoying showing him around, but he found it hard to get excited about seeing a herd of cattle or a watering hole. He could appreciate that the cattle were dollars on the hoof, but the heat, the filth, and the smell left him yearning for his gentleman's club back home. He'd seen absolutely nothing on the ranch that seemed the least bit civilized, and he understood more clearly than ever why Emmie's mother had left and never returned.

When Emmie finally said it was time to head back, he was hard put not to celebrate openly—even though he was returning to the bunkhouse. He looked over at Millie, who seemed to be completely at ease riding across the long miles with Emmie.

"So, you're having a good time in Texas?" Kenneth asked, finding it hard to believe that she was.

"Yes," Millie answered him. "It's been a true adventure. I love it here." She was thinking of George when she said the last.

"You'll certainly have a lot of tales to tell everyone when you get back home."

"Yes, I will." But even as Millie said it, she wasn't certain she would be going back to Philadelphia. She missed her family, but she loved George, and she wanted to be with him.

They rode up to the stable and left the horses there before returning to the house to find Miss Harriet sitting out on the porch waiting for them.

"Did you have a nice ride?" she asked, her gaze on Kenneth.

"It's a big ranch. That's for sure," he answered.

"Yes, it is," Miss Harriet agreed, noticing that he hadn't praised anything. "Kate said dinner would be ready in about an hour."

"Good, I'm hungry," Emmie said. Looking at Kenneth, she explained, "Kate's the best cook around, and we're lucky she works for us. You'll be finding out for yourself real soon."

"I'll be looking forward to it. For now, though, I think I'd better wash up."

"Be back up here in an hour."

"Oh, I will," Kenneth promised.

# Chapter Twenty-three

Kenneth spent the next few days trying to acclimate himself to ranch life, but it wasn't easy. He had little interest in cattle and even less in horses. The ranch hands had tried to get him to saddle-break one of the horses, but he wasn't about to put himself at risk that way. He was a competent horseman, but he had no desire to try to ride a bucking horse.

When Kenneth had learned Emmie had to move to Texas and run a ranch, he'd never imagined just how much work that actually entailed. He'd thought she would simply direct things from the house and leave the actual physical labor to the hired hands. Now he saw how mistaken he'd been. He'd watched her rope and brand cattle with the men, and, to his disgust, she'd even helped deliver a foal when the mare had suffered complications and was close to dying during the delivery. He'd never seen anything so messy in his life. Still, he told himself he could come to accept the harshness of life on the Rocking R, knowing at the end of the two years they could escape back East.

It was on the evening of his third day on the ranch, after Miss Harriet and Millie had retired, that he sought Emmie out in her father's study, where he knew she was going over the books. He knocked quietly on the door and opened it.

"Mind if I come in?" Kenneth asked as he found her sitting at the desk poring over the ledgers.

Emmie looked up at him. "No, I'm almost finished here." Emmie was hoping that he was coming to tell her that he would be returning home soon. She had spent time with him over the last few days, but had not encouraged him romantically in any way, and she frankly couldn't wait for him to leave. She was missing Josh. He'd ridden out to check stock the day before, and she hoped he would be returning soon.

"Good, because I wanted to talk to you tonight," he said as he came to stand beside her chair. "Emmie . . ."

Kenneth reached down and took her arm, gently drawing her up to him.

Emmie stood and looked up at him, hoping to hear him say that he was leaving.

"Emmie, I . . ." He stopped in midsentence and bent to kiss her. "I love you, Emmie, and I want you to marry me. That's why I came out here to be with you. I knew you needed me, and I wanted to be here to help you."

"Kenneth—"

As she started to speak, the door Kenneth had left slightly ajar opened and Josh walked in.

"Emmie, I wanted to . . ." As he saw her standing

in Kenneth's embrace, he stopped abruptly. The look in his eyes hardened. "Sorry."

He turned and left the room, shutting the door behind him.

Emmie was so miserable, she wanted to scream. Josh couldn't have picked a worse moment to walk in on her. She jerked herself free of Kenneth's hold.

"Kenneth . . ."

Kenneth was completely surprised by her flustered response. What did it matter if Josh saw them together? They would be married soon.

"Emmie, I'm sorry Josh walked in that way. Does he always do that?"

"Yes."

"Then we're going to have to put some locks on these doors after we're married." He was smiling.

"What?"

Kenneth continued. "What I was about to say to you . . . Emmie, marry me, and we'll never have to worry about someone walking in on us again, or Miss Harriet checking up on us."

Kenneth had no idea that mentioning Miss Harriet would conjure up memories for Emmie of her time with Josh at the line shack and make this moment all the more embarrassing and painful for her. "Kenneth, stop."

"What?" he asked, puzzled.

"I'm sorry, Kenneth. I'm sorry, but I can't marry you," she told him, feeling fiercely determined. There was only one man she wanted to marry, and she had to go find him—now.

"What are you talking about?" he demanded in

open irritation. "I made the trip all the way out here to be with you. Back in Philadelphia you said you couldn't think about marriage because everything was so confusing for you after your father's death, but you're here now and all settled in, and I'm here with you, too. There's no reason we can't get married just as soon as we can arrange it with the minister." Kenneth was speaking with confidence. "Then I'll be here to help you run the ranch and take care of things."

Emmie couldn't believe how egotistical Kenneth was. This was the second time she'd told him she couldn't marry him, and yet he still believed otherwise. She knew in that moment that her future was with Josh, and she had to make that clear to Kenneth once and for all.

"Kenneth, you don't understand," she began in a sharp tone.

"What don't I understand? I know that I love you and I've given up my life in Philadelphia to come here and be with you."

"Kenneth, I don't love you," she said firmly. She knew her words were blunt, but since he was so wrapped up in his own desires, she realized it was the only way to get his full attention.

"What?" he demanded angrily.

"You heard me, Kenneth. I don't love you. I never have, and I'm not going to marry you."

Without another word, Emmie turned and left the room. She knew Kenneth well enough to recognize that he wouldn't just let things rest, but she didn't care. It was Josh she loved, and she was going to find him right now and tell him so. She went outside and disappeared into the night, looking for the man she loved.

Josh's mood had been as dark as the storm-clouded night as he strode from the house. The lightning and thunder matched his anger as he faced the fact that Emmie and Kenneth obviously meant a lot to each other. Kenneth had come all the way to Texas just to be with her.

Images of Emmie haunted his thoughts—Emmie holding the gun on him in the study, the sight of Emmie swimming, their passionate kisses at the line shack, and the way she'd felt in his arms when they'd danced at the social. He loved her. He'd been trying to deny that reality for some time now, but he finally faced it, and he wondered what he was going to do about it. He knew he had to do something. He'd never known another woman like Emmie, and he couldn't let her get away. He was, after all, a bounty hunter, and she was on his wanted list.

Josh smiled grimly in the darkness as he found himself standing by Hank's grave. Hank had been his friend, and he knew he could have used the older man's help to bring in his daughter. He heard the rumble of thunder in the distance again and gave a shake of his head, wondering whether she would want to ride up to the line shack with him that night.

Emmie had no idea where Josh had gone. His house was dark, so she knew he wasn't there. She skirted around the stable and then went out behind the house. A flash of lightning split the distant sky, and she caught sight of him standing near her father's grave. She wasted no time hurrying to him.

"Josh," Emmie called his name softly as she drew near.

He turned around, surprised to see her. The threatening storm had masked the sound of her approach. "What are you doing out here? You should get back up to the house before the weather breaks."

"Why? I like being caught out in storms with you," she said brazenly.

"Go on," he urged.

"No, I'm not leaving—not until we've had a chance to talk. I want to explain what—"

"There's no need for you to say anything," he cut her off. "I shouldn't have walked in on you that way."

"Josh Grady, I'm glad you walked in on me that way."

"You are?"

"Yes, I am," she insisted, moving forward to stand with him. "Kenneth proposed to me tonight, and I turned him down. I said no. I don't love him, Josh." She stepped closer and looked up at him, all the love she felt shining in her eyes. "I love you."

Josh gazed down at her, seeing the woman who had come to mean so much to him. Ever so gently he took her in his arms and told her, "I love you, too, Emmie."

"Oh, Josh." She sighed his name and gave herself up to his embrace.

Josh kissed her hungrily, wanting to tell her with his lips just how much she meant to him. "Now tell me, woman, if you aren't going to marry Kenneth, will you marry me?"

"Oh, yes!" She kissed him again, thrilled.

"What are you going to do about Kenneth?" Josh asked. He could well imagine how angry the other man was right now.

"I'll have a talk with him in the morning and make arrangements for him to go into town and stay there until he can leave for Philadelphia."

"If he gives you any trouble, just let me know."

"I can handle Kenneth," she assured him.

Josh wasn't quite so sure, but he didn't say any more; he just kissed her again. At that moment the rain started to fall, and they broke apart, laughing.

"Come on, let's get you up to the house." Josh took her hand to walk her back.

"I'd rather go with you to the line shack," she said seductively.

"Be careful what you wish for, woman; you just might get it," he responded, more than tempted to carry her off with him in the night. "But we're not on our honeymoon yet."

"That's too bad."

The look Josh gave her sent a shiver of pure excitement through her, and she stopped and pulled him back to her.

"I need one more kiss."

"Happy to oblige, ma'am," he said, and they shared one last passionate embrace before hurrying to get out of the rain.

* * *

Kenneth had stayed in the house for a while, trying not to lose his temper. He couldn't believe Emmie had turned him down after he'd made such a great sacrifice—leaving his home and traveling to Texas just for her. How dared she reject his marriage proposal! His humiliation and anger overcame him as he finally went outside to try to find her.

This wasn't over between them—not yet.

Kenneth saw that a lantern was burning in the stable, so he decided to start looking there. His search turned up only Burley.

"Have you seen Emmie in the last few minutes? She came out here to check on something, and I'm getting worried about her with the storm coming in," he lied.

"No, she didn't come out here, but I wouldn't worry too much about her and the storm," Burley said, grinning at the city slicker.

"Why? It sounds like a bad one."

"Not too long ago she was out riding with Josh and they got caught up in a real bad one. She was thrown and her horse ran off, but our Emmie's a tough one, and she came through it okay. They couldn't ride back in the middle of a storm, so they ended up spending the night in a line shack. They made it back just fine the next day."

Kenneth was staring at the ranch hand, trying to digest what he'd just heard. Emmie had spent the night alone with Josh at some line shack! His anger turned to full-blown fury. He could only imagine what had gone on between the two of them during all those hours alone. He managed to keep his voice calm as he told Burley, "Well, I'll just wait for her up at the house, then. Thanks."

He returned to the house and went into the parlor. The storm had moved in now, and the rain had started coming down. He knew that any minute Emmie would be returning to the house, and he couldn't wait to confront her.

With a pounding of feet and breathless laughter, Emmie and Josh ran up to the porch.

"I'll see you in the morning," Josh promised. He gave her one last quick kiss before heading off to his own house.

"Good night." She hurried inside, thrilled with Josh's proposal. She was eager to find Millie, and hoped her friend was back from seeing George. She had so much to tell her.

Emmie saw that there was still light coming from the parlor, and thought Millie might be there waiting for her. She was smiling as she went in.

But her smile didn't last long.

Kenneth was standing across the room near the window, glaring at her.

# Chapter Twenty-four

"Oh, Kenneth!" Emmie gasped.

Kenneth heard the note of surprise in her voice and he smiled coldly. "You didn't expect to find me here?"

Emmie looked him in the eye. "Actually, no. I thought you would have gone on to the bunkhouse by now."

"Hardly, my dear," he sneered. He walked slowly toward her. "I think you've got a few things to answer for."

Emmie stood taller. "I don't answer to you or to any man."

"Not even your friend . . . Josh? I understand you spent the night with him at a line shack."

"What I do is none of your business," she said. "We are not engaged. In case you don't remember, I did not invite you here."

"You slut!" he raged in a low, threatening tone as he made a move to try to grab her by her upper arms.

"Don't touch me!" she ordered, backing away.

When he kept coming, she slapped him as hard as she could. "Get away from me!"

Kenneth was shocked as he reached up to touch his cheek.

"Why, you little bitch!" He reacted in fury, backhanding her as hard as he could.

The force of his blow knocked Emmie backward. She managed to catch herself on the arm of the sofa as she looked up at Kenneth. "Get out of my house!"

Kenneth didn't say a word. He just took another menacing step toward her.

At that moment, Josh's voice, cold and commanding, came to them from the doorway.

"Get away from Emmie right now, Kenneth, if you value your life."

Kenneth froze and looked up to find Josh standing there with his gun drawn and aimed straight at him.

"I said *move!*" Josh repeated, stepping slowly into the room. Millie was right behind him.

Millie had been in the upstairs hall on her way to find Emmie when she'd heard Kenneth surprise Emmie in the parlor. She'd rushed after Josh, knowing there might be trouble. She was glad Josh was there now. She didn't know what might have happened if he hadn't shown up.

Kenneth was glaring at Josh, but he finally had sense enough to back away from Emmie.

Josh still didn't let his guard down. He kept his gun trained on Kenneth. "Millie, go get Burley—fast!"

Despite the rain, Millie didn't waste any time running from the house.

"You're going to get off the Rocking R tonight, Kenneth, and I don't ever want to see your miserable face around here again!" Josh ordered. "Do you understand me?"

Kenneth looked from the gun up to the man holding it.

"Yes," he muttered.

Josh could see the man was physically shaking in fear, and he was glad. He wanted Kenneth to be afraid—very afraid.

Emmie ran to Josh. He put one arm around her in a protective embrace as he kept his gun on Kenneth.

"Thank you," she whispered.

"Are you all right?"

"I think so." Her cheek was sore, and she knew it might be bruised in the morning, but as long as Josh was there, nothing else mattered.

Emmie looked up at Josh as she clung to him and saw his fierce expression. She knew then what all the men he'd tracked down had felt when he'd confronted them—they'd known their days of running wild were over.

Burley and George both came rushing in with Millie.

"What's going on?" George asked, looking in disbelief between his brother and the Easterner. He'd been out in the stable talking to Burley when Millie had come frantically running down from the house.

"What did he do?" Burley asked. He knew it had to be bad for Josh to have pulled a gun on him.

"He hit Emmie," Josh ground out. "And I want him out of this house and off this ranch now!"

"Right away. Do you want me to use the carriage or the buckboard?" Burley asked, trying not to smile. He already knew the answer.

"Since it's raining, use the buckboard. George, go over to the bunkhouse and have the boys pack up his things real fast."

They both hurried to do as Josh had ordered. Millie went to Emmie and took her hand to reassure her.

"Millie, go on upstairs with Emmie," Josh suggested, "while I take care of Kenneth."

Millie and Emmie started up the steps just as Miss Harriet was rushing down them in her robe.

"What happened?" the chaperone asked, looking at the two girls nervously. She'd been reading in her room when the sound of Josh's voice had caught her attention. The sight of Emmie's face, which was red and slightly swollen, had her even more worried.

"We'll tell you upstairs. Come on," Millie said, and Miss Harriet accompanied them to Emmie's room.

Alone in the parlor, Josh faced Kenneth and smiled slowly.

"You're quite a man, aren't you? Do you always go around hitting defenseless women?"

"Emmie's no defenseless woman! She's nothing but a slut! I know all about the two of you spending the night alone together out at the line shack!"

"You're not a very smart man, are you, Kenneth?" Josh challenged, slowly holstering his gun as he walked forward. "That's my fiancée you're talking about," he said furiously.

Kenneth's eyes widened at the news as he sneered, "She's going to marry you?"

"That's right," Josh said with a slow smile.

Josh was glad that Kenneth was trying to back away from him, because it proved what a coward he was. Josh reached out and grabbed him by the front of his shirt, jerking him close.

"I think you need to go outside and cool off for a while."

Josh shoved him toward the front hall, and Kenneth stumbled and fell on the floor. Josh moved past him and opened the door, then grabbed Kenneth up and threw him bodily from the house.

He followed him out and stood over him where Kenneth was cowering on the porch.

"I don't ever want to hear another word out of you about Emmie. Do you understand?" Josh ordered.

Kenneth didn't respond.

"I asked you a question."

"Yes," Kenneth muttered, knowing he had no choice but to answer if he wanted to get back to Philadelphia in one piece.

"If I ever hear you've said anything to hurt Emmie's reputation back East, you'll have to answer to me."

"All right, all right." Kenneth was in a panic. He didn't know what Josh was going to do to him next.

"Get up. Burley's on his way," Josh ordered.

Kenneth got to his feet and went down the steps

to stand in the rain. He wanted to put as much distance between himself and Josh as he could.

Burley drove up in the buckboard with Kenneth's bags already thrown in back. Burley was wearing a slicker, but he deliberately hadn't brought one for Kenneth. He thought a soaking would do the Easterner some good. George had ridden back up to the house with Burley, and now he jumped down to join his brother on the porch.

Kenneth quickly climbed up and sat next to the ranch hand, eager to get away from Josh and everything that had to do with the Rocking R.

"You think you'll be all right?" Josh asked Burley. He knew that if the ranch hand was worried about making the trip, they could tie Kenneth up somewhere and take him into town after daylight.

"Oh, yeah. We'll be just fine," Burley assured Josh, grinning at the already drenched Kenneth. He pulled his own hat lower across his face. "The going will be slow, but I'll get him there—eventually."

"Be careful," Josh said.

Burley nodded. "I will. You take care of Emmie." Burley cast a disgusted look at Kenneth before slapping the reins on the horses' backs and driving off into the night.

Josh stood there on the porch, watching until they were out of sight. Getting Kenneth off the ranch was all that mattered to him. Josh wanted him far away from Emmie after what had happened.

He looked at George. "I need to check on Emmie."

"Do you think she's all right?"

"Yes, but I want to make sure."

"I'll go tell the rest of the boys what happened, so they'll know. I'm sure a few of them are wondering what's going on after seeing Burley ride out in the buckboard."

"I'm going to spend the night up here at the house, just in case. I can sleep in the study and make sure the girls are safe."

"All right. I'll see you in the morning."

George left, and Josh turned and went back inside, closing the door behind him.

Miss Harriet left her bedroom window and came to stand before Emmie and Millie, who were sitting on the side of the bed. Her expression was one of indignant outrage now that she'd heard the whole story from Emmie. "Burley just hauled Kenneth off in the buckboard. I don't know where he's taking him this late in the rain, but it had better be far away from me. If I ever see that—"

"I know, Miss Harriet," Millie interrupted her. "I feel the same way about him."

"The good news is, he's gone," Emmie said, relieved that she would never have to deal with Kenneth again.

"Thank heaven Josh showed up when he did," Miss Harriet said.

"You were right all along, Millie," Emmie offered, finally relaxing and smiling at her friend.

"About what?"

"About Josh being my guardian angel. And . . ."

Both women looked at her expectantly, waiting to see what she was going to say next.

"And although I turned down Kenneth's proposal tonight, I did accept Josh's."

"What? Josh proposed?" Millie asked joyfully.

"That is wonderful news!" Miss Harriet was beaming with pleasure. "You've got yourself a fine man in Josh."

"I know," Emmie agreed.

"Emmie?"

They heard Josh calling from the front hall, and Emmie hurried out of the bedroom.

"Kenneth is gone. It's safe for you to come down now," Josh told her as he stood at the foot of the stairs looking up at her.

Emmie didn't hesitate. She flew down the steps into Josh's waiting arms and kissed him.

"I love you, Josh," she said.

"I love you, too." He took her by the shoulders and held her gently away from him so he could get a good look at her. "Are you sure you're all right?"

"Now that I'm with you, I am," she told him as she went back into his arms and rested her head against his chest.

Josh looked up the steps to see Miss Harriet and Millie standing there. "I was just telling Emmie that Kenneth is gone. I had Burley take him into town. Kenneth won't be back."

"Good," both women said in unison.

"Well, we'll leave you two alone now," Miss Harriet pronounced.

"What?" Millie was shocked as the chaperone took her arm and pulled her off down the hall.

"I think they deserve a few moments of privacy, don't you?" Miss Harriet asked with a twinkle in her eye.

Millie just smiled at her and gave her a quick kiss on the cheek. As they both retired to their bedrooms, Millie couldn't help wondering if Miss Harriet would allow her to be alone with George so late at night. She knew it would be worth a try in the coming days, for there was nothing she would like better than to be in George's arms, kissing him. Sighing and feeling lonely, Millie took one last look out her bedroom window at the stormy night and then went to bed.

Josh and Emmie went into the parlor and sat together on the sofa. The sound of the storm outside only made the moment all the more intimate. Josh kissed her, and it was an inviting, tender caress that left Emmie breathless.

"Oh, Josh." She sighed, loving him.

He drew her onto his lap and cradled her against him as his mouth claimed hers in a deeper, more passionate exchange. Josh pressed her down onto the sofa, covering her body with his, wanting her, needing her. Emmie arched against him in love's age-old invitation as he trailed searing kisses down the side of her neck. Her wanton move tortured Josh, for he knew he had to stop—now, or he wouldn't be able to stop at all.

"I love you, Emmie," he told her as he smiled down at her. "I know! Do you want to elope tonight?"

"We could," she purred. "And then, since we'd want to be alone on our wedding night, we could ride up to the line shack, and you could carry me over the threshold again."

"In the rain," he added as a rumble of thunder echoed in the night.

"Maybe we'd better wait until the storm passes. What do you think?"

"I think you're right."

Josh kissed her softly one more time and then sat back up and held her close.

# Chapter Twenty-five

"*I* wonder why you haven't heard back from your mother," Miss Harriet said to Emmie as they enjoyed breakfast a few days later. She knew Emmie had sent her a telegram informing her of Josh's proposal and their plan to marry.

"Do you think your mother will make the trip out here for the wedding?" Millie asked.

Emmie looked at her friend. "No. When she vowed never to come back here, she meant it."

"It's such a shame, what happened to your mother," Miss Harriet said. During her stay at the Rocking R, she'd tried to imagine the horror that Sarah must have witnessed all those years ago. Judging from what they'd experienced during their time at the ranch, the risk of Indian attack seemed to be small now. True, she had heard the men talking about rustlers, and there had been Millie's run-in with Steve, but for the most part, it had been rather quiet.

"Yes, it was. I'll just have to convince Josh to make

a trip back to Philadelphia with me so he can meet her."

"Just make sure when you take Josh back to Philadelphia to meet your mother, he doesn't attend any social events where Kenneth might show up," Millie said with a grin.

Emmie couldn't help smiling, too. "That would be interesting, wouldn't it? Now if we could just get George to propose to you, we could have a double wedding."

"I wish he would, too." Millie sighed.

"He'll come around. You'll see," her friend assured her.

"I hope you're right. I've never known another man like him. I love him very much, but I don't know if he's the kind of man who would ever settle down in one place."

Miss Harriet looked at Millie. The girl had adored George since the first moment she'd set eyes on him after he'd saved her from Steve. "I have no doubt you're the woman who can make the difference in his life."

"I hope so," Millie said, smiling. "He's certainly made a difference in mine."

"Who would have thought when we came west that you girls would find the men of your dreams?" Miss Harriet said, still a little amazed by all that had taken place. "Now, back to the matter at hand. Did Josh say how soon he wants the wedding to take place?"

"We've been thinking in a month or so. We'll

have to talk with Reverend Hunt and see what we need to do."

Miss Harriet offered, "I'll be glad to help you with the wedding plans."

"Do you think you'll be staying that long?" Emmie looked at Millie.

"I'm not about to miss your wedding! And since my mother hasn't sent any ultimatums, Miss Harriet and I are not going anywhere."

"That's right," Miss Harriet put in. "We all know Millie's mother isn't one to be reticent about expressing her wishes. We certainly would have heard from her if she had disapproved of our staying longer. Now, about this wedding . . ." Her eyes lit up with delight as she prepared to plan a most elaborate affair.

"You don't think we need to talk to Josh about any of this?" Emmie asked.

"Heavens, no," the chaperone insisted. "He's a man. What would he know about such things?"

They all laughed.

Emmie's mood was light, but she couldn't help but feel a bit sad that her mother wouldn't be a part of her wedding day.

The bounty hunter was feeling good as he rode into Shotgun. The Rocking R Ranch was nearby, and he was certain his days of hunting down Josh Grady were just about over. He had made his plan. It wouldn't be long now before he'd be bringing Josh in for the five-hundred-dollar reward.

He reined in out in front of the saloon and went

inside to have a drink. He wanted to relax for a while and listen to all the talk in the bar. He usually learned what was going on in town that way, and he hoped today would be no exception. He dismounted and strode inside, ready to close in on his wanted man.

"Whiskey," he said as he sidled up to the bar.

"Coming right up," the barkeep said. He served the drink quickly and took the money the tall, lean stranger shoved across the bar to him.

"Thanks."

"You're new in town."

"Yep, my name's Jones—Rod Jones."

"Well, it's nice to meet you, Rod Jones. Drink up; there's plenty more where that came from."

Rod did just that. The talk in the saloon was uneventful, so he knew things had been quiet there in Shotgun for a while. He finally decided to bring up Josh Grady's name himself.

"I wanted to ask you, what's the best way out to the Rocking R? I'm a friend of Josh Grady's, and I wanted to stop off and see him while I'm passing through," he said to the barkeep.

The other man thought nothing of giving the stranger directions to the ranch. It was common knowledge. "So, you're an old friend of Josh's?" he asked as he wiped down the bar in front of him.

"We go back a ways," Rod lied.

"He's done a fine job taking over the running of the Rocking R."

"It'll be good to see him." And Rod knew it would be good—real good and real profitable.

Rod drained the rest of his drink and walked out. It was time.

He rode for the Rocking R.

About an hour later one of the ranch hands saw a stranger riding in and went to get Burley. Burley left the stable where he'd been working and went out to see who the man was and what he wanted.

"Afternoon," Burley greeted him, feeling decidedly uneasy about the stranger as he looked up at him. There was something about the fellow that seemed almost dangerous.

"Howdy," Rod returned, taking a casual look around for Josh. He saw no sign of his quarry anywhere, but he knew he couldn't let his guard down for a moment. "Nice place you got here."

"Yes, it is. What can I do for you?"

Rod introduced himself and then asked, "Is Josh Grady around?"

"Why do you want to know?"

"We're friends from Josh's old days. I'm a bounty hunter, too. I was in the area and hadn't seen him for a while, so I thought I'd stop by and say hello."

After learning about the man's past, Burley understood why he'd been on edge. He relaxed and said, "Josh isn't here right now. He and George rode out earlier this morning to check the north range. I expect they'll be back by sundown. You're welcome to stay and wait for him, if you want."

"Any chance I could catch up with him there?"

"You can try," Burley said, and he told the bounty hunter the general area where Josh and George had been headed. "You want one of us to ride with you?"

"No, I'll find him. I'm pretty good at tracking," Rod said with a confident smile.

"I'll just bet you are."

Rod rode away, feeling more certain than ever that he would soon be on his way back to Sundown to claim his reward.

"Who was that?" a ranch hand asked as he came to stand beside Burley.

"An old friend of Josh's who was just passing through."

The two men thought nothing more of the visitor and returned to work.

Rod was ready. As soon as he was out of sight of the ranch buildings, he stopped long enough to take the wanted poster out of his saddlebag. He unfolded it and studied the picture on it again. Having never seen Josh in person, he wanted to make sure he got the right man. Satisfied that he would recognize his quarry at first sight, Rod folded the poster up and put it in his shirt pocket.

Rod couldn't believe his luck when, after an hour of riding in the direction the ranch hands had told him to go, he spotted a lone horseman in the distance. But the fact that the rider was by himself troubled him. The men at the Rocking R had said Josh had ridden out with someone named George, and he couldn't be sure this was his man.

The rider hadn't seen him yet, so Rod quickly took cover near a rocky outcropping and waited until the man drew closer so he could get a better look at him. He didn't want to ruin the capture by acting rashly.

Josh and George had split up to go after some strays and had agreed to meet back at the watering hole. Josh had finished first and decided to relax in the shade while he waited for George to return. He was thinking he'd obviously had much better luck than his brother when he heard the sound of gunfire coming from the direction George had ridden. Fearing George had run into rustlers and was in trouble, Josh wasted no time getting back in the saddle. Gun drawn, he galloped toward the sound to see what was wrong.

Rod had gotten his shots off with practiced ease. His first shot had missed, but the second shot had hit the rider, and he'd watched as the man had fallen from his horse to lie unmoving on the ground. Rod mounted up and headed down to claim the wanted man. He knew he had to move fast, just in case the other ranch hand who had ridden out with Josh was somewhere close by.

Rod reined in next to the man he believed to be Josh Grady and dismounted. He knew he had to catch Grady's horse and load the man up. He'd have to take the body back to Sundown in order to claim the reward. He was hoping Josh was already dead, so he wouldn't have to worry about doctoring him. Gun in hand, Rod went to the fallen man.

It was at that moment that Josh topped the low rise nearby and saw a man walking toward his fallen brother, holding a gun on him. Fury filled

Josh, and, believing the man was a rustler, he began to fire as he raced toward them.

Rod was a fast gun, but, caught unprepared, he had no chance. The bullets slammed into his chest and he collapsed, his gun flying from his hand. He lay facedown in the dirt, his life's blood draining from him.

Josh dismounted and ran to his side. He turned the unknown gunman over to stare down at him.

"You!" Rod choked, gazing up at him in disbelief.

"Who are you? What are you doing on the Rocking R?" Josh demanded, but the man went limp.

Once Josh was certain the stranger wouldn't be ambushing anyone else, he holstered his gun and rushed to his brother, fearing he was dead. He knelt down beside George to check his wound.

"George . . ."

Josh was flooded with relief when his brother gave a low groan and half opened his eyes. "What?" he managed weakly as he came around.

"Don't try to talk," Josh ordered.

"Who was he?" George didn't always do what his brother told him to do.

"I don't know. I'd never seen him before. Must have been a rustler. Now be quiet. Save your strength. You're going to need it to make it back to the ranch."

He tore open George's shirt to find that the bullet had hit him in the shoulder and passed cleanly through. He fought to get the bleeding under control, then took off his own shirt and cut it into strips to tightly bind the wound. George said nothing, but Josh could tell he was in a lot of pain.

"We'll ride back double. I don't want to take the chance that you might fall."

"All right," George ground out as he fought to control the pain.

Josh tied the dead gunman's body on his horse before helping George up onto his own. He climbed up behind him and took hold of the reins. They started back to the house at a slow pace, with Josh leading the other two horses.

"I'll bet the last time you rode double, you probably enjoyed it a lot more," George managed weakly, trying not to laugh because it hurt too much.

Emmie was working down at the stable when she saw them coming.

"Oh, my God! Burley! Get some of the boys! Josh is riding back in, and it looks like there's been trouble!"

She dropped what she was doing and ran out to meet Josh, with Burley and several ranch hands right behind her.

"Josh! What happened? And George!"

"George was ambushed," Josh quickly explained. "Burley, you'd better send for the doc."

Burley immediately ordered one of the men to town.

Josh carefully dismounted, and then, with Burley's help, they managed to get George down. George couldn't help groaning as the two men each put an arm around him and half carried him up to Josh's house.

They were just going inside when Kate came outside to see what was going on. She took one look and came running down to help.

"What happened?"

"George was shot," Emmie told her.

"I'll be right back." Kate rushed up to the main house to get all the medicine and supplies she had. As she was going indoors, she came face-to-face with Millie.

"Is something wrong?" Millie asked, seeing the other woman's stricken expression.

Kate stopped to tell her the news. "It's George."

Millie panicked. "What about him?"

"He was shot."

Millie was almost hysterical. "Is he—"

"He's alive, and one of the boys is already on his way to town to get the doc."

Millie didn't say another word. She just ran from the house to do whatever she could to help.

"George . . . ! Where is he?" she demanded as she came through the door of Josh's house.

"He's in here, Millie," Emmie called from the back bedroom.

Millie hurried to stand in the doorway and watched as Emmie and Josh helped make George as comfortable as possible in his bed. She bit back a cry when she saw how pale he was and the bloodied bandage on his shoulder. She went to stand at his side and took his hand.

The moment she touched him, George opened his eyes and looked up at her. He managed a half smile. "We ran into a little trouble."

"Hush—don't even try to talk. I'll be right here. The doc's on his way," Millie said as tears threatened.

"There is something I need."

"Anything." She wanted to ease his suffering in any way she could.

"A kiss."

Millie didn't hesitate. She leaned over him and gently pressed her lips to his. "I love you."

"I love you, too," he said, and he closed his eyes.

Josh brought a chair up to the bedside for Millie, so she could sit with him while they waited for the doc to show up.

"I'll be back," he told her.

Josh started from the house and Emmie went after him. She'd heard the fierce determination in his voice and wanted to know where he was going.

"Josh?"

"Stay here." Josh strode toward the stable.

She did as she was told.

Kate came hurrying to Josh's house then, with Miss Harriet right behind her.

"What can we do to help?" Miss Harriet asked. Kate had already told her that George had been hurt.

"Let's go see," Emmie said, casting one last look Josh's way before going back inside to help take care of George.

# Chapter Twenty-six

Josh went out to where Burley was taking care of the horses.

"How's George holding up?" Burley asked.

"It's a clean shoulder wound. He should be all right."

"Thank heaven." Burley nodded toward the gunman's body, which was still tied on the horse. "What do you want to do with him?"

"We'll take him into town to the sheriff, but first I want you to go through his things. I need to know who he is," Josh said in disgust. "Let me know if you find anything. If he's in with the rustlers, there may be more of them out there." Josh's expression was grim as he lifted his gaze to look out across the endless miles of Rocking R land.

"I will."

"I'll be with George." He left Burley and the hands to their gruesome search.

The moment Josh came through the door, Emmie went to embrace him. She could feel the tension in him as he held himself rigidly in control.

The realization that something might have happened to him, too, left her trembling.

"Are you sure you're all right?" she asked, looking up at him.

"I'm not going to be all right until I find out who was behind this."

"How did it happen?"

He quickly explained, then said, "The boys are checking his belongings for me now. With any luck, we'll find something that will help—"

Before he could finish, they heard Burley shouting his name. Josh moved out of Emmie's embrace and went to see what he'd found.

Burley was running up to the house waving a piece of paper in his hand.

"Wait till you see this!" Burley said, still shocked by the discovery he'd made in the dead man's pocket. He handed the folded sheet of paper to Josh.

Josh took it from him and opened it up. He found himself staring down at a wanted poster.

# Wanted!

### Dead or Alive

### Josh Grady

### $500

### For Murder

### Sundown, Texas

Josh lifted his hardened gaze. He knew now that the dead man had been a bounty hunter, and he had mistaken George for him. Josh looked down at the poster again.

"Sundown," he muttered.

"Josh, what is it?" Emmie asked, coming to his side. The moment she saw the wanted poster he was holding, she gasped in horror. "Oh, my God! Why are you wanted for murder in Sundown?"

"I don't know, but I intend to find out." Josh knew there was something sinister going on.

"What can we do?"

" 'We' can't do anything," he told her, his expression grave. "As soon as I'm sure George is going to recover, I'll be riding to Sundown to track down the man who put up the bounty."

"Can't you let the law handle this?"

"In Sundown there is no law."

"But if one bounty hunter was able to find you, won't there be others looking for you, too?"

"That's why I have to go."

"We'll ride with you," Burley offered, and the men who were gathered around agreed.

Josh looked at them. "I appreciate your offer, but this is my past. I'll handle it. I need you to stay here and keep the ranch going."

Burley didn't want him to go alone. "Then I'll come with you and—"

Josh fixed him with a look that stopped him. "I work alone."

Josh Grady, the bounty hunter, was back.

Emmie said nothing as they returned to his house

to await the doctor's arrival, but there was no way she was going to let him do this by himself.

Millie heard the doctor enter the house, and she left George's bedside to go speak with him. The elderly gentleman had just come in with Josh.

"I'm so relieved that you're here."

"We were lucky. It's been a quiet day in town—up until now," Doc McKinley said as he walked into the bedroom and set down his black bag. "How are you doing, young man?"

George had watched him come into the room, and he managed a slight smile. "I've been better."

"I'll just bet you have. Josh, here, was telling me you were ambushed."

"That's right. I was out chasing strays, and the next thing I knew, Josh was hauling me back to the house."

"Well, let's see how this looks." The doctor glanced over at Millie, Josh, and Emmie, who were all standing in the bedroom doorway. "Why don't you ladies wait out in the sitting room?"

They moved off, and Josh came in.

"Sit him up for a minute," the doc directed.

Josh did just that, and Doc McKinley dug in his medicine bag and pulled out a bottle of whiskey. "Take a deep drink. You're going to need it."

George followed the doctor's orders while the doc spread clean towels behind him.

"All right, let's lay him back down," he told Josh.

Once George was as comfortable as he could be

on the bed, Josh stood back and Doc McKinley went to work. He carefully cut away the bandage.

George was glad for the whiskey as the doctor worked on cleaning out the wound. When at last his shoulder was wrapped in a clean bandage, George smiled at the doctor in relief.

"You were lucky. An inch or two over and you'd have been dead."

George hadn't thought about being lucky, but he supposed when he looked at it that way, he was. "Thanks, Doc."

"I'll be out to check on you again in a day or two," Doc McKinley said as he got ready to leave. He looked at Josh. "Make sure he gets a lot of rest, and let me know if he develops a fever."

"We will."

"If he's in pain, just let him have some whiskey. That should help."

Josh walked the doctor out as Millie and Emmie came back into the bedroom to sit with George.

Miss Harriet and Kate had been hovering nearby, and when they saw the doctor drive off in his buggy, they hurried over to find out how George was. They caught up with Josh on the porch on his way back inside.

"What did the doctor say?" Miss Harriet asked worriedly.

"George should be fine in a few weeks."

"Thank heaven," Kate said. "We'll go tell Burley and the boys for you."

"Thanks."

Josh went in to see his brother. George was still pale, but he looked better than he had earlier.

"How are you feeling?"

"You don't want to know," George growled.

"That good, huh?"

George gave a miserable groan that was as close to a laugh as he could muster.

"Do you need another drink?" Josh asked.

"Yes," George answered quickly.

"I'll get it for you," Millie offered. She asked Josh, "Do you have some whiskey here?"

"In the cabinet by the sink," he answered.

Millie and Emmie both left the bedroom to give the men some time alone. When they'd gone, George looked up at his brother.

"What did you find out?"

"It's not good."

"What?"

"He wasn't a rustler."

"Then, who was—"

"He was a bounty hunter," Josh said tersely.

George was shocked. "A bounty hunter? How did you find that out, and why was he after me?"

Guilt assailed Josh as he answered, "He wasn't after you. He was after me."

"What are you talking about?"

Josh pulled out the wanted poster and showed it to George.

"Who would have done this?" George looked up at his brother, angry and confused.

"That's what I'm going to find out—now that I know you will be all right."

"What are you talking about?" George asked worriedly.

"I'm going to Sundown."

"You can't," George started to protest. "You don't know what you're riding into."

"It won't be the first time."

"No, I don't suppose it will be." George was well aware of the dangers Josh had faced during all his years working as a bounty hunter, but he also knew how good Josh was at bringing wanted men in. "How soon are you leaving?"

"In a day or two. I've got a few things to straighten out around here first."

"What can I do to help?"

"Get well." Josh met his brother's gaze. "And pray."

"But what about Emmie and your wedding?"

"She already knows what I have to do."

"Josh, think about what you're doing."

Josh looked down at his brother. "I already have."

"Be careful."

"I will."

Josh left George to get some rest and went out to the small sitting room. He'd expected to find Emmie there with Millie, but Millie was alone.

"Where did Emmie go?"

"She didn't say," Millie answered as she got up to go back to George's bedside.

Josh had a good idea where Emmie had gone. He left the house and made his way around back. He saw her there in the distance, sitting on the ground near her father's grave.

Josh knew in that moment that leaving Emmie was going to be the hardest thing he'd ever done in his life, but he also knew he had no choice. George had almost lost his life today, and Josh feared that no one around him would be safe until he'd confronted those responsible in Sundown.

"Emmie." He called her name softly as he went to stand behind her.

She looked up at him, and he could see that she'd been crying. Without another word, he sat down beside her and put his arm around her.

Emmie leaned against him, feeling his strength and love in his embrace.

"Thank heaven George is going to be all right," she told him.

"I know. When I heard the gunfire, I thought he'd run into some rustlers. I never dreamed it was a bounty hunter, or that there was a wanted poster out on me."

Emmie turned to him and drew him down for a kiss. "None of this is your fault."

"I know, but I'm the only one who can put an end to it."

"Do you have any idea who would have done this? Or why?"

"It's obviously someone out for revenge. I just have to find out who."

"Take someone with you."

"Like I said earlier, I don't want anyone else involved."

"I'm already involved. It's horrible enough that George was wounded, but if that had been you . . ."

He held her close to reassure her. "It's going to be all right."

Emmie hoped that was true.

"What are we going to do?" she asked.

"We're going to get married as soon as I get back."

"Then you'd better hurry back fast."

"Believe me, that's exactly what I plan to do—especially since I know you're going to be here waiting for me."

Josh kissed her again, and they stayed there a while longer, treasuring this time they had alone together.

Emmie was playing her part perfectly. She knew Josh believed she was going to just sit there and wait for him to come back, but that wasn't going to happen. There was no way she was going to let him ride into a wild town like Sundown alone. She wasn't sure how she was going to do it, but when Josh left to track down the men responsible for the wanted poster, she was going to be riding with him. He was, after all, her partner.

## Chapter Twenty-seven

In the day and a half since the shooting, life had been tense on the ranch. Everyone had been keeping a careful watch to make sure there was no more trouble coming as Josh got ready to leave.

When the time finally came for him to ride out, Josh went into George's room to tell him good-bye.

George was sitting up in bed, watching his brother carefully as he came in carrying his saddlebags and rifle.

"I'm heading out now," Josh announced.

"Are you sure you have to do this? Isn't there some other way?"

"No. Not with the killers I'm dealing with." His mood was dark and determined. "Take care of Emmie for me."

"I will," he assured his brother.

Josh nodded and managed a tight smile. "I'll be back as soon as I can."

"We'll be waiting for you," George said, angry because he was too weak to accompany his brother. If he'd been physically able, there was no way he would have let Josh ride out alone.

Josh said nothing more as he turned and left the house. He had said good-bye to Kate and the ranch hands, but now came the hard part. Emmie was waiting for him in front of the house with Millie and Miss Harriet.

Leaving Emmie was one of the most difficult things he'd ever had to do, but he had no choice. He set his saddlebags and rifle aside and looked at her. Their gazes met but for a moment, neither of them spoke. Josh took her in his arms to hold her close.

"Oh, Josh." Emmie held on to him, never wanting to let him go. She lifted her lips to his and kissed him desperately.

Josh didn't care who else was there. He crushed her to him, savoring this moment of closeness with her that he knew would be his last for too long. When finally they broke apart, he looked down at her.

"I'll be back as fast as I can."

Emmie's heart was aching. "I'll be waiting."

Josh moved away and picked up his gear. He bade Millie and Miss Harriet good-bye and then mounted. He looked down at Emmie one last time before riding away, headed for Sundown.

Emmie was in tears as she watched Josh go.

Millie went to Emmie and put a loving arm around her shoulders as they proceeded inside to see George, while Miss Harriet went up to the main house.

Emmie was discovering that she was quite a good

actress. She played her role perfectly, staying on with George and Millie for a while before going on about her ranch business, working with Burley and the boys down at the stable. Emmie knew it was going to be tricky to get away without anyone realizing what she was up to, but she was certain she could do it.

This was the first time in her life that she'd really appreciated the tracking skills her father had taught her. Today being able to follow a trail was really going to come in handy. One thing she knew for certain—she had to be careful not to follow too closely behind Josh, for he might see her and send her home. Then again, she didn't want to risk being too far back either, for fear of losing his trail. Emmie looked up at the clear sky and said a silent prayer that there would be no rain anytime soon.

Emmie left the stable and went up to her room to pack the few essentials she would need to take, as well as extra ammunition, just in case. She made sure no one saw her carry the saddlebags out or hide them near her father's grave. She returned to her room and wrote letters to Millie and Burley, explaining what she had done and asking them to take care of everything for her. Emmie knew that what she was about to do was the most dangerous thing she'd ever done in her life, but she didn't care. Being with Josh and helping him were all that mattered. She hid the notes under her pillow, certain they wouldn't be found until later that night. She didn't want anyone coming after her to bring her back to the ranch. She was going with Josh to Sundown.

It was just after lunch when she went out to the stable and saddled up. There was only one hand there working, and she told him she would be back in a few hours, that she was just going out for a ride. He warned her to keep a lookout for trouble, and she told him she would.

She wasn't lying.

Trouble was what she was after.

With no one watching, Emmie was free to leave. She rode past her father's grave and stopped long enough to retrieve the gear she'd hidden there. She climbed back in the saddle and left the ranch to follow the man she loved.

Josh made camp at dusk that night and ate the bacon and biscuits Kate had wrapped up for him. The sparse meal was a far cry from her usually delicious dinners, and he realized how spoiled he'd become living on the Rocking R. Josh knew it would be a while before he got the chance to enjoy one of her meals again. He was just spreading out his bedroll near the campfire when he thought he heard the distant sound of someone approaching. Tossing dirt on the fire to smother the flames, he grabbed up his gun and took cover behind some rocks and brush nearby.

Emmie was feeling good. True, she was exhausted, but the hours of hard riding had paid off. She had almost reached Josh's campsite, for she could see the soft glow of his campfire in the distance ahead. She could hardly wait to be with him. When she suddenly saw the glow disappear, she began to worry that something had happened to Josh. Drawing her gun, Emmie urged her horse to a gallop.

"Josh?" she called out as she charged into the campsite.

Josh couldn't believe it when he saw Emmie come flying into the small clearing with her gun in hand. He quickly holstered his own sidearm and, swearing under his breath, stepped out from where he'd been hiding.

"What are you doing here?" he demanded angrily.

"Josh!" Emmie spotted him right away and stopped. Relief flooded through her as she slid her gun back into her holster and jumped down from her horse to run to him. "You're all right?"

"Why wouldn't I be?"

"I saw your fire go out, and I was worried about you."

"Don't you realize you could have been killed? I put the fire out because I heard someone coming. What if this hadn't been my camp?"

"But it was. My father taught me how to track, and I've been following you all day. I knew it was yours."

"But I could have shot you!"

"Or I could have shot you!" she countered. Then she realized just how deadly the situation could have turned out, and she went into his arms. "I'm sorry."

"You should be. I told you to stay at the ranch and wait for me there."

"I couldn't stay behind and just worry about you constantly. I love you, Josh."

Josh gave a miserable half groan and kissed her. When they broke apart, she looked up at him.

"So you thought I was trouble?" she asked, smiling up at him.

"I know you are," Josh declared. He was torn between being angry with her for not staying behind and his desire to take her into his arms and never let her go. He gave in to the last urge, pulling her into his embrace and kissing her again, even more passionately.

At the touch of his lips on hers, she forgot everything but the pleasure of being in his arms. She quickly melted against him in sweet surrender. She was with Josh. . . .

It took a major effort on his part, but Josh finally managed to get control of his runaway desire. He lifted his head to look down at Emmie in the moonlight. "You should go back home. What I have to do is too dangerous."

"I can't just wait there, never knowing if you're safe. If you force me to go back, I'll just come after you again," she said defiantly.

Josh was frustrated. Emmie was so hardheaded, he knew she would do exactly what she said. "What am I going to do with you?"

"Kiss me again?"

And he did.

When they finally moved apart, he rebuilt the campfire and then helped her take care of her horse. They spread their bedrolls out close together.

"Have you eaten?" he asked.

"No."

"Here's some of Kate's bacon and biscuits," he offered.

"Sounds wonderful." She sat down with him by the fire.

They were quiet for a few moments as she ate some of the biscuits and bacon.

She spoke first, breaking the silence between them. "What's your plan?"

"I don't have one yet. Sundown is a wild place—real wild—and the sheriff there is known for being on the wrong side of the law."

"Have you had run-ins with him before?"

"No, that's why I'm sure there's someone else behind this."

"We'll find them."

Josh looked at her, accepting that she would be with him on this hunt. "Yes, we will."

"Where could she be?" Miss Harriet asked frantically as they all stood together in front of the house.

They had been waiting for Emmie to come home for several hours, and now that night was falling and there was still no sign of her anywhere, they were getting deeply worried.

"One of the boys told me she rode out around midday, and nobody's seen her since," Burley said.

"Did she leave a note anywhere?" Millie asked, looking at Kate.

"I looked around the house, but I didn't find anything."

"Do you think she might have left deliberately?" Burley put in.

"No, not unless . . ." Millie suddenly realized what her friend might have done. "Wait here; I'm going to take another look around her room."

Just then George appeared in the front door of Josh's house. Millie had told him earlier that they couldn't find Emmie, and when he'd heard all of them talking outside, he'd managed to work up enough strength to get out of bed and investigate.

"Has she shown up yet?" he called out.

"No," Millie answered. Then she turned to Burley. "Can you get him to sit down somewhere? I'll be right back."

Burley and the others went to tend to George as she rushed back up to Emmie's bedroom.

Millie wasted no time. She searched through every drawer of Emmie's dresser and her washstand. She found nothing until she tore the bed apart. It was there that she found the hidden notes. She opened hers immediately and read, *Dear Millie: Forgive me for sneaking off this way, but I have to be with Josh. Please tell Burley and George to take care of things on the ranch for us. We'll be back. Love, Emmie.*

Millie hurried back to where everyone was now waiting with George, to let them know what she'd found. "Nothing's wrong. Emmie's not lost or in trouble."

"What are you talking about?" Burley asked.

"She's gone after Josh," she announced, handing Burley his note.

The ranch hand opened the letter. " 'Dear Burley,' " he read to the others, " 'I've gone to help my partner. Please take over running the Rocking R with George for us. We'll be back. Emmie.' "

Millie knew Emmie was a remarkably strong-willed, capable woman, but she was still worried. She looked at Burley. "What are we going to do?"

The ranch hand was frowning. "They've got a full day's head start on us. There's no way we can catch up with them. There's only one thing we can do," he said seriously.

"What's that?" Millie asked.

"First thing in the morning I'll ride into town and send a wire to the Texas Rangers to let them know what's going on."

George met Burley's gaze and nodded.

"How early do we have to ride out in the morning?" Emmie asked as they got ready to bed down for the night.

"The earlier the better. We want to get as many miles in as we can before it gets too hot."

"How long do you think it will take us to get to Sundown?"

"If the weather holds, we should be there in a week, but there is one stop we have to make first."

"Where?"

"Tomorrow we'll be near San Luis. We can stop there and find a justice of the peace."

"Oh, Josh!" Emmie went into his arms.

"You don't mind not having a fancy wedding?"

"I've never cared about that—I just want you."

Josh bent to her and kissed her then. "Come on. Let's get some sleep. We've got a big day coming tomorrow."

Emmie didn't need any encouragement. They stretched out on their bedrolls and she went into his arms. Just being close to him was heaven for her.

"Are you sure you want to go to sleep right now?" she asked, rising up on one elbow to look down at him.

Josh needed no further encouragement. "No . . ." He drew her down to him and claimed her lips in a hungry kiss. Emmie melted against him as his lips left hers to trace a fiery path down the side of her neck. Josh worked impatiently at the top buttons on her blouse and brushed the garment aside as he pressed heated kisses to the tops of her breasts where they were exposed above her undergarment. Emmie gasped in delight, thrilling to his touch. In her innocence, she just wanted to be closer to him, unaware that her passion was tormenting Josh. He sensed that she was his for the taking in that moment, but he forced himself to rein in his desire for her before he lost all semblance of control.

Emmie was trembling as he shifted away from her all-too-tempting nearness. "Josh . . . ?"

"Tomorrow night, love. Tomorrow night," he managed. He kept her close to his side as he gave her one last tender kiss and struggled to restrain his need for her.

Josh knew the morning couldn't come soon enough.

# Chapter Twenty-eight

The heavyset, balding bartender at the Wild Times Saloon looked up as the stranger walked in.

"Afternoon," the bartender said as the man came up to the bar. "What can I get for you?"

"I'm looking for someone," Josh said.

"And who would that be?" The bartender eyed him, wondering what business he had there in San Luis.

"I'm looking for Paul Williams. I was told I'd find him here."

The bartender smiled as he cleaned a glass. "You're looking at him. I'm Paul Williams."

Josh smiled. "It looks like you're holding down two real important jobs in town—justice of the peace and barkeep."

"That's right. Which one you looking for?"

"Whichever one can marry me to the woman I've got waiting outside." Josh laughed.

Paul laughed, too. "I reckon that would be the justice of the peace. Annie Belle, keep an eye on things for me. I shouldn't be gone too long."

The saloon girl came over to tend bar while Paul left to perform the wedding.

Another saloon girl, Lucy, joined her there, and they watched the bartender leave with the tall, dark-haired stranger.

"I don't know who's marrying him, but she is one lucky girl. He's a mighty fine-looking man."

"You're right about that," Annie Belle agreed, regretting that there weren't any men like him in their rough little town.

As Paul went outside, he saw the young woman who was waiting for them. She was a pretty little gal, even though she was dressed in pants and boots for riding, and he knew she would have been downright lovely if she'd been wearing a wedding dress.

"This is Emmie Ryan, my fiancée, and I'm Josh Grady," the stranger told him.

"Nice to meet you folks. Let's go on over to my office and get you hitched," Paul said. He led the way down the street and into his small one-room office. "Come on in."

They followed him inside.

The room was dark and cluttered, and Emmie looked around herself, knowing that in all her wildest imaginings, she'd never dreamed she'd be getting married in a place like this. She glanced down at the clothes she was wearing and almost felt like crying. She'd always believed she would be wearing a beautiful white gown at this most important moment in her life, not trail-dust-covered clothes and boots. She'd fantasized, too, that she would be swept away by her handsome husband in a fancy carriage after the ceremony for a romantic honeymoon. Somehow, another night by the campfire wasn't quite what she'd envisioned.

And then Emmie cast a glance up at Josh.

She found his gaze upon her, the look in his eyes one of deep and abiding love. A thrill went through her, touching her heart and her soul, and she knew in that moment that nothing mattered except being with Josh. The fancy ceremony and beautiful dress meant nothing. What was important was love—and she'd found it with the tall, handsome man at her side. She loved him, and in a few moments she would be bound to him forever. She would be his wife. She smiled up at him as tears of happiness filled her eyes.

"If we can begin . . ." Paul said.

He made short order of performing the ceremony and concluded with the final vows.

"Do you, Emmie Ryan, take Josh Grady to be your lawfully wedded husband?" he asked.

"I do," Emmie said.

"Do you, Josh Grady, take Emmie Ryan to be your lawfully wedded wife?"

"I do," Josh vowed, his dark-eyed gaze warm upon her as she stood by his side.

"Then I now pronounce you man and wife," Paul said. "Do you have a ring?"

"No, I didn't have time to get one."

"Well, that don't matter none. You can get a ring anytime. Go ahead and kiss your bride."

Josh needed no further encouragement.

He kissed her, a sweet, chaste kiss there in front of the justice of the peace, and then paid the man.

"Thank you," Josh said, shaking his hand.

"You're welcome, Mr. and Mrs. Grady," Paul said, and congratulated both of them.

Emmie smiled at the sound of it—Mr. and Mrs. Grady. She was now Emmie Grady. She looked up at Josh as he walked out of the office beside her, and she knew she wanted him to be there always—right beside her.

They stopped only long enough to pick up more supplies at the general store in town. Josh bought a few things that surprised Emmie, but she said nothing while they were in the store. She knew there would be time for questions later.

"I have to ask," she said as they were headed out of town. "Why did you buy henna?"

Josh looked over at her. "With the wanted posters out on me, I'm going to need to change the way I look. I won't be shaving for the next few days, and you can help me dye my hair."

Emmie was surprised by his plan, but realized how smart it was. "So my tall, dark, handsome husband is going to disappear?"

"He'll be back. Don't you worry."

Josh was familiar with the area, having ridden through it before. He knew exactly where he wanted to camp that night. Since it was their first night together as man and wife, he would have preferred to be back at the ranch in the privacy of their own bedroom, or in a clean, fancy hotel somewhere, but that wasn't possible, so he'd come up with another idea. He just hoped she liked it.

It was late afternoon when they reached the secluded spot.

"What do you say we spend our wedding night here?" he asked as he reined in on the top of a hill near a small lake.

Emmie stared down at the scene before them with open delight. "It's beautiful."

"I thought you might like it. Come on," he said, kneeing his horse forward.

They rode down to a grassy area near the shore. Josh took care of the horses while Emmie set up their campsite. When he came to join her, she was standing at the water's edge, staring out across the lake.

"Are you thinking what I'm thinking?" Josh asked.

She looked up at him, grinning. "Too bad Millie's not here to go swimming with me."

"She's not, but I am."

Emmie giggled and wasted no time starting to undress, but Josh was there, brushing her hands aside to help her.

"I've been wanting to do this for a long, long time," he said in a low, seductive voice.

"You have?" she asked.

"Ever since that day I found you in the water at the ranch."

With care, he unbuttoned her blouse and helped her shed it, then pushed the straps of her undergarment from her shoulders. Unable to resist, he bent to kiss her and crush her against him. Any thoughts of moving slowly or swimming were lost in the heat of the moment. Emmie reached up to free him from his shirt, caressing the hard-muscled width of his chest and shoulders. Josh swept her up in his arms and carried her to their bedrolls.

They lay together on their makeshift honeymoon bed and quickly took off the rest of their clothes, removing the last barriers between them.

"I want you," he murmured.

With each kiss and caress, he showed her just how much she meant to him, and Emmie responded without reserve. She had never known such excitement. She wanted him, too. When he moved over her body to make her his own, she opened herself to him, and with one long thrust they came together. Ecstasy seemed to fill Emmie as they sought the perfection of their loving . . . and found it. In the aftermath of their passion they clung together, savoring the beauty of the gift of their love.

"I never knew . . ." Emmie said, still in awe of his lovemaking as she nestled against him.

"I love you, Emmie," Josh said, knowing what a lucky man he was to have her.

"I love you, too." She remembered then the temptation of the cool waters and asked with a smile, "Are you ready for a swim now?"

He grinned at her. "If you are."

They got up and went into the cool, welcoming water together. It was a sensual experience for Emmie to be in the lake with Josh, and she loved every minute of it. They left the water only as the shadows of night claimed the land, and passed the rest of the night sharing their love under the star-spangled canopy of the sky.

Josh awoke first, just before dawn, and lay quietly, watching Emmie sleep. He loved her with all his heart, and he knew these next days were going to be hard for her. He was tempted to go back to the ranch and just stay there, to pretend that the encounter with the bounty hunter had never happened, but the reality was that if one man could find him, someone else with the same wanted poster could, too, and he didn't want anyone on the ranch in danger. He thought of George then and hoped his brother was making a good recovery.

"You're awake already?" Emmie asked in a sleepy voice.

"It's almost time to move out," he said regretfully.

"I know, but I'd like to just stay here."

"Don't tempt me."

"Josh, what's going to happen once we get to Sundown?"

"With the wanted posters out, I've got to be real careful going into town. That's why we'll have to work on changing the way I look tonight. When we do get to Sundown, I'm going to find the sheriff and have a talk with him."

"Aren't you worried that he'll try to shoot you when he realizes who you are?" she worried.

"He's not going to get the chance." Josh knew that straightening this mess out wasn't going to be easy, but he'd been in worse situations in the past. His greatest concern was keeping Emmie safe.

Emmie heard the edge in his voice and knew he was ready for whatever might come. She silently offered up a prayer that he would be safe.

A short time later, after eating a hasty breakfast, they were heading out. Emmie cast one last look back at the serene setting. It had definitely been a memorable wedding night.

"As soon as we get back home, we're going swimming at my favorite place," she told him with an inviting smile.

"With or without Millie?" he joked.

"Without!" She laughed.

"I was hoping you'd say that."

They rode on toward Sundown.

# Chapter Twenty-nine

After six days of hard riding, Josh and Emmie finally reached the outskirts of Sundown. They waited until it was dark to make their move.

Emmie was as ready as she would ever be. She'd stuffed her hair up under her hat so she would look like a boy if anyone noticed her on the ride in. Josh had gone over every step with her, and she knew exactly what she had to do. Their plan was simple. They were going to sneak into the sheriff's office when no one was around and wait there for the lawman to return so Josh could surprise him. Josh figured that if he got the drop on the sheriff, he could quickly find out who was behind the bounty that had been put out on him. Emmie would be going with him into the office, but she was planning to stay out of sight, just in case there was trouble.

They rode into town and left their horses in the alleyway behind the sheriff's office. Josh moved easily out onto the night-shrouded street to take a look around. He found the saloons were noisy and obviously doing some business, but the streets were deserted. The sheriff's office was dark, giving him just the opportunity he was looking for. With no one around to see him, he let himself into the office and closed the door quietly behind him.

Josh didn't know if there would be anyone locked up in the jail, but when he checked he was glad to find the cells were empty. There was a back room with a bed in it and some gear, but he figured that belonged to the lawman. He let Emmie in the back door and found her a safe place to hide while he went to sit in the darkened outer office to await Sheriff Dawson's return.

The time passed slowly. Minutes seemed like hours as he anticipated the confrontation to come. It was well after midnight when Josh saw the sheriff walk up to the front of the building.

Sheriff Dawson stood there for a moment looking up and down the street and then came inside. He hung up his hat and moved wearily to light the lamp on the small table nearby. He had just blown out the match and started to turn around when he heard a harsh order.

"Don't do anything stupid, Dawson. Just pull down the shades and turn around real slow."

Sheriff Dawson had frozen in place. He was shocked at having been caught off guard this way and couldn't imagine who would be there to ambush him in his own office.

"Who are you? What do you want?" the lawman asked without moving.

"I told you what I wanted. Pull down the shades— now!"

Knowing he had little choice, the sheriff did as he'd been ordered.

"Good," Josh said in a low, threatening voice. "Now, real slow-like, turn around and put your gun on the desk."

Sheriff Dawson obeyed the order again.

"Keep your hands where I can see them now," Josh said as he picked up the lawman's sidearm. "I wouldn't want to accidentally shoot you right here in your own office."

Sheriff Dawson stared down at the mustached, red-haired man who was sitting at his desk holding a gun on him. He had no idea who the stranger was or what he wanted from him. "There's no money here, if that's what you're after," he began.

"I'm not after money. I'm after information," Josh said coldly.

"What do you want to know?" Dawson was nervous, quite nervous. He'd been involved in a lot of shady deals over the years and had no idea which one was coming back to haunt him.

Slowly, very slowly, Josh set the lawman's gun aside and pulled out the wanted poster, tossing it on the desktop for him to see. "Who put this wanted poster out on me?"

"You're Grady?" Dawson did a double take, trying to reconcile the image of the man in the picture with the reality of the one sitting at his desk. With the mustache and changed hair color, Dawson would never have recognized him.

"That's right, I'm Josh Grady, and I've never been

on the wrong side of the law. So why am I 'Wanted—Dead or Alive' here in your town?"

The fierce look in Josh's eyes terrified the lawman.

"Well, um, I, um . . ." Dawson stammered, knowing that no matter what he said or did there would be a terrible price to pay.

"You're not answering my question," Josh snarled.

Sheriff Dawson swallowed hard. "It was—"

"It was me." Ned laughed evilly as he came out of the cell area with his gun drawn. "I'm the one who put him up to it, Grady."

"Barton!" Josh was startled to see the outlaw standing there. The last he'd heard, the man had been serving time in the penitentiary. It made sense to him now to learn that Sheriff Dawson and the outlaw were working together.

"That's right. I'm the one who put the bounty on you, and it couldn't have worked out any better. I figured somebody else would just bring in your body to claim the reward, but now I'm the one who gets to decide whether you're going to be turned in dead or alive to our friendly sheriff here." Ned was chuckling as he moved forward. "And I think we know the answer to that."

"Whatever your answer is, it's wrong," Emmie said fiercely from behind the outlaw. She'd been hiding in the back room. When she'd heard the back door to the jail open, she'd known it meant trouble—someone was sneaking in that way.

Emmie's unexpected appearance surprised Ned and caused him to turn and look behind him. That interruption gave Josh the opportunity he needed to make his move. Ned was a cold-blooded killer, and Josh had to act fast. He launched himself at Ned, hitting his gun from his hand and slamming him violently up against the wall. Ned tried to scramble back to his feet, but Josh hit him with his gun, knocking him unconscious. The outlaw collapsed on the floor.

Dawson started to go for his own revolver, where Josh had left it lying on the desktop, but Emmie drew her pistol.

"Don't even think about it!" she yelled at him as Josh was busy grabbing Ned's gun.

The sheriff froze again to stare at the person he thought was a boy standing there holding a gun on him.

"Thanks," Josh told her.

"What do you want to do now?" she asked.

"I'm going to lock them up."

Emmie nodded and kept her gun on Dawson as Josh hauled Ned's limp body back into one of the jail cells. He checked the outlaw over quickly to make sure he didn't have any other weapons on him and then locked him in before going back for the lawman.

"Let's go, Sheriff," Josh ordered.

"You can't do this! This is my jail! This is my town!"

"You can walk in the jail cell or I can carry you in like I did your friend. It's up to you," Josh told him.

Dawson was swearing vilely as he moved into the other jail cell and heard the door slam shut behind him and the key turn in the lock. "You're not going to get away with this, Grady."

"I already have," Josh replied.

Certain that the two were unarmed and not going anywhere, Josh took Emmie out into the front office.

"Emmie, I want you to go over to the telegraph office and wake the operator up if you have to. Tell him we need to send a wire to the Rangers."

Emmie couldn't believe that it had all happened so fast, and without a shot being fired. She found she was trembling as she looked up at him. "You did it."

"*We* did it," he said. Her timing had been perfect, coming up on Ned that way. "But we still have to notify the Rangers about what's happened."

She nodded as she slipped out of the sheriff's office. Emmie pounded on the locked door of the telegraph office, and after a few minutes an elderly man came to the door.

"What is it?"

"I need to send a telegram right away. It's important. I need to wire the Texas Rangers. We need a Ranger here in town."

The man had never seen this boy around Sundown before and wondered what he was doing there. Still, if the boy was looking for a Ranger, he knew he could help him.

"There's no need to send a wire," the telegraph operator said.

"But—"

"There's a Ranger already here in town," he interrupted. "He rode in yesterday, and he took a room down at the hotel."

"Thanks!" Emmie couldn't believe it as she ran off to try to find the Ranger.

Texas Ranger Bob Tackett had just settled into his room for the evening when someone started pounding on the door.

"I'm coming," he called out. He opened the door to find a boy standing there.

"Are you the Ranger?"

"Yes. What can I do for you, son?"

"We need you down at the sheriff's office."

Bob was instantly alert. "Has there been trouble?"

"An escaped prisoner was just caught."

Bob strapped on his gun belt and left the hotel with the boy.

Emmie and Bob reached the sheriff's office to find Josh pacing the room, waiting for her.

Josh looked up, completely surprised to see Emmie coming through the door with a Texas Ranger. He'd thought they were going to have to wait for days before one would show up.

"I'm Texas Ranger Bob Tackett," the man said, coming into the room. He'd met Sheriff Dawson before and wondered who the stranger was standing before him. "I understand you've got some trouble here?"

"I can't believe you're in town," Josh said.

"Neither could I," Emmie added.

"We got a telegram from someone named Burley in Shotgun, telling us that there might be trouble here in the next few days, so I rode in," the Ranger explained.

Josh looked at Emmie and managed a slight smile before turning to the Ranger. "It's good to meet you. My name's Josh Grady, and I've got a story to tell you."

# Epilogue

*Two months later*

Emmie gave Millie a big hug as she fought back the tears gathering in her eyes. "I can't believe you're leaving me!"

"I can't either." Millie was openly crying as she got ready to get on the stagecoach.

"You'll send us your wedding information as soon as your mother gets everything arranged?" Emmie asked.

"Oh, yes. I know it will be hard for you to make the trip, but if you can, it would be so wonderful," Millie said.

Emmie knew she had to get Josh to Philadelphia to meet her mother, and going back East for Millie and George's wedding seemed the perfect time. "We'll find a way."

George and Josh were standing off to the side, watching the women. Josh looked at his brother and they shook hands.

"Have a safe trip," Josh said.

"Thanks. I'll send you a wire and let you know when we get there."

"Good. Do you think you're going to like working for Millie's father in their family's business?"

"I guess we'll find out." George chuckled. "That is, if he approves of me and lets me marry his daughter."

"He'll approve of you," Miss Harriet put in from where she'd been watching everyone say their good-byes. "Have no doubt about that."

"With your recommendation, I can't go wrong." George smiled at her.

"Everybody get on board," the stage driver shouted.

"It's time," Millie said, hugging Emmie one last time before she let George help her into the stage.

George gave Miss Harriet a hand climbing up, too, and then turned back one last time. "I'll be seeing you."

He joined them in the stagecoach, and Emmie and Josh stepped back as the stage pulled away. They watched until it had gone out of sight.

Josh looked at his wife. "Are you ready to go home?"

Emmie smiled at him. "I'll go anywhere with you."

"In that case . . ." He took her arm as they walked to where they'd left their carriage. "How would you feel about stopping for a swim on the way back?"

Emmie looked up at her husband with a twinkle in her eye. "That sounds like a wonderful idea."

Josh stole a quick kiss before helping her up into the carriage. He joined her there and they started for home. They were both smiling at the prospect of what lay ahead.

**Turn the page for an exciting preview of**
*THE SILVER QUEEN*
**by award-winning author**
**JANE CANDIA COLEMAN**

Augusta Tabor may have been the first woman in the Colorado silver-mining camps, but she never dreamed of making the big strike. She labored hard to support her family, while her husband went out prospecting for months at a time and gave away their store credit to just about anyone who asked. And then one of his schemes finally worked out. Suddenly they were the richest folks in Colorado Territory and Haw Tabor was elected lieutenant governor. But untold wealth and power led them to a scandal that shocked the country—a scandal that would push Augusta's strength to its limits. . . .

# Chapter One

*Maine, 1855*

"There will be bloodshed. And it will end in civil war." My father's words echoed in my head as I stood in the Augusta station and said good-bye to Horace Tabor on a bitterly cold spring morning.

I clasped my hands together for warmth and to keep them from trembling. "You'll be careful? Father was right, you know. The Abolitionists and the pro-slavers won't ever compromise. You . . . you might be hurt." *Or even killed some place in Kansas.* Bleeding Kansas was what they were calling it then, a name that only increased my anxiety.

But I didn't say those words aloud. To speak them would be tempting fate. Besides, over the last two years I'd supported Horace's decision to join the New England Immigrant Aid Company, a group of Abolitionists whose intent was to populate Kansas and by sheer numbers defeat those who would vote to bring another slave state into the Union. Instead, I bit my lip to keep from crying.

Horace was impatient—a young man in search of his fortune, lured by the idea of adventure and conquering the unknown territory of Kansas. He had no qualms about leaving his future bride behind to wait and worry, and wanted no part of tears or mournful farewell.

"There's not a pro-slavery squatter born who could lick me, Gusta. This is my chance for a place of my own. Our chance, and I'm taking it." He put his big hands on my shoulders and pulled me close.

Actually my entire family approved of his idea. Like the rest of New England, we'd heard and read about the impassioned speeches of Eli Thayer as he toured the North in search of support for his army of immigrants, and we'd applauded when Amos Lawrence, a Pierce distant relative, began pouring huge amounts of money into the Immigrant Aid Company's coffers.

We Pierces were Unitarians, and we believed in the rights of men—and women—believed that slavery was unjust and a crime before God, and that it was our human duty to do all that we could to bring the evil practice to an end. Only a few years before, the publication of Harriet Stowe's *Uncle Tom's Cabin* had roused not only our town but much of the North. Mrs. Stowe was, at that time, living in Brunswick, Maine, in belief and heart one of us, an Abolitionist with a spine of granite and a way with words. And, though it was mentioned only by inference, it was understood that there was a house by the Kennebec River in Augusta with a secret room built solely to harbor runaway slaves.

Everyone we knew, with the exception of our

cousin, President Franklin Pierce, was opposed to slavery in any form, but so far, at least in Maine, the opposition had been verbal. In Kansas men were killing each other over the right to own slaves, and, according to Father, Cousin Frank was to blame. The passage of the Kansas-Nebraska Act, which repealed the earlier Missouri Compromise, was, as Father put it: "Frank's way of avoiding his responsibility. No fight in him. None at all, damn his hide!"

In the end, he predicted, only war would solve the slavery problem. War and bloodshed. And the man I'd loved from my first glimpse of him was off to do battle.

Two years before, my father, William Pierce, had been awarded the contract to cut the granite and rebuild the Augusta State Asylum. On the train to Boston to hire more workers, he'd met Horace Tabor and his brother John, both of them master stonecutters in search of jobs, and both of them also fellow Abolitionists and excited by the promise of free land in Kansas and the chance to strike a blow for their belief.

Was it fate? I've often wondered. Is the tapestry of our lives already stitched and in place, so that all we can do is follow the threads that bind us? Whatever the answer, I fell in love at my first sight of Horace as he jumped down from the wagon and stood staring up at our big, white house. He was tall, with broad shoulders and a stonecutter's massive but careful hands, and at dinner that night his dark eyes twinkled whenever he caught me looking at him. Twinkled, as if he knew what I was feeling and felt the same.

That night, and every successive night, the talk at the table was of slavery and abolition, and I can still see Horace's face when he realized we were related, both to our weak President and to Lawrence, the fierce philanthropist.

"You've chosen the right side," he boomed, barely restraining himself from pounding a huge fist on my mother's well-laid table. "By gad, sir, the South, with Pierce's blessing, will split the country in half!"

Father paused in the act of carving the roast. "The country is already split. If and when you go to Kansas, I believe you'll find the war has already begun. On a small scale," he added, "but war, nonetheless."

I folded my hands in my lap and prayed Horace wouldn't go. Surely there was enough to keep him here, safe and well employed, and in no danger. It wouldn't be the last time I uttered such a prayer, only to find it useless in the face of Horace's determination. But I was helpless in the throes of my first adult emotion.

Something of my intensity must have reached him, for he leaned across the table and said: "What do you think of all this, Miss Augusta? Give us a woman's opinion."

He'd picked me out! Me! I unfolded my hands and dropped my napkin on the floor, but when I answered, my voice didn't waver. "It's written that we're all created equal, Mister Tabor. And I believe that's so. Not only men, but women as well. What equality means is not that we're all born with the same strengths, but that we should all have a chance in life to use those strengths, and the freedom to fight for that chance."

This was nothing more than what we all believed and lived by, but Horace was impressed. As he told me later, he'd not met many women who'd been educated or who were even able to express themselves. He reached for his water glass and raised it in a toast.

"Well said. I salute you." Then he swallowed the contents in one gulp.

Father raised his glass, too. "My daughter has spoken for all of us. We believe in the rights of man. And woman," he added with a nod toward Mother and my sisters.

Stunned by the unaccustomed praise, I said nothing, but from that night on Horace sought me out at every opportunity. My sisters teased me about my beau, my mother in her roundabout fashion urged caution, and I ignored them all. At times I believed I'd die, if not from love then from the sheer excitement of being with Horace and listening as he talked about his dreams, wrapping my whole family up in his enthusiasm. That was one of his greatest charms—that boundless, fevered way of dreaming and making the achievement of those dreams sound both practical and assured. Even when he walked, he seemed to be filled with energy, always headed somewhere and sure of what awaited him.

From that first day, my health, which had kept me bedridden for so much of childhood, began to improve. I willed it to improve with all the strength I had. From that day my life took on meaning. And it was with my family's blessing that Horace was now leaving Maine in search of a homestead, a place in which he and I could make our home.

"Write me," I whispered. "And . . . and remember your promise not to drink very much."

As soon as the words came out, I regretted them. He frowned at me, his eyes dark. "You worry too much about nothing."

Well, I did. I knew his weaknesses as well as his strengths. He loved the company of men, the adulation of women. He loved politics and the idea that he was striking a blow against slavery. And he never hesitated to speak his mind to anyone who'd listen.

"Take care," I said, my voice drowned out by the whistle of the train.

He bent and kissed me, his lips warm in the cold air, and I clung to him, attempting to memorize the feel of his strong arms and how he towered over me, blocking out the gray sky.

"Stay well." He let me go, and picked up his bag. "I'll write. I'll be back as soon as I can. And"—he grinned—"I'll try to be moderate in all my bad habits."

Then he was gone. I stood watching till the train was out of sight, then walked slowly back to where my brother Frank was waiting with the team.

He tucked a robe around me, and we headed back to the house that would, I knew, feel empty without Horace to bring it to life.

*Keep safe, keep safe, keep safe*, I prayed all the way home, but there was, of course, no way to know if my prayer had been heard, or if it would be answered.

# Bobbi SMITH

It hadn't been easy growing up half Comanche in the small ranching town of Two Guns, Texas. But Wind Walker had always managed to keep his self-respect…and the attention of pretty Veronica Reynolds. After being sentenced to prison for a murder he didn't commit, Walker had managed to escape, and only Roni could help him track down the real killer. He hated the idea of putting her in harm's way, but still worse was the thought of going to his grave without tasting her sweet lips one more time….

# WANTED: The Half-Breed

ISBN 13: 978-0-8439-5850-8

# *Fallen*

"If you haven't read the Wind books, I suggest you do so; you won't be disappointed." —Fresh Fiction

# Cindy Holby

*Fallen…*

He was the product of illegitimacy, son of a noble house with no claim to its title or riches. For John Murray, the only hope of a decent life was his career as a British officer.

*Fallen…*

Had she lost her heart when he rescued her from ruffians, or when she first looked into that face like a golden angel's? No matter when it began, Isobel knew there was no hope of a happy ending for a rebel Scottish lass and a red-coated Sassenach.

*Fallen…*

Betrayed by the girl he loved, disgraced before his commander, wounded in battle and left for dead, John thought he'd hit rock bottom. But the sweet touch of a lover he'd never thought to see again taught him that no matter how far a man falls, with the right woman at his side, he can always stand tall.

ISBN 13: 978-0-8439-6026-6

# PAMELA CLARE

*MacKinnon's Rangers: They were a band of brothers, their loyalty to one another forged by hardship and battle, the bond between these Highland warriors, rugged colonials, and fierce Native Americans stronger even than blood ties.*

# UNTAMED

Though forced to fight for the hated British, Morgan MacKinnon would no more betray the men he leads than slit his own throat—not even when he was captured by the French and threatened with an agonizing death by fire at the hands of their Abenaki allies. Only the look of innocent longing in the eyes of a convent-bred French lass could make him question his vow to escape and return to the Rangers. And soon the sweet passion he awoke in Amalie had him cursing the war that forced him to choose between upholding his honor and pledging himself to the woman he loves.

ISBN 13: 978-0-8439-5489-0

# ☐ **YES!**

Sign me up for the Historical Romance Book Club and send my FREE BOOKS! If I choose to stay in the club, I will pay only $8.50* each month, a savings of $6.48!

NAME: _____

ADDRESS: _____

TELEPHONE: _____

EMAIL: _____

☐ I want to pay by credit card.

☐ **VISA**        ☐ **MasterCard.**        ☐ **DISCOVER**

ACCOUNT #: _____

EXPIRATION DATE: _____

SIGNATURE: _____

Mail this page along with $2.00 shipping and handling to:
**Historical Romance Book Club**
**PO Box 6640**
**Wayne, PA 19087**
Or fax (must include credit card information) to:
**610-995-9274**

You can also sign up online at **www.dorchesterpub.com.**
*Plus $2.00 for shipping. Offer open to residents of the U.S. and Canada only.
Canadian residents please call 1-800-481-9191 for pricing information.
If under 18, a parent or guardian must sign. Terms, prices and conditions subject to
change. Subscription subject to acceptance. Dorchester Publishing reserves the right
to reject any order or cancel any subscription.